Praise for Sophia Bennett's books

Great fun. It goes at a cracking pace and girls will love it.
JACQUELINE WILSON, AUTHOR

. . . a must read . . .
INDEPENDENT ON SUNDAY

Miss it, miss out.
MIZZ MAGAZINE

Bang on trend . . .
TBK MAGAZINE

A treat . . . elegant and funny and has real narrative verve.
DAVID ALMOND, AUTHOR

Intelligent chick-lit with lots of heart.
THE BOOKSELLER

. . . one word, BRILLIANT.
CATHY CASSIDY, AUTHOR

*[Bennett] writes about what really matters to teenagers
with zest, warmth and sympathy.*
THE TIMES

. . . well plotted and crisply and humorously written . . .
THE TELEGRAPH

*. . . funny and thoughtful, glamorous and sensitive, romantic
and down-to-earth in equal measure . . .*
BOOKS FOR KEEPS

A MESSAGE FROM CHICKEN HOUSE

So the biggest stars started out as music fans just like us – moved and inspired by love and beauty to rock and roll!

Sophia Bennett takes us on a voyage beyond the lights, to find a bunch of boys who need to remember the truth behind their music – and the only girl who can help them rediscover why it really matters to them, and a waiting world.

Thanks from all of us, Sophia – love rocks!

BARRY CUNNINGHAM
Publisher
Chicken House

Love SONG

SOPHIA BENNETT

Chicken House

2 Palmer Street, Frome, Somerset BA11 1DS
chickenhousebooks.com

Text © Sophia Bennett 2016
First published in Great Britain in 2016
Chicken House
2 Palmer Street
Frome, Somerset BA11 1DS
United Kingdom
www.chickenhousebooks.com

Cover and interior design by Helen Crawford-White
Cover photographs:
hands © Annette Shaff/Shutterstock;
pedals © optimarc/Shutterstock;
microphones © bogdanhoda/Shutterstock
Typeset by Dorchester Typesetting Group Ltd
Printed and bound in Great Britain by CPI Group (UK) Ltd, Croydon, CR0 4YY
The paper used in this Chicken House book is made
from wood grown in sustainable forests.

1 3 5 7 9 10 8 6 4 2

British Library Cataloguing in Publication data available.

ISBN 978-1-910002-72-8
eISBN 978-1-910655-56-6

*For E, who plays rock guitar
and writes love songs*

INTRO

The first time I hear The Point I'm fourteen, sitting with my boyfriend at the back of the bus, talking about the Himalayas.

'What's that?' I ask, distracted for a moment by the music.

He has his phone in his jeans pocket, with the earbuds split between us. It's a new song and he can't remember the title, so he eases the phone out of his jeans to look. I'm mesmerized by that pocket. I can't take my eyes off those rivets and seams …

'"Amethyst",' he says, checking the screen. 'This new band. Yeah, it's OK.'

It doesn't move him the way it moved me. But if he doesn't like it, then I don't care either. It was only background music anyway.

'In Nepal there's this sacred mountain they call the Fish Tail,' I continue. 'No one's allowed to climb it, but you can watch it from the nearby trails. You should see what it looks like with the sun setting on the snow.'

He gives me the sideways look I love. His name is Jez Rock-ingham and he's the best-looking boy in our year by miles. He's funny and clever, and captain of the football team. I think he's teasing me, and it's delicious.

'And there's the Chitwan National Park. You can see black rhino.'

'Rhino? Mmm *hmmm*?' Sideways glance at me again.

'It's got tigers and dolphins. Can you imagine?'

'Tigers *and* dolphins?'

'Stop it!' I dig him in the ribs. 'Aunt Cassie told me all about it. She wants to photograph the wildlife there. It sounds incredible.'

He grins, flashing perfect white teeth. 'You're getting in such a state, Nina! It's not as if you're going to go there anyway. Nepal's in *Asia*. You live in *Croydon*. You've still got GCSEs. Don't fuss about it. You'd only get malaria anyway, or mugged, or something ...'

He puts his hand gently on my neck, and his thumb rests on my collarbone. It's on the tip of my tongue to point out that the risk of malaria in Nepal's high mountain districts is very low, but he's looking into my eyes now, and his lips are getting closer, and the 'OK' music makes me want to wrap my arms around his neck and pull him in tight.

When his lips reach mine, I know I won the boy lottery, first time I tried. We are perfect together.

For ever starts now, and it is beautiful.

And that's how it was.

For a while.

In the year that followed, I had Jez, and he had me, and our love dipped and soared, and I was happy. Meanwhile, The Point's third single, 'Unlock Me', went to number one in America and from then on there was no stopping them.

Their new song, 'Eden', was the song of the summer as our first anniversary approached. I had a surprise to show Jez, and all the plans in the world. I'd even spent a month writing a poem to encapsulate my love. Dare I share it with him? Probably not. He'd laugh at me, but then, Jez laughed easily. His laugh was one of the things I loved most about him.

I was still working on the final lines when I heard Mum screaming.

And so how did you get here today?'

It was a warm summer's day, and my sister Ariel and I were standing in a meeting room in one of the poshest hotels in London. A huge banner with a red and black target logo dominated the back wall, illuminated by a couple of dazzling spotlights. 'Eden' was playing in the background. I still knew every note, every word, every minor chord. I hated it.

The room was full of excited girls. Next to us, a perky interviewer in a green T-shirt was talking to a platinum blonde with a Taylor Swift body, sticking a microphone under her nose.

'So, like, when the concert dates were announced I got, like, ten friends to help me,' the blonde girl answered with an American twang, 'and we all spent, like, forty minutes on our laptops, pressing refresh as soon as the tickets came out. I couldn't get one for the O_2, but then they announced this extra meet-and-greet for the mega-fans and I spent, like, four hundred dollars on this ticket, plus my air fare from Cincinnati, and here I am.'

She said the whole thing without a flicker of a smile, like one huge 'duh' to Perky Girl – because that was exactly the normal procedure for getting your hands on an Ultimate VIP meet-and-greet ticket to meet The Point these days – and I decided I liked her deadpan attitude.

'Well, that's very interesting,' the interviewer gulped, looking slightly intimidated. 'And how do you *feel* right now?'

'What? Seriously?'

I grinned. If it was possible to distil the essence of *What do you think?* into one raised eyebrow, Deadpan Blonde had mastered it. But once she started talking, her expression changed. Her eyes welled up. Her lips twitched. I watched her try to control herself, but she couldn't help it.

'OK, so I'm excited, obviously,' she said. 'I've met them before, in Chicago, and that time I got to hold Jamie's hand. Which was …' She looked away. '… so …' Whatever it was, she couldn't bring herself to say the words. '… but I didn't really get to say hi to Angus, and I want to tell him … that I … he … he means a lot to me. That's all. The music …'

She bit her lip. The interviewer nodded sympathetically. 'Uh huh. Angus has that effect, doesn't he? They're all so … *scrummy.*'

Yeah, because *scrummy* just perfectly captured all the complicated feelings Deadpan Blonde was struggling with just now.

I tried to catch her eye to offer some sympathy but that moment Ariel grabbed my arm.

2

'Nina! They're coming!'

She was right. After a flurry of activity in the corridor outside, two massive bodyguards moved in to stand either side of the nearest doorway. Moments later the boys were walking past us in a blur of famous, surrounded by their entourage. Four iconic hairstyles glinted in the light. Last year we studied *A Midsummer Night's Dream*, and this motley crew reminded me exactly of Oberon and Titania and their attendant fairies. Ariel squeezed my arm more tightly. We'd seen so many news videos like this – the busy entourage, and the band captured fuzzily behind them. Now they were real, and it was weird to see them in 3D.

As they swept towards the far end of the room, an assistant said something to Jamie Maldon, the singer, and as he turned to answer, he happened to catch my eye. He looked straight at me and smiled. He has the most beautiful lips, all curves and curlicues, and three moles on his left cheek, which Ariel says he hates, but which every Pointer Sister would sell her soul to kiss. He looked at me like he knew me, half questioning, half laughing.

For a moment, all the fame just fell away, and I felt a connection. It was as if he knew me, and he liked me, and he wanted me to like him too. We smiled at each other and …

I was an idiot. One second later, he was giving Deadpan Blonde exactly the same look, and she practically cooed with excitement. Jamie Maldon was famous the world over for that smile. It was one of the reasons he was the superstar of the band, and not Connor Clark the bassist, with peroxide locks and sharp-angled cheeks, who was so uncannily beautiful that it almost hurt to look at him. I couldn't believe I fell for it.

3

Beside me, Ariel sighed. 'Did you see the way he looked at me?'

'Who?'

'Jamie.' She glowed with happiness.

Goodness, the boy was a male Mona Lisa. Whoever you were, his eyes seemed to follow you round the room. I was even more of an idiot than I thought.

Ariel's eyes glazed over and I could tell she was in the middle of her very own fanfic story. The one where you meet the band, your favourite member spots you across a crowded room, falls instantly in love with you and spends the next twenty chapters trying to win your affections. Ignoring the fact that she's thirteen and he's nineteen. Oh, and like me, she's a schoolgirl and he's a *rock star*. And another minor detail: Jamie was engaged. Taken. Spoken for.

Without another glance, the boys walked over to stand in front of the banner. I still had an image of them in my head from three years ago, when 'Amethyst' came out. They all had a schoolboy-rebel look about them then – tight jackets, white shirts, scruffy trousers and James Dean hair. Now they were glossier and more designer. Their faces had developed sharper lines, their hairstyles were more extreme. Close up, they looked frailer than I'd expected, and tired too, despite their cheerful smiles.

Meanwhile, the door to the corridor opened again. Two girls entered. One was tall, pretty, serious and dressed in sober black. The other was a tiny, curvy figure in a white cotton dress with trailing cut-out sleeves.

'OMIGOD!' she announced, beaming at us all. 'I've never

DONE this before! You must be all Jamie's little meet-and-greet fans! You guys are just BEYOND!'

I stared at her, then looked at Ariel.

'Is that ...?'

My sister nodded.

Sigrid Santorini was a Hollywood rom-com star who had started going out with Jamie at Christmas. Three months later, they were engaged. *Backstage with Sigrid*, her reality TV show, was required viewing at school. If you didn't know that Sigrid's chihuahua was called Ryan, or that she once skydived for charity in a pink bikini, then you wouldn't understand half the conversations in the sixth-form common room.

And here she was, grinning at us all as if it was really her we'd come to see. It was fascinating how the room seemed to refocus around her. She was more compact, thinner and some-how brighter than the rest of us. In the flesh, she was even more spectacular than on TV. She seemed to glow, from her tumbling black hair to her lightly-freckled, golden skin and clear blue eyes that sparkled almost as intensely as the utterly ginormous diamond on her left hand. She was like a slightly-smaller-than-lifesize perfect doll.

Next to me, Deadpan Blonde groaned. 'I don't believe it. It's like she's following Jamie everywhere these days.'

Several of the Pointer Sisters turned to glare at Sigrid as she stalked over to stand near her fiancé in teetering heels. When you've paid four hundred dollars for an Ultimate VIP ticket, you don't want to be labelled as a 'little meet-and-greet fan'.

'Did you see the diamond?' Deadpan Blonde whispered to us.

I nodded. The rock on Sigrid's engagement ring was impossible to miss – the size of a Malteser and glittering on her hand like a distant star.

'Isn't it beautiful?' Ariel sighed.

Um … Large, yes. Beautiful … maybe. For me, in order to be beautiful, something has to be more than just very, very big and shiny. It has to produce an emotion, and the only emotion it made me feel was worry about what would happen if she lost it.

'Did she choose it?' I asked.

'Oh no!' Ariel said. 'Didn't you hear? About the proposal?'

I shrugged. 'It was at night, wasn't it?' I remembered something about moonlight. Also a car.

Deadpan Blonde and Ariel shared a look. The Proposal was obviously a Pointer Sister story. Something you had to know about in all its gory details if you were a true fan.

'Sigrid turned twenty-two in March,' Deadpan Blonde recounted. 'She had a crazy party at this big hotel in Las Vegas.'

'The one Prince Harry stayed in,' Ariel added breathlessly.

'But Jamie whisked her away from it, like, secretly, and flew her to the California coast, and he'd hired this car …'

'A pale blue vintage Mustang convertible,' Ariel specified. (Truly was she our father's daughter.) Oh yeah – the Mustang. I liked the Mustang.

'And he took her to her favourite restaurant,' Deadpan Blonde went on, 'and he'd hired the whole place, so it was just them and this pianist playing jazz …'

'And he proposed to her on the terrace, overlooking the ocean,' Ariel concluded. 'With the diamond.'

6

As you do.

'And she said yes,' I assumed.

As you would. If you were a rom-com star like Sigrid and still believed in heartfelt proposals from nineteen-year-old rock gods with Mona Lisa smiles, who would never, obviously, cheat on you, and seriously intended to spend the next seventy-plus years of their lives hooked up to you and only you.

'It was just … so … romantic,' Ariel sighed dreamily. 'He's such a wonderful person.'

This made me smile. While the details were hazy, I did remember that after the news was announced, many of the Pointer Sisters had queued up to hate Sigrid online, or threaten to kill themselves, or her. But my little sister just saw the good in his proposal.

It was Ariel's soul that was beautiful, I thought. She'd never said so out loud, but I'd seen her practise her signature in the back of her notebooks: *Ariel Maldon, Ariel Maldon, Ariel Maldon.* There had been hope. Crazy hope, but hope. Now there was none. The rest of the family teased her about her passion for Jamie, but not me. I'm an expert in heartbreak. A black belt in unrequited love. I know it hurts enough as it is, and it takes all your energy to heal.

'Why don't you tell him you're happy for him?' I suggested at the time. 'Nobody else seems to be.'

And so she did – in a long video, describing all her favourite Jamie moments, culminating in the-diamond-by-the-ocean. And by some miracle he saw it, and wrote back saying how touched he was, and how he'd noticed she'd said she couldn't get tickets for any of his shows, and so he was sending her a couple for the special meet-and-greet today, with his love.

With his love.

And his signature, and a kiss.

Ariel had been walking on clouds ever since. She wore the paper with his signature on it in an old locket, hanging near her heart.

It made her feel … 'happy'.

God.

By now, the boys were in position at the back of the room, ready for the fans to file past them for the meet-and-greet. The two bodyguards stood nearby, arms folded, making it clear that nobody was getting close unless they wanted it to happen. Meanwhile, dark-dressed members of the entourage bustled about, getting us all into something approaching an orderly queue.

Ariel and I were about halfway down, which gave us plenty of time to watch the boys in action. They certainly weren't painful to look at, though they didn't look like any real boys I knew. Over the years each of them had developed his own sense of style. Connor used to look like an angel who'd just stepped out of a Renaissance painting. Then he had his peroxide hair cut super short and now he was more like a visiting alien. He emphasized the effect in a silver T-shirt and spray-on jeans. Angus, the guitarist, was black and moody from slicked-back quiff to biker-booted toe. George, the frizzy-haired drummer, wore a sleeveless vest to show off his bodybuilder physique. Jamie's loose silk shirt was probably a one-off by a designer mate of his. I knew this because Ariel and Mum had

had a long conversation about it over breakfast.

The Point were famous for their jokey friendship, and it was one of the things Ariel loved most about them. There was lots of laughter and silly gestures, kisses, hugs and stupid faces. They hit their mark for every photograph – eyes front, smiling – and all the fans walked away beaming.

'I feel sick,' Ariel moaned, clutching her tummy as we moved forward.

'Not long now,' I murmured.

'I know. That's why.'

It was Deadpan Blonde's turn. She sauntered across the floor, handed her details to the photographer's assistant and walked over to the spot where the band were standing. She already had Connor Clark's full attention. He was looking her up and down like she was a lobster in a restaurant and he'd just ordered lobster.

She posed between him and Angus, legs casually crossed, doing a peace sign. They spoke to her briefly and that strong emotion from earlier suffused her face. Whatever they said, it had obviously made the four-thousand-mile trip worthwhile.

'Go. GO.'

Ariel was being lined up to go over already, and I hadn't even noticed.

It didn't take a big detective to work out who was here for the band, and who was just here as a chaperone. Ariel was wearing an oversize blue T-shirt she designed herself, with handwritten lyrics from her favourite Point songs, surrounded by glitter doodles of their signatures. Her hair was dip-dyed sky blue from waist to shoulder – because Jamie often said his favourite colour was blue – and blonde from the shoulders upwards, because once he said it was yellow. I was in one of my old painting shirts and the first pair of shorts I could find.

'Go on. Have fun!' I said, pushing her forwards.

She hesitated, looking terrified. 'Come with me?'

For the sake of speeding things up, I took her hand and we walked across the brief expanse of carpet towards the band.

The boys looked over at us and smiled. 'Where d'you want us?'

And there we were, face to face with the most famous faces on the planet, and I kind of got why Ariel was so nervous. I wasn't a fan and even I was practically having an out-of-body experience. It was like meeting the Queen, or walking on the Moon: definitely happening, and yet somehow impossible.

Ariel was lost for words, but the band had done this a thousand times before. Angus and Connor scooted up one way and Jamie and George went the other, leaving spaces in the middle for Ariel and me.

'Oh, I'm not in this,' I explained.

I had just spoken to the collective Point. Weird. Weird. I said human words to them, and they understood.

'Sure you are,' Jamie said, with a sultry grin, motioning me next to him.

'No, really. I'll just take a picture.'

He shrugged, moved in a little and put his arm around Ariel. She stared blankly ahead. Anyone else might think she was brain dead, but I could see her emotions were in lockdown: she was too overwhelmed to think.

While the photographer lined up the official shot, I got busy with my camera. I got into position in front of them and framed the shot so the boys and Ariel filled the screen. It looked bizarrely familiar after seeing their faces, just like this, on countless videos and posters. Now here was my sister's face right in the middle of them, as if I'd Photoshopped her in.

'Loving the hair,' Jamie said, picking up a strand of it and laying it across his upper lip like a moustache. 'Great colour.'

'I know,' Ariel breathed, happily.

Meanwhile, George gave her bunny ears, Angus scowled seductively, and Connor did his 'Connor-face' thing, which was his mysterious middle-distance stare. The photographer snapped the official picture. I took mine. And it was over.

Except it wasn't.

As soon as the photographer nodded that she'd got the shot, Ariel suddenly got her courage from somewhere.

'Thank you for the tickets,' she said shyly, turning to Jamie.

'Um ... the tickets?'

'The ones you sent for today. I did the video about your proposal.' He still looked blank. 'The one saying how romantic it was. And you wrote back, remember?'

'Um ... yeah ... sure.'

My heart lurched. It was obvious, to me at least, that Jamie didn't remember at all. Getting his note was the greatest moment of my sister's life, but to him, she was just another loved-up girl in a long queue of them – not as glamorous as his fiancée and not even as cool as Deadpan Blonde. My heart ached for her.

Move on, Ariel. Jamie clearly has no idea who you are.

'Come on,' I said, gently. 'Let's go.'

But Ariel stood there, glowing with the joy of standing next to her idol. Nothing would make her move if she could help it.

'Did I hear you right?' said a voice from behind me. I spun round. Sigrid Santorini was directing the beam of her film-star smile straight at my sister. 'You did a *video* about us?'

'Yes,' Ariel whispered, staring at her shoes.

'Well, aren't you *THE MOST*?' Sigrid laughed, fluttering her fingers, so the diamond flashed in the light. I caught sight of Angus watching it with the faintest hint of a sneer.

'What's your name?' Sigrid asked.

'Ariel,' she breathed.

'And where are you from?'

'Croydon.'

Sigrid's eyebrows shot up. 'Croydon? Really?'

Yeah, that area of South London Sigrid would so *obviously* have heard of. But she seemed intrigued, or faked it well.

'You're so *fascinating*,' she said. 'Jamie, baby, we must get a picture. Us two with little Rachel here, with that beautiful blue hair. Isn't she charming? Would you like that, Rachel? My assistant can take it and put it on Instagram. Pamela!'

The girl in dark clothing emerged from the shadows and dutifully took Sigrid's phone. While Pamela nudged me out of the way so she could get a good shot, Sigrid squeezed herself next to Jamie, manoeuvring Ariel in front of her. Standing to one side, I glanced back at the queue. This was all taking precious time from the meet-and-greet. The remaining girls did not look happy. Nor did Angus, whose moody pose was morphing into something like disgust.

Sigrid adjusted her hair so it cascaded over one shoulder,

and her pose so she was perfectly three-quarters on. She sucked in her cheeks and turned on her million-dollar smile. *Wham!* It was like switching on floodlights. She radiated joy. It was almost as if there was an aura of light around her.

In fact, there *was* an aura of light around her, bright and flickering. And a strange, unpleasant smell.

'Fire!'

The word was out of my mouth before I knew I was shouting.

'OMIGOD! WHERE?' Sigrid yelled.

I gasped. It seemed to be all around them. Somehow, the banner behind the band had caught light. It was disintegrating super-fast, sending gossamer-light, glowing specks of fabric floating through the air.

Adrenaline pumped through me. *Nononono* ...

I'd been here before. My little sister in a flimsy witch's cape, going up in flames in front of me. Not now. Not again.

I thought of Aunt Cassie, and how quickly she'd reacted all those Halloweens ago when Ariel's cape had brushed the top of a burning candle. For an instant, I pictured Mum howling Cassie's name, but I pushed the image away. What now mattered was to make sure Ariel was safe.

I reached forward, grabbed her by the arm and pulled her out of the way. With lightning speed, the lurking bodyguards did the same for the boys, taking two each and bundling them through the crowd to the nearest exit. Around us, the meet-and-greet descended into chaos. Alarms went off. Girls screamed. People started running in a stampede for the doors. I was about to follow them when behind us, somebody shouted.

'HELP ME! SOMEBODY, HELP ME!'

I looked back. Sigrid was still rooted to the spot, paralysed with shock. The banner had almost burnt itself out but she was staring down at the trailing sleeves of her white dress, where little flames were licking upwards, burning their way through the cotton like advancing armies of light.

'WATER!' she screamed. 'I NEED WATER!'

As I glanced around for something to put out the fire, I noticed that at the back of the stampede, several people had paused to get their phones out and video the scene. *Way to go. Don't help – just put it on the internet, why don't you?* Meanwhile, Sigrid whirled her arms in terror, and the flames rose higher, like burning wings.

There was a table nearby, covered with a big dark cloth and set with bottles of mineral water. The girl who'd taken the Instagram picture grabbed one of them and sprayed it in Sigrid's direction. Only a few drops reached her and they did no good. The girl reached for a second bottle, but before she could get hold of it, I'd grabbed the cloth underneath and sent the lot flying.

'WHA—?' Sigrid gasped, horrified to see the precious bottles falling.

I rushed over to her with the tablecloth held out in front of me, and wrapped her in it, wrestling her to the floor as I went. I rolled her over inside the cloth and threw myself on top of her for good measure.

'OW! GET OFF ME!' she shouted. 'HEY! What are you *doing*?'

'I need ... to stop ... the air ...' I panted, straddling her with my body. After Ariel's Halloween terror, I knew more than I wanted to about how to put out a person on fire. The best way was to wrap them in something thick and heavy, fast, and keep it there until all the flames were out.

The ground shuddered under the weight of heavy footsteps.

'Oi! You!' a gruff voice shouted. 'Get away from her.'

Sigrid's frightened eyes flicked to something in the distance behind me. I glanced back through falling flecks of ash to see a bodyguard the size of a small hatchback bearing down on us both. Beyond him, Jamie hovered anxiously, helpless and terrified.

'You! *Move!*' the guard repeated.

'I can't!'

But before I could explain what I was doing, his strong hand had hauled me off Sigrid and dumped me face down on the ground beside her. My shoulder hit the floor with a crack. A big, heavy knee dug firmly into the small of my back.

It hurt. A lot.

'Get off my sister!' Ariel yelled desperately, trying to pull him away.

He ignored her, and kept the knee where it was. 'You all right, miss?' he asked.

Well, obviously not. But he wasn't talking to me, he was talking to Sigrid.

'I ... no. OW. My hand ...' she moaned.

'Don't worry. It's under control now,' he said, pressing down on me even harder.

With my head squished against the carpet, my vision went blurry. All I could really see was flashes of coloured light bouncing off the Malteser diamond as Sigrid flexed her fingers to

15

check her left hand was OK, while Jamie crouched consolingly beside her now the big, bad teenager was out of the way.

At least I hadn't paid four hundred dollars for the privilege of being here today. I made a mental note never again to try and save the life of a celebrity.

It sucked.

2

As anyone who watches *Backstage with Sigrid* knows, Sigrid Santorini lives in a house in the Hollywood Hills, with views over the twinkling town and a new swimming pool recently built in the shape of Jamie Maldon's favourite guitar. Ariel and I went home, eventually, to Croydon. Famous for Kate Moss and car parks. Home to South London's branch of Ikea. Things are a little different in the real world. Just saying.

Our house was a little white box with a shed in the back garden and a garage beside it, and as long as he had a shed and a garage, my dad was happy. He was on the front drive working on the Mini when we arrived. It was an original Mini – one of the really tiny ones that look like they're probably run by pedal power. Dad looked quite ridiculous underneath it, with his long legs encased in overalls sticking halfway down the drive.

He slid himself out and glanced up at us, wiping his hair out of his eyes with an oily hand.

'You're back late. Was there a problem?'

'Yeah,' I sighed. 'Jamie Maldon's girlfriend caught fire.' I rolled my aching shoulder.

Dad looked at it in alarm. 'You weren't caught up in it, were you?'

I was about to say 'no', because it was a long story and I really needed a shower, but Ariel butted in.

'She was brilliant. Nina was the one who put it out. You know? Like Auntie Cassie did with her coat? A guard jumped on Nina first, but they realized what she'd done and they were really grateful. Sigrid just had this teeny weeny burn the size of a 5p and Nina made her put it under cold water like Aunt Cassie told us and while she sat there she talked to me for ages about our family and all sorts of stuff and she was really nice, and they offered us tickets for *any* of their shows at the O$_2$ and you've got to take me, Dad, seriously, because ...'

I'd forgotten Ariel's ability to remember things the best way possible. Dad calls it 'retrospective optimism'. She only talks about the best times with Aunt Cassie. Sometimes it feels like being related to a helium balloon.

'Whoa!' Dad flicked his gaze from her to me. 'You put out a girl on fire?'

I shrugged. 'It was either that or take a video of it.'

'Well, I'm proud of you, Nina, love.'

'And now we've got to decide which day you're taking me to the O$_2$,' Ariel chattered on. 'Because Nina doesn't want to go and—'

'Hey, hey, hey,' Dad smiled. 'Slow down, love. We can talk

about that later. Nina, now you're back, can you look after the twins until Mum gets in? Michael's making their tea, so God knows what state they're in. Josh has had an interesting day. I'd come and help but I just need to work out where this oil leak's coming from ...'

He smiled at me hopefully.

'Sure.'

I was used to helping out. As the eldest of four, with two extra toddlers in the house and Mum and Dad both working, I could either live in total chaos most of time or fix some of it myself.

Ariel rushed inside to text her friends about our day. In the kitchen my fifteen-year-old brother Michael was stirring something on the stove, but his attention was mostly focused on a girl with tumbling red ringlets sitting on the kitchen table, her legs elegantly crossed for maximum display. She was idly feeding chocolate biscuits to my twin cousins, Aunt Cassie's boy and girl, who were strapped into booster seats at the table. There was a strange, sickly-sweet smell in the air.

'Neenie Neenie Neenie!' the twins called out, reaching for me with crumby fingers and chocolate-smeared faces.

I went over and bent forward for a kiss and a hug, while each of them in turn squeezed their chubby arms around me, getting chocolate on my lips and crumbs in my hair.

'Pip! Lara! Did you miss me?'

'We always miss you, Neenie,' Lara said reprovingly.

'It's been extremely tedious without you,' Pip joined in. He'd learnt 'extremely tedious' from a TV show and came out with it in the bath two days ago. Mum practically levitated with pride.

Now he said it all the time.

While I disentangled myself from them, I gazed in surprise at the red-headed girl, who grinned at me.

'It has indeed been extremely tedious without you, babe. I've been waiting for half an hour. Luckily, your brother kept me entertained me with his brilliant impersonation of Jamie Oliver.'

This was my best friend Tammy. We've known each other for ever and I'm not sure I'd be alive without her. She nursed me through all my Jez fiascos and I've helped her through some better-managed heartbreaks of her own. I gave her a squeeze and went over to the stove to check what was happening in Michael's pan. It wasn't a pretty sight. They might have been baked beans once, but you would never know. Now they looked like the kind of thing a special-effects team would use to portray the aftermath of a deadly disease. That explained the smell.

'I'll take over,' I suggested. It was good to be in control again.

Michael nodded gratefully. He, girls and cookery don't mix. We learnt this long ago. He can just about manage to focus on one or the other, but never both at the same time. Especially if the girl is someone like Tammy, who demands a man's full attention at all times.

'Thanks,' he said, rushing out of the room at full speed, with one last backward glance in Tammy's direction.

'I think he's just a little bit afraid of me,' she observed, twirling a ringlet around her fingers.

'I should think he's practically terrified,' I agreed. Michael is a sensitive computer geek with a love of classical music and a fondness for playing the trumpet. Whereas Tammy is a force of nature.

'So listen,' she said. 'I came straight over. Everyone's saying there was some kind of fan invasion at this Point thing you went to. You weren't involved, right?'

'Everyone who?'

She pointed at the phone beside her on the table. 'The internet. Everyone. Some crazy person apparently threw herself on Sigrid Santorini. There was a girl-fight. It was intense.'

'That girl-fight would be me,' I admitted. 'And it was not "intense" – I was just trying to stop her dress from burning her to a crisp. Anyway, she wasn't happy about it. Then this gorilla landed on me.' I rolled my aching shoulders again and stretched my neck.

'There was a *fire*? Where were the boys?'

'Right next to us, to start with. Until the bodyguards caught hold of them and they ran away. I hate to break it to you, but they're not exactly action heroes.'

But Tammy was less concerned about the running-away part, and more interested in the fact that The Point had been there in the first place.

'So what does Jamie Maldon actually smell like, close to?'

I had to admit that I hadn't noticed. I was concentrating more on the smell of his girlfriend's burning clothes, and then on trying to get home, once I'd got out from under the bodyguard.

Tammy pouted over the bread knife. 'You might have hung around a bit longer, Neens. You never know – maybe Jamie could have offered to help you with your poorly shoulder ...'

'Don't even go there! The boy wouldn't have noticed my

poorly shoulder. He hardly noticed Ariel's whole body when she'd dyed her hair both his favourite colours and was standing right in front of him. He's going out with a movie star, remember?'

She sighed, and changed the subject. 'So – are you coming to the party tonight? You can tell everyone all about it.'

'No,' I said firmly. 'I told you before. I need to work on my art assignment. And I'm tired.'

'Oh, come on. It's at Angelle's house. I helped her decorate. It's the last big party before exams. You should be celebrating being an independent woman.'

'I like being an independent woman. Which is why I want to nail this assignment. And I don't like big parties.'

It's true, I don't. I don't like people getting drunk and being sick on carpets. I don't like feeling that I wore the wrong dress, and not knowing who to talk to, or where to sit. I don't like people casting sideways glances at me, wondering if I'm going to bump into my ex-boyfriend snogging another girl and go to pieces. Even though the last time I did that was practically a lifetime ago, and anyone who wants Jez Rockingham these days is welcome to him.

Tammy knew this well enough by now. Reluctantly, she left me to it while she went home to get ready. Once she'd gone, I quickly checked on Josh, my little brother. He was half-asleep on the sofa in the front room, curled up under a blanket and watching an old recorded episode of *Murder, She Wrote*. His pale skin and purple-shadowed eyes showed the signs of a busy day. So did the fact that every chair cushion, book, toy and ornament had been thrown across the room.

Josh used to have behaviour problems when he was little and even at the grand old age of seven he still completely lost it sometimes. It never lasted long, but the results could be impressive. Nothing was where it should be. It looked as if a hurricane had recently passed through.

While the twins chased each other up and down the hallway, I picked each object up and put it back, slowly clearing a path for myself as I went. Piece by piece, the room came back together. As it started to look like a home, not a war scene, I realized I was starting to breathe more deeply again.

'Sorry, Neenie,' he murmured sleepily, as I put one of the cushions behind his head.

'It's OK. I know you didn't mean it.'

'No. I was just sad. Can I sleep in your bed now?'

He looked up at me pleadingly. How could I say no? Josh always preferred my bed to his, even though I had deliberately tried borrowing one of Ariel's old Little Mermaid duvet covers to put him off, and Josh was 'allergic' to anything Disney or 'girly'. If he went down in my bed, he'd sleep, which he needed to.

'Course, Joshie. Come on.'

While I bathed the twins, to the sound of Michael practising Purcell on the trumpet, Ariel set the smoke alarm off twice making cheese toasties, then Dad did for a third time, 'doing a bit of soldering while I had my tools handy'.

I opened the bathroom window to let some of the steam out and clear my head a little, and I caught sight of a boy in the next-door garden, throwing a ball for his dog to catch. He looked up, alerted by the light, and our eyes locked for a moment – he from the peace of his garden, me from the madness of my house. Then he looked away.

'Robbie! Robbie! Here, boy!'

He threw the ball high in the air and the terrier practically turned somersaults trying to get it.

Jez Rockingham had hardly spoken to me in the year since our final break-up, but that was OK. I got over him a long time ago. I was even grateful for the scars.

I looked at myself in the misty bathroom mirror. My hair is thick and unruly, like Aunt Cassie's was, and Dad says my heavy fringe always makes him think of a Shetland pony caught in a Highland breeze. Thanks, Dad. My eyes are mud brown and there's a gap between my front teeth. I used to hate it, but not any more. Mum says it reminds her of Jane Birkin, the British actress who sang with Serge Gainsbourg and made it big in France and became super-cool. Mum's better at the 'you remind me of' game than Dad. It comes from running a hairdressing salon – if you tell your customers they remind you of wild animals of the British Isles, you're not going to get much repeat business.

Then, as always, my eyes travelled to my neck, to make sure it was suitably covered by the collar of my shirt.

Ariel thinks she invented crazy-in-love, but that's not the case. As Jez and I approached our first anniversary, he told me this was 'the longest I've lasted with a girl'. He gave me a pendant with my initial on it, but it was really *his* initial I wanted to wear. So a few days later, while he was away, I found a tattoo parlour that didn't ask questions and had a little black 'J' tattooed on my neck, just above my collarbone. I wanted the world to know how strong our love was, and it was one of the

24

surprises I wanted to show him when he got back.

I should have realized, of course. 'The longest I've ever lasted with a girl' is not the beginning of for ever – it's the beginning of the end.

I was innocent then. I've learnt my lesson now.

Two years ago, the day after I came home with my new tattoo, Mum got the news – Aunt Cassie was dead.

Drowned, off the coast of Scotland. Twenty-nine, and dead.

That's when the screaming started.

We couldn't bear it. We couldn't believe it. She had two babies who needed her. Cassie, hair like straw, eyes like blue fire, was life personified. Her pictures sang with it.

Lying on the beach. Seaweed tangled in her hair.

I needed Jez so badly. But he was on holiday with friends from school. Not answering his phone. He was staying at a villa owned by some rich girl's parents. Mum wouldn't let me go.

The day he got back there was a party. Everyone was going to be there. I knew Jez was home, because I saw his bags in the driveway. But still no answer.

I called around our friends to find out if anyone knew where he was. I knew I sounded desperate, but my aunt was dead and I had to talk to him. Now. Only Jez would do. Only he and I had that connection.

Night-time. Party. Wandering through the low-lit rooms, looking for my boyfriend. People avoiding my eye. I understand – I am bereaved. Nobody knows what to say.

'Eden' in the background. Jamie Maldon's voice, hopeful

25

and haunting, and the sound of rock guitar. I want to dance with Jez. I need to hold him. Skin on skin. I need this nightmare to be over.

And there he is, in the darkest corner of the darkest room. Slow-dancing with a girl I don't recognize. He raises his eyes from her long, dark hair and looks at me.

Jamie Maldon sings a love song and Jez's eyes meet mine. Blue gaze, long and unblinking. I get the message.

'For ever' is a relative concept, like time.

He couldn't even be bothered to text.

For several months, I was a wreck. Was it Jez, or Aunt Cassie dying? I don't even know.

Jez broke up with Ria, the girl he was dancing with, and got back with me for a while. I took him desperately, gratefully. I was pathetic. Then another girl came along. It happened again. And again. I crashed through my GCSEs. At school, I became a joke.

Until I lost myself in art and books and gradually learnt some self-respect. Mum adopted Cassie's twins, Pip and Lara, whose dad had gone out of Cassie's life long before they were born, and I got infinitely more pleasure and unadulterated love from them than I ever had from a boy. My heart mended. Slowly and messily. But it mended eventually. I am like Mum and Dad: I'm practical and I can fix things. Including myself.

And here we are.

I used to think that Ariel was the crazy one – saving all her deepest emotions for four boys who didn't know she existed, while my boy bought me presents and hung around in my room, showing me the funniest YouTube videos, and stroked the skin on my neck with his thumb. Two years on, though, she is as much in love as ever. The Point, she says, give her life its purpose. Her happiest moments have come from loving them.

I am ... cured.

3

For about a week, a grainy clip of a girl leaping on Sigrid Santorini and being squashed by a security guard became a minor hit on the internet. Some people knew it was me, but others didn't believe it. I didn't bother to correct them. I didn't exactly want to become famous for starring in a comedy video.

Dad took Ariel to the concert at the O$_2$ and she said it was 'the best night of her life'. Tammy said I'd missed an epic party at Angelle's house. Two couples got together that night, and four broke up. Of the two that got together, one had already split, while two of the broken-up ones had swapped partners and reconnected. Relationships in our school were like a complicated maths question. I didn't get the impression I'd really missed that much.

I was in the kitchen the following Saturday, feeding tomatoes from the allotment to Pip and Lara. They wouldn't touch the red ones, but I'd managed to persuade them that the yellow and orange ones had special magic properties and if you ate enough of them you might get to spot the invisible unicorns hiding in the gro-bags. They both swore they'd seen them a million times.

'I know they're there because they're sparkly and they look at me,' Lara said solemnly, holding a cherry-sized tomato in each pudgy little hand.

'I saw twenty the last time I had an orange tomato,' Pip announced, stuffing one in and letting the juice run down his chin. 'Ashlly, i' 'as 'wenty-four.' He swallowed. 'And a half.'

'Wow, Pip.'

'I saw them too!' Lara insisted. 'And a lady unicorn!'

'Blimey!' Dad said, walking in and wiping his face with an oily rag. He'd been working on the Mini again. 'There's a twin-cam MGA roadster outside, in spanking condition. 1959 or '60, I'd say. Original leather interior. It's a classic. Oh, and there's a man here to see you, Neenie. I've put him in the front room. Very tall. Hat.'

I couldn't think of anybody I knew who wore hats and drove classic sports cars. Or was ever likely to.

'Sorry to leave you,' I told the twins, kissing them on their curly heads. 'Dad'll look after you for a minute. I'll be back.'

In the front room, Josh was curled up in his usual spot, engrossed in an old episode of Columbo. Perched awkwardly next to him was a blond, bearded man in an immaculate cream linen jacket, with a huge green scarf wound several times around his neck, and clutching an old-fashioned peaked cotton cap. He had gold-rimmed spectacles, and the air of an absent-minded professor, or an artist from the 1970s, or perhaps the next Doctor Who.

'Ah! Miss Baxter! Hellooo!'

He leapt to his feet as soon as I walked in, and bashed his head on the ceiling lampshade. He was absurdly tall.

'Um … hello?' It came out as more of a question than a greeting.

'Rory Windermere,' he said, holding out his hand. If his top half was 'eccentric gentleman', his bottom half was 'hipster businessman', consisting of designer jeans and bizarrely bling Nikes, which looked like he'd borrowed them from Jay Z and forgotten he was wearing them. 'Pleasure to meet you. I hope you don't mind me popping by. I had one or two things to do at the BRIT School. People to see, you know … So handy it's round the corner from here.'

'Erm, yes,' I said, confused. The BRIT School for the Performing Arts was indeed close by, as attended by Amy Winehouse, Adele, Jessie J and various other famous people. But I didn't go there. I'd never even visited it. What did that have to do with anything?

He saw my face. 'So I happened to be passing, and I offered to come and see you. I … we … have a really very excessive favour to ask.'

'Um, OK,' I said. 'I'm sorry, but who are you?'

He seemed slightly surprised to be asked. 'I manage The Point. I'm sorry, I should have said.'

It took a moment or two for this information to sink in. Assuming this bizarre person wasn't lying, he was either sadly deluded or he was in charge of the world's biggest rock band.

Standing in my front room, with the fringing of the purple lampshade resting on his head.

'Really?'

'Absolutely. Scout's honour.' His face crinkled into a smile. Without another word, he pulled out his phone. (Big, fancy, latest model.) He searched for himself on Wikipedia and showed me his entry. There it was, with a high-definition picture of him standing with his arms around the band. Better than a business card.

'Oh. Wow.'

The smile became a grin. 'Known them since they were fifteen. Best bunch of lads in the world.'

'I think it's my sister you want,' I told him. 'She's the Pointer Sister. I can get her for you, if you like.'

'Thank you, but you're Nina, aren't you?'

'Yes.'

'Then it's you I came to see. Is there somewhere quiet we could talk?'

With no idea, still, why could possibly be here, I did a quick mental tour of the house. The kitchen was full of toddlers, Dad and squashed tomatoes. Here in the front room, Lieutenant Columbo was about to confront the murderer. The back room was too full of toys and ironing to sit down anywhere. Upstairs was … worse.

'This isn't a great place for a conversation,' I admitted.

'Outside somewhere, then? A cafe? A hotel?'

Yeah, right. Like *that* was going to happen. I meet up with rock managers in hotels *all the time*.

*

Fifteen minutes later, we were sitting at a corner table in the restaurant at Ikea. The manager of the biggest band in the world looked slightly stunned to be sitting in a furniture store, which made me want to laugh. He must be used to waiter service and cordon bleu, not Swedish meatballs and a view of the car park. But this was Croydon, not the Soho Hotel, or wherever The Point were currently residing. It was quiet enough for a conversation. And the apple cake was good.

We'd arrived by taxi, leaving the manager's low-slung sports car parked outside our house. I'd decided to bring Ariel with me for moral support, and his car wasn't big enough for three.

Ariel was now staring at us wide-eyed, with the kind of excitement she normally reserved for a new video on the band's YouTube channel. Mr Windermere took a thoughtful sip of coffee, while I dug into my cake.

'This will sound rather odd,' he began.

I nodded. Anything a rock band manager had to say to me in a furniture shop in Croydon was going to sound odd. Literally anything.

His eyes twinkled behind his glasses. 'First of all, I must tell you how grateful we are.'

I blinked. 'For what?'

'For what you did for Miss Santorini. I'm so sorry about the confusion afterwards. Our security team are top notch, but they can be a little ... enthusiastic sometimes.'

'Oh, that. It's OK. My shoulder's better now.'

'You seem like a useful person to have in a crisis.'

'She *is*,' Ariel agreed cheerfully. 'Nina's perfect in a crisis.

32

She's saved Josh's life a million times. And when the twins had this sick bug and pooed everywhere last week, she—'

'I'm sure she was brilliant then too,' the manager interrupted, turning slightly green and pushing his cake away.

'So ... *is* there a crisis?' I asked.

'Not exactly,' he said. 'But Sigrid's latest film project has fallen through. A hazard of showbiz, I'm afraid. So she's decided to accompany the boys on the last few dates of the tour. Paris, Verona, Berlin and so on. We're *delighted* to have her, of course.'

He wasn't – that was obvious. If she went around calling people 'little meet-and-greet fans' all the time, I wasn't surprised.

'And ... me?'

'That's why I'm here. She'd like you to help her. As her assistant. The last girl had to go. Family problems, I believe.' Again, he looked momentarily shifty. 'Sigrid asked specifically for you.'

Across the table, Ariel gasped and raised her hands to her lips. I frowned. A million things about this made no sense. I picked on the first one that came to mind.

'But I hardly know her. We only met for, like, five minutes.'

'As I say, you made a big impression.'

'I don't know anything about being an assistant.'

'It's not rocket science, I promise you. Just managing her diary. Keeping track of her luggage ... There will be plenty of people to show you the ropes and help you out.' He seemed to take it for granted that I would say yes.

'I'm still at school. I have exams,' I pointed out.

Girls like me do not become assistants to Hollywood stars. It's pretty simple. This was obviously a mistake.

'I hope you don't mind, but we checked,' he said. 'Sigrid was really *so* insistent on hiring you. You're doing these AS level things, I gather? And in between, you don't have classes? We can fly you back for the exams if necessary, but we can almost certainly arrange for you to take them wherever we are. I can get supervision for you and that sort of thing.'

He saw the look I was giving him. Really? *Really?* Sigrid Santorini sounded pretty freaky. She had me *checked out?* Who does that? I'm supposed to take my exams in some random country? And she got the *manager* to ask me to work for her? All this so I can help her keep track of her *luggage?*

He met my look with a smile. 'I manage a rock band. A big one. I solve problems bigger than this before breakfast. You haven't been on tour before, I take it?'

'Well, no.' Obviously.

'Try it. It's the opportunity of a lifetime, Nina, I promise you. Take it. You won't regret it.'

His steady, smiling eyes met mine. He was very persuasive. If only what he was asking me to do wasn't quite so ridiculous.

Back at home, after we'd waved him off in his little sports car, Ariel danced me around the front lawn.

'Oh, Neenie,' she squealed, hugging me. 'This is the best thing *ever!* Just think – you'll be on tour with Jamie.'

'I'm not doing it!' I assured her. 'That's *your* dream, Lellie.'

She looked at me pleadingly. 'I know. But if I can't do it, you're the next best thing.'

'There are a million girls who could look after Sigrid better than me.'

34

'But they don't have me as their sister! Please, Nina! Please! You can tell me everything about Jamie – what he wears, what he says, all those cute little things he does all the time. Maybe he can have a nickname for you. That would be so cool. You can check that ...' She paused and chewed at her bottom lip for a moment.

'Check what?'

'That Sigrid's ... really looking after him. I mean, I'm sure she is, but ... I just want to be super-sure. That it's true love, and they're going to be happy for the rest of their lives.'

'Ariel,' I said gently, reaching out to stroke her hair where the blonde met the blue, 'this is not one of Sigrid's rom-coms. I mean, not everyone gets a happy ever after every time.'

'Mum and Dad did.'

Typical, helium-balloon Ariel. Her thoughts floated straight to our parents, who've always been stupidly happy together, and past Aunt Cassie, for example, who had a string of boyfriends who were horrible to her. Past me and the boy next door.

'Mum and Dad were lucky,' I pointed out.

'Jamie must be lucky too,' she said, her eyes ablaze. 'He's changed my life. I need it to be perfect for him.'

Oh boy. I didn't pretend to know the future, but this girl was going to get her heart broken so badly one day. It made mine hurt just thinking about it. First by proxy, when Jamie Maldon messed up his love life, as he inevitably would. (Teenage rock star; engaged way too soon; tragedy inevitable.) Then directly, when some ordinary boy would break it in some ordinary way, because that's what they do.

'Even if I went with the band,' I said, 'I couldn't protect him.'

'I don't want you to. Just keep an eye out for him. Please, Neenie.'

'It's not my decision anyway. Mum and Dad would never let me go.'

Ta-dah!

Why hadn't I thought of that before? I'd been wasting my breath trying to reason with her, when Mum and Dad could simply do it for me. I mean, what parent lets their seventeen-year-old daughter go travelling with a *rock band*?

4

'Over my dead body. I was in a band once myself, don't forget. I know exactly what they get up to. Never in a million years.'

God, I loved Dad.

'You're right, Bill, obviously,' Mum agreed, as she went through work stuff on her laptop, while Dad washed up the twins' tea things.

Yesssss!

I'd saved this conversation until she was home from the salon. I thought it would be kinder if we presented a united front to Ariel: all three of us – not just me.

'Although,' Mum added, looking up from the screen with a mischievous look in her eye, 'as I remember, the way you originally told it, you weren't *in* the Massive Kegs. You just helped them shift their kit around.'

'Well, that's technically true,' Dad agreed sniffily, wiping bubbles on his nose. 'But, you know, we were all in it together.'

'I'm sure you were. Touring Europe. In those little camper vans. I still don't understand how you all fitted in.'

'Neither do I,' Dad said with a nostalgic grin. 'We were all huge. Nobody under six foot two, except Danny on bass, who was about the same height as you, Nina. The Midget, we called him. Midge.'

'Charming.'

'I usually slept on the floor, between the bunks. On a couple of guitar cases. With a Marshall amp for my pillow ...'

'Where did you go?' I asked. Dad had told stories from his roadie days many times, but they usually revolved around technical issues that he had brilliantly fixed, not the bigger picture.

'South of France. Italy. Greece. Croatia. Anywhere with beaches and beer. All those nights we'd sit on the sand dunes, chatting up strapping Danish girls in bikinis, while Dave and Midge played guitar. Those were the—' He caught himself fondly reminiscing, then remembered why we were having this conversation, and stopped short. 'Long time ago,' he muttered. 'Different times. And those Danish girls got up to things I don't want my daughter even thinking about.'

Mum caught my eye and hid a smile. I had a nasty feeling she knew exactly what daughters think about. Whether their dads want them to or not.

'And how old were you again?' she asked, oh-so-casually. I wondered where she was going with this. Something was starting to make my skin prickle, and I wasn't sure why.

'Nineteen ... twenty? I'd just finished my apprenticeship. I met you, what, a year later?'

'That's about right, she said, closing her laptop and looking wistful. 'I planned to go to Morocco with Cassie, remember? She had friends there. It sounded so exotic. Camel trekking in the desert. Shopping in the souk … We had this whole trip organized. But then, well, I met you, and Nina came along. Then Michael. Then Ariel. Which of course I don't regret for a moment. But I never did go to Africa.'

She gazed dreamily out of the window. Nobody said anything. It was becoming increasingly obvious where Mum was going with this. And where she was going was weird.

Dad turned his back on the soapy water, wiped his hands on a tea towel and scratched the back of his neck.

'What are you saying, love? Surely you don't want Nina to …? I mean … surely …?'

Mum looked from Dad to Ariel to me, and took a deep breath.

'You'll think I'm mad. If it was any of my other children, I'd say no. But Nina … well, I wish I *could* worry about you a little, sweetheart. You're the most sensible person I know. Which is lovely, but … you need to get out. You need to breathe.'

'Not surrounded by rock-star love gods!' Dad protested.

'Nina would be fine with rock-star love gods,' Mum retorted. 'She doesn't even find them remotely attractive. Do you, Nina?'

'No,' I shrugged. Which wasn't exactly true. I mean, I'm a straight human female. I found them attractive, obviously. I just didn't obsess about them like my sister.

'She's a sensible girl. And this is a tour we're talking about, not an orgy.'

Dad huffed. 'In the music biz, there's not necessarily much difference.'

'Oh, don't be silly. And she'd get to see Paris. And Berlin. She's always wanted to travel. She's got the same bug as Cassie and me. You got it out of your system, but I didn't. And Cassie …'

Her eyes flicked spontaneously to the picture of two freckled girls in sunhats on a beach, with their arms around each other's shoulders, squinting shyly into the camera. Mum was eleven when it was taken, and Cassie was seven. The same age difference as between Ariel and me. They fought all the time and they were 'as close as Velcro', Mum always said.

'What's that thing with the fish?' she asked, frowning at Dad.

'What?'

'A saying. With a fishy name. Cassie's thing. You know.'

'Cod? Mackerel? Goldfish? Koi?' Dad suggested, looking baffled.

'Carp – that's it. *Carpe diem*. Seize the day, Nina. That's what your aunt used to say. She had it tattooed on her ankle.'

Mum's eyes drifted down to my collarbone, where my 'J' was safely hidden under my shirt, and gave me a kindly smile. She'd never minded about the tattoo as much as I'd expected her to. Maybe it was because Cassie died so soon after, and we had more important things to think about. Then she pushed my fringe out of my eyes with gentle fingers.

'You used to have a sparkle in your eye, my love. I miss it. If this Mr Windermere can sort out your exams, then let him. How glamorous is that? God knows you've revised enough this year.

Go and have some fun. See the sights. Live a little. Find out if there's any Berlin Wall left. Go and see Juliet's balcony in Verona, and tell me if it's incredibly disappointing, like they say it is.'

This was worse than useless. Sometimes I forgot that Mum fell in love with Dad about two weeks after she met him, and was pregnant with me soon after. She was an unpredictable mix of practical and impulsive – never regretting the things she did do, only the ones she didn't. Though getting pregnant with me so young meant there was a stack of things she didn't do.

My last hope for anyone with a grain of common sense was Tammy. To be honest, Tammy and common sense didn't always fit in the same sentence, but surely she would understand how mad this idea sounded? She was 'revising' with her boyfriend that night, but I grabbed her over a coffee in the sixth-form common room the next morning.

'I mean, why did Sigrid pick on me? What schoolgirl's going to skip off during the exam season to go touring with The Point?'

I realized that didn't sound right as soon as it came out of my mouth.

'*Any* schoolgirl!' Tammy exploded, spraying cappuccino everywhere. 'Any single one. Me. Anyone in our year. Are you *crazy*?'

'No. Sigrid Santorini is. Have you seen her on that show?'

'She's mad as a box of frogs,' Tammy conceded, 'but did you get the other bit? She's going *on tour. With The Point*. She wants you to *travel with them*.' She said the last bit very slowly,

41

like she was explaining it to one of the twins.

This was Mum all over again, but louder, and with coffee froth.

'I can't just drop everything. I have exams. Mum needs me to help at home. I have a life!'

Tammy shook her curls at me.

'You don't have a life,' she said. 'You haven't had a life for over a year, Nina Baxter, and you know it.'

'That's not fair!'

'It is, and somebody has to say it. I know you're over Jez, but I keep telling you to get back on the horse again, and you never do.'

'"Getting on the horse again", as you so delicately put it, doesn't have to involve mixing with a bunch of smug rock-star millionaires and their film-star fiancées.'

'You lost me at "millionaires", babe. What better way could there possibly be? I can't believe I'm even having to point this out to you. Go! And if the pressures of fame mean Jamie and Sigrid split up while he's touring … you know … you can invite me over. I can help him overcome his devastating loss. I'm very spiritual that way.'

She did her 'spiritual' face, like a smoky-eyed nun, praying. It made me laugh so hard I started to hiccup.

'You mock me,' she said. 'But believe me, I could comfort that boy. I could *totally* comfort him.'

'I'm sure you could.'

'Oh, speaking of. Here he is.'

'Jamie Maldon?'

'No, idiot. Jez. With Clementine. Act natural.'

'Don't tell them about—'

But before I could finish, my ex and his latest, leggy girl-friend were wandering over to say hello. Since me, Jez had worked his way through half the girls in our year, and some in the year above. Clementine was a showjumping grade-A student who occasionally modelled for her father's sportswear business. They paused in front of us, Jez's arm slung casually around her shoulder.

Tammy bristled all over, like a flame-haired porcupine.

'How's it going?' Jez asked. 'You two look as if you're having fun. Anything you can share?'

'No,' I informed him coldly.

Tammy looked him up and down. She was one of the few girls the boys all lusted after not to have gone out with him. (Out of loyalty to me – even Tammy admitted he was hot.)

'Yeah, actually,' she said. I gave her my don't-go-there glare. But she ignored me. 'Nina's been invited to go touring around Europe. With—'

'Oh, *has* she?' Clementine butted in, with a sickly-sweet smile. 'That's such a coincidence. That's what we're going to do, as soon as the exams are over. Well, not Europe, exactly. Asia. My dad's taking us to Nepal. We're going trekking in the Himalayas, then visiting a wildlife reserve in the jungle ... We might even get to Bhutan. It was all Jez's idea.'

Oh, *was* it? My chest felt tight. The Himalayas? *Really*? Bhutan? He wasn't so keen three years ago. He'd changed his tune now.

'Yeah, we're in luck,' Jez grinned. 'Clem's dad's sold his company, so he's taking the whole family. We're going on an elephant safari and we might even get to work with some of the animals in the reserve.'

'Nepal's so cool,' Clementine chimed in, wrapping a possessive arm around his waist. 'And it'll help with our applications to vet school. They're *so* competitive.'

Her smile was the perfect combination of smugness and pity. She knew I'd crashed my GCSEs after the last break-up.

'Oh, so you're going on holiday with your dad. How *lovely*,' Tammy deadpanned. She paused for a beat. 'Nina's going on tour with The Point.'

Silence. Perfect silence. Every conversation in the room seemed to stop. Clementine gawped at me. Suddenly, the Himalayas didn't seem quite so tall.

'As in the band?' Jez asked, eventually.

'No, the breakfast cereal. Of course the band,' Tammy snapped.

'But … I didn't think … you liked them,' he said, staring at me.

He'd taken no interest in me for months. How would he even know?

Tammy nudged me.

'Big fan,' I said, looking him squarely in the eye. '*Love* them.'

'We saw them at the O_2, of course,' Clementine announced, recovering her composure. 'Dad managed to get us front-row seats. We were so close we could nearly touch them. How many shows are you going to?'

'I don't think you get it,' Tammy said, cutting across me. 'Nina's not going to see the band, she's travelling with them. In their entourage. She'll be touching them every day, I imagine.'

'But how—?'

'She saved the life of Jamie's fiancée,' Tammy said airily. 'Didn't you hear? You know what Nina's like. They want her to start as soon as possible, so she might have to fly back for exams. It'll be *such a bore*.' She flicked a superior glance at Clementine, who was doing a reasonable impression of a goldfish. Or possibly a carp.

By now, four more sixth-formers had clustered around to listen, and others were heading over. For once, they were looking at me with curiosity, not pity. I began to imagine Nina Baxter 2.0. I could be 'the girl who went to Paris with The Point', not 'the girl who went to pieces'. I'd no longer be defined by Trek Boy, and that moment couldn't come too soon. I'd moved on ages ago, but nobody had noticed.

'It's the opportunity of a lifetime,' I quoted. Oh my God. I was actually doing this.

Tammy's face was one big, satisfied smile.

'*You win*,' I mouthed to her when nobody was looking.

Her smile grew wider. '*I know.*'

5

Tricky issue: now I somehow had to persuade Dad to let me go.

'I'll sort it out,' Rory Windermere said when I called him.

'I don't think it'll be as easy as that,' I warned him. 'Dad's been in a band. He knows what it's like. And he seems to think I'll be in …' *Danger*, I wanted to say. But it sounded so ridiculous.

'Over your head?' the manager suggested. 'Don't worry. You won't be. And they'll look after you, trust me.'

Meanwhile, I looked up the details of the *Right On Target* tour. So far this year, The Point had already visited Australia, New Zealand, the Philippines and Japan, and most of the major stadiums in the UK. Before that, they'd travelled around South America and done dozens of gigs across the States. They'd been on the move for about two years, it seemed.

At the moment, they were in Scandinavia and they still had a month of other European dates to do. Lisbon, Barcelona, Paris, then Switzerland ... As Rory Windermere had mentioned, they were even heading back across the Atlantic for one night only, to perform at Madison Square Garden in New York. Apparently, it was their favourite venue, and they'd take any opportunity they could to play it. The more I researched, the more travelling with them didn't seem like such a bad idea after all.

Dad got an email from a man called Steve Grange, who was The Point's tour manager, in charge of all the logistics while they travelled the world. He assured Dad that I'd be looked after. I'd travel with the band, not the crew. Sigrid didn't drink, and would make sure I didn't either. Everything I needed would be provided for.

Steve described the tour itself and it sounded nothing like the Massive Kegs and the camper van. The Point visited capital cities and stayed in the best hotels. For as long as I could remember, I'd wanted to get out of Croydon and see the world. What better chance would there ever be? True, it wasn't the Himalayas, but it was *Paris, New York, Berlin* ... I pictured myself ordering *frites* in French cafes, and finally seeing the wonders of the Metropolitan Museum. Mum said I'd got my sparkle back, and though it was the cheesiest line I'd ever heard, I kind of knew what she was getting at.

'All right,' Dad sighed, finally broken. 'If you really want to, you can go.'

'What would you have done?' I asked. 'If you were me?'

'I'd be there now,' he admitted, his lips twitching. 'I'd have sneaked out and joined the tour the first minute I could. What – miss a chance like that?' He shook his head. 'D'you think I'm mad?'

It was arranged that I'd join the band in Barcelona, after my art exam. Ariel hugged me tight in the hallway as Dad waited to take me to the airport. She looked up at me with mournful eyes.

'You'll be gentle with Jamie, won't you?'

'Lellie! I doubt I'll even get close to him!'

She ignored my protests. 'He's had a really hard life, you know? His dad left home when he was young and his mum was an addict. He had to look after her when he was growing up. It's why he doesn't drink or do drugs. Nor does Angus. He looks like he's got it all, but he's really vulnerable inside.'

'Vulnerable. Got it.'

'And Angus's dark moods are just an act. You should see the way he smiles … but he's had a tough time too. His dad … well, I don't know the details, but Angus doesn't like to talk about it, so that's got to be bad, right? And he's just split up from his girl-friend. It was painful.'

'You want me to be gentle with him as well?'

She nodded seriously. I promised I would be gentle with the *world-famous rock stars with film-star fiancées and millions of screaming fans*, and Ariel thanked me with zero sense of irony.

'What about Connor?' I asked. 'More family problems?'

'No-o,' she admitted. 'He's had a really happy life. He grew up in a big house with his brother and sister. But everyone knows he's a bit sensitive about his bass playing. I mean, he's *brilliant*, but he seems to think he's not the best ever. So be nice to him, OK?'

Again, I promised not to damage the confidence of one of the richest, best-looking, supermodel-dating boys on the planet.

'And George?'

'Isn't he lovely?' she sighed. 'He's got this really sweet girl-friend called Kelly in Texas, and he talks about her all the time. He looks manic, but he's just so adorable.'

'Adorable. Got it.'

She was starting to sense that I wasn't entirely taking this seriously.

'Look after them, Neenie. Promise me.'

'All right. I promise.'

Tammy had come over to say goodbye.

'I just want you to know that I am completely jealous,' she said, fishing something out of her bag. 'And I will never speak to you again.'

'Thanks, Tam.'

'I got you this.'

She handed me a journal. It was bigger than average – more of a scrapbook size, really – and she'd personalized the cover with a collage of cut-out pictures of The Point, with Sigrid's face beaming beatifically from the middle.

'Hmm. Tasteful.'

'I thought you'd like it,' she grinned. 'I worked on it all last night. You can use it to write down all your deep and meaning-ful thoughts about Jamie.'

'I promise that if I have any, this is exactly where they're going.'

For once, Tammy looked serious. She threw her arms around me and hugged me as tightly as I'd let her.

'They're lucky to have you,' she murmured into my hair.

Yeah. Something like that.

'We'd better go,' Dad said gruffly. 'Don't want to miss that flight.'

Despite what he'd said before, I think he might have been very happy if the plane had gone without me. He dropped me off at the airport with the grizzled air of a man who, without knowing quite how it happened, has agreed to let his daughter play in the lions' cage at the zoo.

'If anything happens, call me,' he instructed, checking for the tenth time that my suitcase was safely on its way into the baggage system, and my passport was in my hand. 'Me, or the police. Or both. Just ... call me. OK? Promise?'

'I promise.'

'If anyone tries to—'

'They won't, Dad.'

'They're boys. They will.'

'I've seen some of their girlfriends. They won't.'

He shook his head and hugged me.

'Your mother is a sucker for adventure. She hasn't had any, so she doesn't know how dangerous they are.'

I laughed. 'I know, Dad. You need to watch out for her.'

'I will.' His mouth turned down at the corners. 'I'd watch out for you too, but ... little girls grow up.'

'I'm not getting married. I'm just doing a temporary PA job.'

'And you'll do it brilliantly. You're the reliable one, Nina. You always were. But if anyone—'

'Like I said, they won't. I'm going now.'

I gave him a kiss and walked off to passport control. If I didn't hurry, I really would miss that plane.

6

By the time I landed in Barcelona, it was already early evening. A driver was waiting for me, with my name hand-written on a cardboard sign, and soon we were heading for the venue in a luxury BMW. It was out of town, so I didn't get to see any landmarks, but I loved seeing the ads at the side of the road, with their strange Spanish accents and upside-down exclamation marks.

We pulled up in a special car park, near to the artists' entrance. Rows and rows of dark, shiny tour buses gleamed under the lights. I checked the time: the band had started a while ago. It looked as though I'd miss at least the first half of the concert – but that didn't matter. There would be plenty more to see.

At the security desk inside, I waited for a long time while the guards phoned around to find out if anyone had any idea who I was, or what to do with me. Meanwhile, the boys were launching into another song, and the whole place seemed to throb with their music. The distant, distorted beat pulsed through me, and the sense of excitement everywhere was palpable – even among the backstage staff, rushing around behind the scenes. I could have been at home, I thought, revising for English. Why had I ever thought that was a good idea? How could I possibly have imagined *that* could be better than this?

Eventually, a stressed-looking young man showed up, dressed in the typical black, casual outfit of the band's entourage, and clutching a two-way radio.

He held out his hand. 'Hi. I'm Oliver. I work for Steve. You must be Nina. You look …'

His brow furrowed as he looked me up and down. I wondered what the problem was. My outfit? I was dressed in black from head to toe, like him, as Dad told me that was what staff wore backstage, so they remained invisible. My hair? Had my face gone puffy after the flight?'

'… younger than I expected.'

'Oh. I'm seventeen.'

The furrows deepened. 'And you've done this kind of thing before?'

'Absolutely not. Nothing like it. Sorry.'

'OK, fine,' he sighed, sagging slightly. 'Let's hope there's method in her madness. I don't have time to babysit, so ask if you've got a problem, but once I tell you how to fix it, you're on your own.'

I nodded dumbly. It wasn't the world's best welcome, but I liked the idea of knowing at least one person who could fix things.

'Have you got your pass yet?' he asked.

I shook my head. He sighed and said something to the guards. Eventually they handed over two of them, with lanyards attached, and gave me a special wristband for good measure. One pass was black, the other red. The guards seemed surprised that I needed the red one, and Oliver had to show them an email from Steve to prove it.

As soon as I was ready, he took my case for me and hurried me down miles of corridors, past stacks of equipment and busy roadies, and several layers of security – all of whom double-checked my red pass as if they couldn't quite believe I was wearing it.

'Look after that,' he said, noticing me staring down at it as it dangled in front of my chest. 'It's Access All Areas. It takes you right inside the dressing room. Only about ten people have this, but Sigrid insisted one of them was you.'

We finally reached an area marked 'BAND – NO ENTRY' and Oliver led me to a door flanked by two enormous body-guards, also dressed in black. They stared at me impassively.

'This is Paul and this is Ian,' Oliver said. 'Be nice to them. They control who gets close to the boys. They like me, because I feed them chocolate. But they can be terrifying when roused.'

He didn't need to remind me. Ian was the same bodyguard who had slammed me to the floor a couple of weeks ago. He frowned at me for a second, as if I looked familiar but he couldn't place me. I decided not to bring it up – it wasn't exactly one of my favourite moments.

'Is she still in there?' Oliver asked.

Ian nodded.

By now, the distorted roar of the music was immense. We couldn't be far from the stage. Ian opened the door behind him.

I didn't quite know what I'd expected (possibly the Tardis, crossed with Rio at Carnival – I had no idea), but it wasn't this – a large, messy room that reminded me a bit of the sixth-form common room, but with less comfortable furniture. It smelt of hairspray, talc, stale food and decades of smelly feet, overlaid with expensive but inadequate room spray. It was scattered with clothes and abandoned plates of food.

Oliver rushed me through it and knocked on a further door at the back. Sigrid appeared in the doorway, in a towelling robe, with her hand to her head. Even with her hair in rollers, with no make-up on, she looked heart-stoppingly beautiful. She glanced from Oliver to me, and practically shouted.

'HOW BIG IS THE POOL? IS IT INFINITY? Well, can they *make* it infinity? And can you see the ocean from it? How far away did you say Jennifer's place was? No, the other one.'

'Gotta go,' Oliver whispered to me. 'I'm needed elsewhere. I'll leave you in her capable hands.'

Looking at Sigrid more closely, I spotted the phone she was holding, tucked next to her ear under one of the rollers. I stood facing her, uncertain what to do, while she carried on talking.

'Send me the details on that one, and the one with the video mirrors in the closets … I totally need those for ass views. ASS views. I can hardly hear you – the reception's *lousy*. Love you, Stan. Talk later. *Ciao ciao.*'

She peered at me in polite confusion.

'Can I help you?'

'It's Nina,' I said. 'Your new assistant. From London.'

It took another second to sink in, but when it did her whole demeanour changed. Her face lit up. 'Oh! Nina! From *Croydon*! Hi, sweetie! I've got so much for you to do!'

She motioned me inside. This room was much smaller than the last, and contained not much more than a mirror, a cupboard and a couple of chairs. As the strains of 'Unlock Me' came over the PA system, I wondered how far the boys were through the set.

'It's lucky you caught me,' Sigrid smiled, sitting at the mirror. 'If it wasn't for my realtor calling, I'd be out there already.'

'Have you missed most of the show?' I asked, concerned.

'No biggie,' she said, examining her face critically in the mirror. 'I know the songs by now. I'll catch the end of it.' She flicked her fingers as if to say The Point's back catalogue could get boring after a while. I imagined Ariel's outrage if she knew.

Over the next three numbers, I watched in the mirror as Sigrid expertly did her hair and make-up, transforming her face from natural, unadorned beauty to cover-ready perfection.

'Bring me that dress,' she instructed, pointing to a doll-sized micro-mini hanging on a cupboard door.

I held it out to her and she stripped to her knickers. (If there is a boss/new employee version of too much information, this was it.) She took the dress from me and wriggled into it.

'Zip.'

She held up her hair as I dutifully zipped up the dress at the back. It looked if it had been sprayed on to her.

'You'll have to do my shoes,' she added, pointing to a pair of strappy sandals on the floor.

For a moment, I was confused. The sandals were right

beside her. Then, as she lifted one foot a few centimetres, I realized that she wanted me to put them on for her. The dress was so tight she couldn't bend over. I knelt down and buckled the straps to her satisfaction. It felt a bit ridiculous, but also very easy. If this was the kind of thing she wanted from an assistant, anyone could do it. I still didn't really get why she'd asked for me.

As she put on a bright beaded necklace, she gave me a businesslike look.

'I got Pamela to make a spreadsheet of duties for the new girl. It's somewhere on my phone. You can find it and email it to yourself. For now, just stick by me and carry my bag. Oh, and since Pamela left I've had, like, a million emails. Why don't we start now? Like I always say, there's no time like the present.' She handed me her luxury phone in its crystal-encrusted case and told me her PIN number. 'Save the ones I need to see and delete the junk, OK? If they're fans, I always reply. Tell them their message means the world to me.'

Next thing I knew, I 'was' Sigrid Santorini online. Wow she had a lot of haters. Mostly people accusing her of boyfriend-stealing (Jamie wasn't the first who'd been going out with someone else when they met), or breaking up The Point. I could see that blocking them alone could be practically a full-time activity.

Over a speaker in the ceiling, the band were playing 'Eden'. I shuddered. My break-up song. Sigrid cocked her head and listened as Jamie's voice floated over the sound of the guitars.

'Time to go. Jamie likes me to be there for this one. I have a little spot near the speaker stacks. It's so cool.' She headed for the door and I went to follow her, but she shook her head. 'You stay here – you're so busy. I'll see you later, OK?'

She left before I could reply.

Oh. OK. So I wasn't going to see the band tonight, which was a shame. I'd been hoping to catch a song or two and tell Ariel about it. However, Sigrid was right: she'd left me with a lot of work to do.

Delete. Delete. Delete. Delete.

> Thank you for your kind words. Your message
> means the world to me.

Was this how Jamie wrote to my sister? Via some intern in an abandoned dressing room? No wonder he didn't remember her.

With my head buried in the internet, I hardly noticed the time go by. Over the PA system I heard screams, then an encore and more screaming. I didn't think much about it until there was a sound like thunder in the room next door and I realized it was filling up with people.

The show was over, and I was sitting in a part of their dressing room. My heart raced.

I was about to get up close and personal with The Point.

7

I took a minute or two to finish the task I was doing. I didn't even bother to try and kid myself – I was stalling for time. The band were *right there*, through that door, and I was about to meet them. I hadn't thought this through. I wasn't ready. I remembered how weird it had felt last time, and then I was just holding a camera. Now I was part of the team.

But I wouldn't be for much longer if I spent my time hiding like this. So I slipped Sigrid's phone into her big leather tote bag, hooked it over my arm, took a deep breath, ran my hands through my hair, checked in the mirror that my eye make-up hadn't smudged (it had – I corrected it), took *another* deep breath, and opened the door.

To a noisy group of people I didn't recognize.

Perhaps I'd misunderstood. Maybe this was a meet-and-greet room, or something, and the band were somewhere else. I felt my heartbeat slow slightly.

And then I caught a glimpse of Connor, the bassist, checking his bleached blond hairstyle in the mirror. George the drummer was sharing a joke with a couple of people who looked vaguely famous, while he glugged champagne straight from the bottle.

Nearby me, Angus, the dark-haired guitarist, was ... undressing.

His skinny frame showed off a set of surprisingly sculpted abs under the sweaty T-shirt he was throwing to the floor. As he stretched up, the tattoo of a snake that wound itself around his right bicep seemed to move like a living creature. He caught my eye and muttered something I couldn't hear above the excited noises in the room. I assumed he was introducing himself.

'I'm Nina,' I said loudly, holding out my hand to shake his. 'Hi.' I tried to look like the kind of girl who meets rock stars every day.

He frowned at me for a moment, then flicked his eyes to the wall behind me.

'Tow-el,' his lips mouthed, slowly.

I turned round. I was standing next to a stack of them. Mortified, I handed him one. He took it without giving me a second glance. The heat from my face would have powered this arena for several minutes. I tried to take my mind off it, and Angus's nearby, naked torso, by focusing on the men that George was talking to. I knew I'd seen them before somewhere.

Oh yes. They were two of Spain's biggest footballers. Tammy had posters of them in her room. If anything, they were hotter than Angus. Or possibly not. This wasn't helping. I was getting very confused.

It was a massive relief when another door opened at the back of the room and Jamie and Sigrid emerged together. She was adjusting a silk scarf around his neck. He'd changed into one of his loose shirts and several colourful beaded bracelets, matching the necklace that Sigrid wore. It wasn't as drop-dead cool as the ripped-jeans-and-school-shirt combos he used to wear in the early days, but he carried it off. To be fair, a boy with that smile could carry off anything.

I was nervous that I hadn't seen the show and had nothing to say, but as they passed by there was a faraway look in his eye and he didn't seem to see me anyway. Sigrid threw me a vague smile, the main door opened, and a moment later they were swallowed by the eager crowd outside. I looked down at the tote bag I was holding for her, with her phone and all her personal stuff in it.

Oh.

For now I had one job: *Stick by me and carry my bag.* Not as easy as it looked. I followed her as best I could, muscling my way through the crowd that now filled the corridor, flashing my red pass at anyone who tried to stop me.

Luckily, they weren't too far ahead. Jamie's progress was slowed down by the endless excited fans and VIPs, eager to hug and kiss him and take a selfie. He was like the still point in a perfect storm.

It was strange to see the world from an almost-Jamie perspective. All the faces around him were extremely happy, extremely excited, extremely in love. Extreme. And everyone seemed to want a picture of their face next to his. His view must be a constant sea of phone screens, capturing every moment of his life for eternity. I would *hate* to be Jamie Maldon. One day, maybe, I'd ask him how he coped.

Sigrid, on the other hand, beamed with happiness, posing for every selfie she could. It took a while before I could attract her attention.

'I have your bag,' I said, panting slightly from the effort of getting through to her. 'Do you want me to hold on to it?'

She barely glanced at me. 'Uh huh.' Then she turned back to Jamie and left me to follow in their wake.

The rest of the night passed by in a blur.

Suddenly remembering my own suitcase, and rushing back to find it, before it was too late ...

Losing Sigrid and Jamie as they got a golf cart without me and were whisked to a waiting limo ...

Sitting in a following car, arranged by Oliver, alongside a PR girl called Jess, who was kind, and three glamorous VIP girls, with perfect hair and perfect nails, who gave us both the evil eye the whole way.

'You get used to it,' Jess whispered. 'They're just jealous of our jobs. Don't take it personally.'

I tried not to.

Not getting into the nightclub with Jess, because the bouncers wouldn't let me. Handing the precious bag to this person I'd just met with a plea to pass it to Sigrid as soon as she could, and a vague sense of doom ...

Taking the car back to the band's hotel. Luckily the driver knew where to go, because I had no idea.

Getting close to the hotel was a memory that would stay with me, despite the blur. The streets became more and more crowded and the car had to slow down until it was only just crawling along. There were girls everywhere, holding signs saying 'KISS ME JAMIE!' and 'TE AMO CONNOR'. Girls with blue hair and glittery T-shirts, chanting in the night air. Girls like my sister. The loyal band of Pointer Sisters never changed.

I checked in at the reception desk and crawled up to the little room they gave me. It was small, dark and poky, and as far from the main areas as it seemed possible to get. The view through the tiny window was of other tiny windows, surrounded by noisy pipes.

All the time, the image was imprinted in my mind of Angus saying 'Tow-el'. So far, it was the only word The Point had collectively spoken to me. And even then, the moment had been an epic fail.

When it came to telling Clementine and the other people in our year about my amazing tour experience, I probably wouldn't start with tonight.

8

The next morning, I met with Oliver in the hotel lobby at seven, as arranged. In the mirrored lift up to the band's floor, he gave me another pass to wear.

'This is for the Hotel California.'

'Is that where we're going later?' I asked. 'I thought that was the Ritz.'

He shook his head. 'It's what the band call their base wherever they go,' he said. 'After the Eagles song. D'you know it? The one about checking out any time you like, but never leaving? Band joke.' The lift doors opened and we stepped out. 'Anyway, right now it's this corridor. Easy to guard. Hard for the paps and the girls to get into – unless invited. Although goodness knows they try.'

Ahead of us stood two more enormous bodyguards, who looked a bit like Ian and Paul, but marginally less friendly. They smiled when they saw Oliver, though, and stood aside to let us pass.

'Angus is *there* …' Oliver indicated, passing one door. 'That's George. Wardrobe *there*. Connor *here*. And Jamie's … this one.' He stopped at the last door and knocked. Oliver seemed to spend a lot of his life knocking. 'Good luck.'

His two-way radio crackled into life. He walked off quickly, holding it to his ear with one hand and waving me a brief good-bye with the other.

Once again, it was Sigrid who opened the door. Today, she was wearing tight white yoga pants and a tiny crop top. It was the kind of look that would only work on a size zero body, and she had one. She didn't exactly smile at me, but she didn't frown either.

'Good morning. I hope you slept well,' I said. Was this the way assistants talked? I had no idea.

'I always do,' she said airily. 'I'm so blessed.'

She stood aside and I walked into one of the most beautiful rooms I've seen in my life. Brightly coloured sofas faced each other across a wide expanse of floor. Pale walls were covered in modern art. Beyond it all was a wall of windows opening on to a full-length terrace, bathed in the rays of the morning sun.

'I'm sorry about your bag,' I said, thinking back to my last hectic hours yesterday.

'Was there a problem? You fixed it, right?'

There was a beady look in Sigrid's eye and a sudden edge to her voice. But I spotted the tote bag sitting on a nearby desk.

'Um, yes. I did.'

Jess must have delivered it, just as I'd asked. Relief flooded through me, making me feel light-headed.

Sigrid's Zen serenity returned. She flicked a hand in the direction of a door behind the dining area. 'Why don't you make me a green tea while I finish meditating? The kitchen's over there.'

Last night, I'd sleepily studied the spreadsheet of duties that Pamela had prepared. It ran to ninety-seven lines, and the correct preparation of green tea was line four. Moroccan mint, brewed for ninety seconds. When I took the cup through to her, she was sitting in the lotus position near the terrace window.

'Mmm. Good,' she said, tasting it and raising her eyebrows in mild surprise. She didn't seem to expect me to have mastered the spreadsheet so fast. 'Better than Pamela's, actually.'

'Thank you.'

She saw me staring at the strange contraption she was sitting under. It was a rickety-looking structure made of bamboo poles, with a white canopy draped over the top.

'This is the peace tent,' she explained. 'It keeps me *present*, you know? Jamie needs it to realign his chakras. He's so *stressed*. Oh, hi, baby!' She switched on her Hollywood smile. 'Isn't it a beautiful day?'

A sleepy-looking Jamie Maldon ambled into the room through the bedroom door, rubbing a hand through his ruffled hair. He was wearing an open hotel bathrobe, boxer shorts and a necklace with a small gold circle on it. His face looked grey and tired.

Beneath the robe, his body was pale and skinny, but there was a thin layer of muscle on his chest. I wondered for a moment if he worked out, or got all his exercise from running around onstage. Then it hit me: *I am staring at the semi-naked*

65

body of Jamie Maldon. *If my sister were here right now, she would faint.*

He stopped in his tracks and peered at me.

'Who's this?' he demanded.

'My assistant, baby,' Sigrid said, smiling sweetly.

He stared at me, confused. 'I thought we got rid of Pamela.'

'This isn't Pamela, it's Nina. Remember? The blanket girl.'

It wasn't a blanket – I'd used a tablecloth to rescue her – but whatever.

'From the fire in London? You *hired* her?'

'Of course. We talked about it, remember?'

'I thought you meant you'd get her in LA. Everyone has an assistant in LA ...' He put a hand to his forehead, as if just the thought of me gave him a headache.

So, this was going well. I smiled politely and said nothing. I got the impression that even a 'Good morning' from me would only make things worse. His chakras clearly needed more realigning.

'Hey, baby,' Sigrid cooed, undoing herself from the lotus position, walking over to him and laughing, 'I need an assistant *everywhere*. Just while things are so crazy. Not when it's just us, when all this is over. Then it'll just be you and me.'

She put her arms round his neck and drew his head down to hers so they were almost kissing. Her fingers wove themselves through his hair. I imagined for a moment what that would be like ... then I stopped. And wished I could magic myself out of this room. There are some places an assistant shouldn't be.

I closed my eyes for a moment. *So, grandkids – the first thing I did to Jamie Maldon was give him a headache. Yes, the moment was that awesome.*

Luckily, they were interrupted by another knock at the door, and Jamie was taken off to get ready. The Hotel California had a separate suite reserved for wardrobe, hair and make-up. I thought Sigrid was fancy to have her own assistant, but Jamie basically had a whole team. The boy didn't even brush his own hair.

Sigrid went off to the bedroom to get changed, and I focused on making her breakfast, or 'fixing' it, in Sigrid-speak. The instructions ran to several lines of Pamela's spreadsheet and I'd stared at them so often last night, marvelling at their weirdness, that I'd memorized them like a poem.

Egg white omelette, served on fresh spinach leaves
(washed in spring water);
Green juice with goji berries
(see special juicer);
eleven almonds on a plate, arranged in a karmic pattern
(see diagram)

Feeling like a cross between Mary Berry and Picasso, I ordered the omelette and green juice ingredients from room service and tracked down the nuts and berries to some large, unsightly catering bags that Sigrid also travelled with. I was just arranging the almonds in their pattern when there was a loud hammering at the door.

Instead of the room-service waiter I was expecting, a figure slumped against the doorway, staring at me with bloodshot eyes from under a frizzy mop of dirty hair. His greenish face clashed with his brown-and-yellow Simpsons pyjamas. His feet were bare.

''S Jamie here?'

'Um, hello, George.'

The drummer's breath smelt exactly like the alley behind the Three Crowns pub at home: stale beer and cigarettes, and the heady whiff of rubbish bins. I took a step back and he took this as an invitation to come inside.

'Jamie? Jamie, mate?' he called plaintively, pushing his way past me and staring around. 'I need to talk about Kelly. Where are you?'

'Jamie's not here,' Sigrid said crossly, emerging from the bedroom. By now she was wearing powder-blue lace-trimmed shorts that skimmed her thighs, with just enough make-up to look as if she wasn't wearing any. 'This is my personal energy space. Get out! You're so gross, you know that?'

'Where is 'e?' George repeated, ignoring the look of repugnance on Sigrid's face. 'I've got to show him something.' He waved his phone around vaguely and looked as if he might fall over.

'He's in wardrobe,' Sigrid snapped crossly. 'Where you were supposed to be twenty minutes ago. Take a shower. Get a shave. We're due in Paris by noon, and you're a mess.'

The theme tune to *Backstage with Sigrid* sounded in the bedroom, and she headed off to answer her phone.

'Get rid of him, Nina,' she called out behind her. 'Give him to security. They know what to do.'

George stared after her, then down at the screen in his

hand. In Ariel's endless posters of the band, his muscles rippled under the sleeveless vests he wore. On video, he always looked like the one most likely to bite the head off a bat. Right now, he looked as if he might cry.

'Is there a problem?' I asked, glancing nervously at the bedroom door closing behind Sigrid. I couldn't throw him out in this state.

He looked at me dumbly for a moment, then held his phone out towards me.

'Kelly changed her status. To single, man. Last night. And look at the pictures. She's there with that guy from two days ago. He's got his hand near her waist, see? I was supposed to call her but things got a little crazy and ...' His voice wavered. Tears risked spilling down his cheeks at any moment. 'It's like, everyone's saying it's over, and she's not taking my calls now. What do I do?'

The drummer of The Point was crying in front of me. This was not how I pictured life with a rock band. I took the phone from him and scrolled through several pictures to see what he was talking about.

A very attractive red-headed girl was posing in what seemed to be a bar, surrounded by a group of young men in suits, one of whom may or may not have been touching her waist. It was hard to tell if this was a gesture of affection, or lust, or sheer accident. The strange thing was, this kind of impossible analysis of blurry photos was exactly what happened in the sixth-form common room every day. The situation was oddly familiar.

'Who's saying it's over?' I asked.

'Like, a million people on Twitter. And some showbiz blogs. And I just got woken up by this journo who somehow got my number, asking questions.'

Oh. Not so familiar.

But I know about break-ups. Hopeless at my own, but good with other people's. Tammy and I have talked about enough of them over the years.

'Don't listen to them,' I said, picturing Tammy at my shoulder, nodding, like she did at school. 'Talk to Kelly. Don't assume anything until you know what she's really thinking.'

'But why did she—?'

'Ask her. And tell her how you feel. Don't trust the internet, George. What do they know?'

'Yeah,' he sniffed, taking his phone back. 'They're wrong about most of the stuff, most of the time. Thanks ... whoever you are.'

'Nina.'

He nodded, but he wasn't listening. His attention was already back on the photos. I felt sorry for him. Long-distance relationships don't work – everybody knows that. I was starting to understand why Sigrid felt it so necessary to stick to Jamie like glue.

'Are you still here?' she called out crossly, re-emerging from the bedroom, eyes blazing. 'I thought I told you to go. Leave poor Nina alone. She doesn't need your dramas.'

George threw her a filthy look and shambled towards the door. 'They're not all *my* dramas, mate,' he muttered under his breath.

I stifled a smile. 'Good luck,' I whispered.

He nodded and disappeared.

'Oh my lord, that boy!' Sigrid groaned, as soon as the door closed behind him. 'He's a walking disaster.'

'I thought they didn't drink,' I said, feeling like an idiot. Just because my sister was an expert on the band, it didn't mean everything she thought she knew was true.

'They don't,' she said. 'Mostly. Angus and Jamie grew up with addiction. They've seen where it goes. But George ... since he turned twenty-one, he drinks by the bottle. Whisky, champagne, you name it. It's so skeezy. Jamie hates it. It's one of the things we have in common.' She put her hands into a prayer position. 'We're very pure.'

Pure, maybe, but not very kind. And the kind of 'pure' it takes a whole team of people to produce. With perfect timing, a room-service waiter arrived with Sigrid's egg-white omelette, accompanied by some toast for me. I hoped she expected me to eat too at some stage, though she hadn't mentioned it. I served her meal with the nuts and juice, and she beamed at me gratefully.

'Well, aren't you *perfect*, Nina? I knew I got the right girl when I hired you. Come talk to me while I eat. Tell me about your family.'

I brought my toast to the table. As we ate, she quizzed me about everyone and everything back home, from the size of our house to Pip and Lara's favourite sayings. I had no idea she'd be so interested. Sigrid was one of those people, I was starting to realize, who only had friends and enemies – nobody in between. As I explained about Mum taking in the twins after Cassie died, I was thankful that I counted as a friend, but I shuddered for anyone Sigrid considered as an enemy.

9

Ninety minutes later, we were flying to Paris.

In my head, I was busy telling half the sixth form, *I AM ON A PRIVATE JET WITH THE POINT AND THIS IS REALLY HAPPENING.* It was a shame about all the confidentiality agreements I'd signed, saying I couldn't talk about it. Because nobody else here seemed to have noticed how amazing the experience was.

Nearby me, Angus was recovering from an argument he'd had with Jamie at the airport. I'd been waiting with them in the ultra-VIP lounge while Sigrid redid her barely-there make-up in the ladies' room.

'Listen, you remember Digger V?' Angus said to Jamie, innocently enough. 'That producer I met in Miami? He's just sent me some of his new stuff. It'll blow your mind. He's said we can have a couple of songs if we want them. I said yes.'

'You said what?' Jamie asked, in a low, dangerous growl.

'I said we'd record them. God knows, we need something new. Windy keeps bugging us about it.'

'You said we'd record them? Just like that? Without asking me?'

'Oh, so I'm supposed to go to you every time I want to do something, am I?'

'That was the general idea,' Jamie snarled. 'We always said we were a band, not a photo opportunity. We write our own songs, remember? We do it *our* way. We don't just cover other people's pap.'

'Pap? What d'you know about pap? Have you listened to Digger recently? He's a genius. But then, how would you even know? You're so busy snuggling up to *Sisi*. When did you last write a decent song, anyway?'

'When did you last listen to one? If you want to be a rap star, go ahead. I'm sure Kanye's quaking in his Yeezys.'

Jamie's lips curled with contempt and he'd walked off without another word, leaving Angus pale and shaking. Now, he was hunched in his seat on the jet with a tablet in his hands, moodily playing some shooter game. Jamie was sitting as far away from him as possible, listening to music on his headphones, looking sullen and remote. George had asked me to sit next to him, and been told off by Sigrid for talking to me. After a few sips of something hidden in a paper bag, he was comatose.

Connor was the only one who seemed truly happy. He spent the flight on his phone, checking out whether the band's arrival was trending in France yet (it was), and telling everyone else what the fans were saying about it. Oh, private jets have Wi-Fi.

That is now something I know.

Having missed all the excitement earlier, Sigrid might as well have been at a business meeting. She sat opposite me at a polished wooden table, poised and perfect, giving me a list of California-based wedding planners she wanted me to contact.

'Also, there are some designers I want to try out in Paris. Have them send something round. If they ask, say I'll give them photo credit – that usually works. Oh that reminds me: I'm going to need new pictures for my Instagram. Do some of me – show me them first – but also my lifestyle. You know, like the view through that window. What's in my closet ... or sunsets. Check out what Pamela did. She was good at sunsets. Don't take pictures of the boys, though. Jamie doesn't like it.' She smiled indulgently at her fiancé, alone on the far side of the cabin. 'He has this privacy thing. He's so shy, it's adorable.'

All the time she talked, Angus glared at us from across the aisle. He'd given up playing his game to listen to our conversation. Jamie seemed to want to ignore my existence, but Angus had definitely noticed me. On the way up the steps, seeing my arms full of Sigrid's carry-on bags, he'd given me his own to look after. Nice. I couldn't help noticing him too, though. Today, there was a skull picked out in tiny, glimmering crystals on his black T-shirted chest. His face had its usual sour expression, but my eyes fell on his right arm, with its snake tattoo. It was more muscled than I expected, like his abs last night.

He caught me staring and his lip curled as I flushed to the roots of my hair.

Stop noticing the hotness of the band, Nina. Step away from the hotness of the band.

74

I tried to focus instead on whatever was going on between Angus and Jamie. Something had definitely gone wrong between them. I had a sense that 'something' liked green tea and employed me. Which was probably the reason Angus obviously didn't like me. Apart from the fact that I didn't seem to understand the word 'towel', and I was taking up valuable jet space that could have been used by a modelicious groupie.

'Nina's so *fascinating*,' Sigrid said, turning to him with a flirtatious smile, as if he was keen for a conversation – which he so clearly wasn't. 'Tell him about your family, Nina. She has so many brothers and sisters I lose track. Aw' living tah-gevver in li'l ol' Croydon.'

She said the last line so weirdly that I wondered if she was about to have a coughing fit. Then I realized she'd been attempting some sort of a Cockney accent. Which felt kind of rude. But her face still wore its angelic smile.

Angus's sneer was very eloquent, however. The extent to which he Did. Not. Care. About my family was written all over him.

'And will you and your *lovely* assistant be travelling with us *all* the time?' he asked. His voice was clipped and tight. I'd never felt such hostility from someone I didn't even know.

'Not all of it,' Sigrid said smoothly, ignoring the menacing edge to his voice. 'I have *such* a busy schedule, don't I, Nina? But I'll be joining you for the interviews. I mean, they're *begging* to talk to me and Jamie together. They practically said they wouldn't do them if I wasn't there.'

She gave Angus a wide-eyed, innocent look, but there was triumph behind it.

'Oh, really?'

'Yes.'

'I *do* look forward to hearing what you have to say. Your presence is so *essential* to our music.'

'It's not about the music,' Sigrid answered smoothly. 'It's about the story. Right now, Jamie and I are the story. Anybody can play guitar.'

Angus scowled so furiously it looked as though his eyes were going to shoot lasers right through her. He glared at Jamie, hoping for a reaction, but either he was asleep by now, or faking it.

I AM ON A PRIVATE JET WITH THE POINT AND THIS IS REALLY AWKWARD.

I picked up Sigrid's phone and buried my head in her Instagram settings, trying to ignore the poisonous atmosphere that swirled in the air like the notes of a thousand break-up songs.

'And so, tell me, how do you find French girls?'

I watched the band squash together on a small black sofa in a Paris TV studio, talking to a female French presenter who was gazing in wonder at each of them in turn. We'd driven here straight from the airport, chased by cars of excited fans.

'I find them everywhere. They're delectable,' Connor said seductively, staring right back at her.

The presenter flushed and checked her notes.

'And do you have any message for your fans here in France?'

'You have the greatest football league in the world,' George said, grinning into the nearest camera. 'No, wait. That was yesterday. Where are we?'

There was laughter in the studio. Connor jabbed George in the ribs. 'You can do this, mate. Concentrate.'

George put a hand in his frizzy hair and gave a comedy frown, as if he was just playing up for the cameras. Although, having seen him earlier, it wouldn't at all surprise me if he really couldn't remember what country he was in. Angus started humming the 'Marseillaise' and the others joined in.

'Oh yeah!' George grinned. 'La France. Home to my favourite drink.' He paused for a beat. 'Orangina. Je t'aime, la France. Also, I've run out of yellow jelly babies. So if anyone wants to bring some to the gig tomorrow ...'

The presenter giggled. And, watching them from behind the cameras, I was impressed. Under the lights, they did a brilliant job of being the band of happy friends the Pointer Sisters dreamt about. It was going to be hard to tell Ariel what they were really like.

'And Jamie ...' The presenter paused, looking into his grey-blue eyes.

'Yeah?' At the mention of his name he fixed his gaze on her. She gulped, and temporarily lost track of what she was saying.

'You ... um ... you have a lot of fans here in France.'

'I believe so.' He switched on the Mona Lisa smile and all the women around me gave an audible sigh.

'You've made many of them very sad.'

'Oh? How?'

'By announcing your engagement.'

'Ah yes. I'm sorry about that,' Jamie said, not looking or sounding sorry at all.

She smiled. 'But it is such a love story. Everybody wants to know about it. And we're lucky to have your fiancée here with us today. Sigrid Santorini! Woo!'

She stood up, raising her hands in the air to applaud, and Sigrid was guided on to the set. She gave the nearest camera her dazzling smile and there was a pause while she waited for the boys to scoot up and make space for her on the sofa. I noticed that even though space was tight, Angus moved as far away from her as he could get.

'So, Sigrid,' the presenter said. 'What is it like to be in love with Jamie?'

Sigrid looked down and batted her eyelashes. 'We don't talk about it much. We're very private.' When she looked up again, her eyes brimmed with sincerity. 'All I can say is, what Jamie and I have is very special. We're so blessed.'

'Aah! You make such a cute couple. You have to tell me, what are your wedding plans? Who will you be wearing? Where will it happen? That's what we all want to know!'

Sigrid smiled a toothpaste-ad smile. 'Oh well, you know … we're so busy … we're still making plans. Everyone says will it be a big Hollywood wedding, but we're so not like that, you know? I picture us on a beach somewhere. Away from the paparazzi. That's what brought us together – our love of the simple life. Isn't it, baby?'

As she talked, the Malteser flashed under the studio lights. Jamie nodded, looking serious. On Sigrid's other side, I saw Angus roll his eyes.

10

Sigrid's idea of the simple life was obviously different from mine. After the visit to the TV studios we travelled through Paris in vans with darkened windows, chased by paparazzi on motorbikes and fleets of girls in cars.

We arrived at the Ritz via the underground car park next door, to avoid the jostling crowds. As usual, the people we did meet turned their phones on Jamie to take a photo. Sigrid made sure they all got her best side.

Upstairs, the silk-lined suite was bigger than the last, with chandeliers and blue velvet sofas everywhere. The balcony doors overlooking the Place Vendôme were slightly open, letting in the sound of Pointer Sisters chanting outside.

'Really – can't those girls just *shut up*?' Sigrid muttered angrily under her breath as we walked inside. 'I can hardly hear myself think.'

But Oliver was already opening the balcony doors wider,

and motioning to Jamie to come and see the crowd. He did, and as soon as the fans outside caught a glimpse of him, their screaming became ecstatic. The other boys heard the noise and came to join him. They stood together, waving to the noisy square, until the hotel management begged them to stop because it was disturbing the other guests.

Meanwhile, I paused in the middle of the room to watch them. If anything, they were even hotter from behind. It was something else to add to my collection of interesting facts about The Point. Along with the fact that one was almost certainly an alcoholic, and two of them were barely talking to each other.

By now it was lunchtime. Oliver announced that a special meal was waiting for them in a private room.

'Forget that,' Angus announced. 'Who wants pizza?'

The others agreed. Yes, we were in France, home of one of the greatest gastronomies of the world, and they had ordered the signature dish of Italy. There were no plans for them to go sightseeing today because the crowds were too big outside. I began to abandon all hope of seeing the city, but the boys didn't seem to mind. Soon afterwards, three of them were busy playing a game called Pizza-Frisbee, which they'd apparently invented in Japan. They hadn't mastered the catching yet – just the throwing. I may not know much about Paris, but I do know the slapping sound fresh mozzarella makes against silk-upholstered walls.

Jamie wasn't around for this part. As soon as he'd eaten, he'd grabbed the nearest bodyguard and disappeared. He did it so subtly that I think I was the only person to notice him go. At least it meant we were spared the tension between him and Angus for a while.

Connor abandoned the Pizza-Frisbee when he spotted a pile of cardboard packages stacked against a wall. 'They're here!' he crowed.

'They' were a pair of drones with mounted cameras.

He saw me staring. 'They used some like these to film the crowd in Barcelona. Cool, huh?'

I agreed they were. He used one of them to mount a hunt for Jamie, zooming from room to room and aiming for anyone who didn't duck in time. After years of sharing the house with five slightly mad younger children, I was used to this level of chaos. In fact, it kind of reminded me of home, but Sigrid retired to bed with a headache.

'I hate it when they get like this,' she muttered. 'It's so child-ish. They only do it when they're all together. The sooner I get Jamie to Hollywood, the better.'

'Is he going to Hollywood?' I asked, closing her curtains for her, as she'd requested.

She paused for a moment before answering.

'It's an option,' she said cautiously. 'I know some directors who can't wait to work with him. Don't mention it, OK? For now he's so into this band thing. Wake me when this is over.' She flicked her hand, Sigrid-style, in the direction of the buzzing and slapping noises beyond the door.

'Of course. Is there anything you need me to do while you're sleeping?'

'Instagram,' she murmured, pulling an eye-mask over her face.

This was good. I'd been taking pictures of my family for as long as I could remember, mixing them with words and images from the internet, making the moments into little collage stories. Every birthday and big event had its artwork. And small events too. These were always my favourites: Ariel hanging out on the sofa in a Dalmatian onesie; the look of shock and joy on Josh's face the moment he learnt to freewheel on his BMX; little Lara blowing a massive bubble the size of her head in the garden and looking up, astonished, as it floated away into the sun-soaked sky.

I used Sigrid's phone to take several shots of shoes and handbags, and snazzily upholstered French furniture. But that got boring after a while. More intriguing, I thought, was the sight of Jamie's acoustic guitar propped up against the bathtub, and the tops of all the Pointer Sisters' heads in the square outside.

Back in the corridor, the Pizza-Frisbee game was over but the mess had yet to be cleared away. I took some shots of that too, but realized that Sigrid would hate them, so I swapped her phone for my camera, which I always carried with me. Once I had the familiar weight of its body in my hand and my eye to the viewfinder, the world seemed to organize itself and settle in my head. Or at least, the craziness became art, not just bad behaviour.

I was careful only to capture details, not people's faces. I knew about Jamie's 'privacy thing' – even though he wasn't here. But the Hotel California was insanely photogenic. Light. Action. Madness. Watching it through the lens, I began to feel part of it all.

Time passed. I rang up designers, as Sigrid had asked, and they fell over themselves to deliver their hottest outfits. Jamie returned and the boys went off to do more interviews and sign merchandise. Actually, they worked pretty hard most of the time. Despite all their fame and money I even wondered whether Dad had had more fun with the Massive Kegs.

I was unpacking Sigrid's goji berries in the kitchen area when I was startled by Jamie's voice behind me.

'I need you to keep Sisi busy this evening, from seven till eight-thirty. Keep her away from the suite.'

I turned around. These were possibly the first words he'd addressed directly to me. He seemed tired and tousled, as if he could do with a sleep. Also, he was looking furtive.

'How?'

'I have no idea. Think of something. Look, I'll text you when I'm ready. What's your number? And don't tell her I spoke to you.'

I did as he asked, trying to play it cool and ignore Tammy's voice in my head pointing out that I'd *just given Jamie Maldon my number*. Yeah – so I could assist him in some nefarious scheme. I didn't want to, but I didn't exactly have much choice.

Not telling Sigrid that we'd spoken was easy, given the way he'd ignored me so far. What was more difficult was to think of some excuse why she couldn't use her own room.

'I have to get ready for tonight,' she complained. 'We're going out to dinner. I need *at least* an hour.'

I'd managed to persuade her to use the hotel health club to recover from a busy afternoon on the phone to her realtor in LA and trying on party clothes. But despite the fact that this place included a Chanel spa and a frescoed swimming pool, she'd finished early, and there were still twenty minutes to kill.

'It's George,' I said, feeling totally guilty. 'He came in to find Jamie and … threw up everywhere. I'm really sorry. They just called. The staff are still getting rid of the smell.'

'*Where?*' she ranted. 'I'll *kill him*! How *dare* he?'

I'd have to apologize to him later.

'I'm sure they won't be long,' I assured her. 'They said they'd call back when they were ready.'

Jamie hadn't texted yet.

'Go now,' Sigrid instructed. 'Make them hurry.' She indicated her flawless, freshly-steamed, film-star face. 'I *refuse* to go out looking like this.'

I left her sipping a wheatgrass shot in the spa, and went back up to the Hotel California to warn Jamie he didn't have long.

My heart was in my shoes, because I had no idea what I'd find. What did rock stars get up to in hotel suites when their girl-friends weren't there? I could think of a few things, and none of them were good. Whatever it was, I really, really didn't want to know.

Tonight, it was Paul standing guard in the corridor.

'Can I go in?' I asked, wishing I didn't have to.

He knocked for me, and nodded. The door was opened. Unwillingly, I stepped inside.

And held my breath.

The room had been transformed.

Hundreds of tea-lights glimmered in mirrored holders. Most of the furniture had been moved aside, and a white-clothed table sat in the centre, set for two. A silver lace dress had been laid out in the bedroom beyond, next to a pair of her favourite shoes. The person who let me in was busy scattering the floor with pink rose petals, leaving a pathway to the door. The air was heady with their scent. Soon the carpet would be thick with them.

A chef in his whites was at work in one corner, putting the finishing touches to a dish. Jamie sat by the window in a dinner jacket and jeans, with a guitar on his knee, strumming an intro to a song I didn't recognize. He looked up when he saw me. A glimmer of candlelight caught the moles on his cheek.

His eyes held mine for a moment and once again I jolted with the same sense of connection I'd felt at the meet-and-greet. But I knew now to ignore it. Girls must feel it for Jamie all the time – it was an accident of his face.

'Special occasion,' he muttered, in answer to a question I hadn't asked. 'She wanted to go out. But I can't. If we do, there'll be a riot.'

'I ...'

I couldn't talk. This whole scene was so ... romantic. Most of all because he wanted to surprise her. He'd certainly surprised me. I stood there, spellbound. For once, Ariel had been right about Jamie. He *was* romantic, even if he went overboard sometimes with Malteser diamonds. He was nineteen, and he could be anywhere, with anyone, and he'd done all this for her.

I stood there for a moment, just taking it all in. Then I noticed he'd stopped playing. I glanced across at him, and he was watching me. He seemed tense.

'Is she annoyed?' he asked. I nodded; he sighed. 'I thought she would be. How long, François?'

The rose-petal-scatterer looked up. 'Five more minutes?'

'Go and get her,' Jamie said to me. 'But come back slowly. We'll be ready by then.'

I backed towards the door, still taking in the flickering light, the scent of roses. Careful not to tread on too many petals, I left the room.

Yet another impressive encounter with Jamie Maldon, I thought to myself as I descended in the lift. *Go, Nina.*

It had all looked so enchanting – like something out of a film, or a dream. I wanted to tell him it reminded me of Shakespeare: Romeo's heart, with a sprinkling of Puck's magic. But as far as I remembered, I hadn't said a word.

11

The next day was a gig day. The boys did more interviews all morning and went to the stadium for the sound check after lunch. Sigrid left the hotel with me and a borrowed bodyguard to 'get a feel for the culture of France'.

By which she meant shopping. For expensive stuff.

She was in a bad mood.

'Huh. *City of romance*,' she grunted a couple of times in the limo, glaring at the Champs-Elysées as we passed.

'How did it go last night?' I asked, sensing she wanted to talk.

'It was our six-month anniversary! I wanted us to *honour* it, you know? He could at least have taken me to a decent restaurant. Fans wanna see that stuff. We could've been *anywhere*.'

'He mentioned there might have been a riot.'

'Tom Cruise managed it. With Katie.'

She arched an impeccably threaded eyebrow. I had no

answer to Tom Cruise.

'And I couldn't even get you to take a picture, because my face was like, *nude*. I was all puffy from the treatment. It was a *disaster*.' She didn't mention the meal, or the rose petals. I sensed from Jamie's tension last night that he already knew he'd made a big mistake. This morning, he'd been grumpier than ever.

The limo stopped and I saw that we'd arrived at Christian Dior. Sigrid's mood instantly lifted. She was never down for long. 'But tonight's gonna be *fantastic*.'

'You mean the gig?'

'No. After. The party.'

When we got back, a hairdresser came to the suite to give her glossy locks his full attention. As he worked, she got me to film a clip for the *Backstage with Sigrid* website.

'I'm not really a party girl,' she told the camera with her wide-eyed look. 'Like Jamie says, all we need is a house, and a view, and each other. But ...' She indicated the sound of singing still coming from the Pointer Sisters outside ... 'I think, omigod, what would those girls do if they could listen to the best DJs and dance with Jamie and really have that *experience*? They'd be so psyched. It would be *incredible*. And I get to live that.'

She paused and smiled a saintly smile.

'So I feel I owe it to them to look my best, and really enjoy it, and let them *see* that, because in a way, I'm doing it for them, you know?'

I pressed the button to end the video.

'Did you get that? Did it work OK?' she checked.

'Absolutely,' I told her, wondering *exactly* how grateful Ariel would be when she saw this.

'Oh, Nina, you're a *marvel*,' she smiled. 'Wha' would I do wivout you?'

She said the last words in an odd voice. But I wasn't concentrating. I didn't think much of it at the time.

Once again, she didn't ask me to come with her to the show, or the party afterwards, which was being held upstairs, back at the hotel.

'We're leaving early,' she said. 'I need the luggage to be ready by six-thirty. That means packing tonight.'

It took me a moment to work out what she was saying. That meant *me* packing for her tonight. She wasn't informing me of her plans – she was giving me instructions. Sigrid could be subtle that way.

'Of course,' I said. 'I'll get on to it.'

'Oh, and I was thinking about a gift for Jamie,' she mused. 'I forgot earlier. I like to get him a little souvenir in every place we visit. Something local. We're in France, so …'

'Cheese?' I suggested. 'A map of the Paris Metro?'

She stared at me, unimpressed. 'I was thinking of a Matisse.'

'Oh.'

She outlined her budget. 'Just a limited edition. Nothing special. Jamie likes modern art. He's so … *cultured*. Matisse is like my favourite French artist now, after Picasso.'

'Erm, Picasso was Spanish.'

The look she gave me would have shrivelled the Eiffel Tower.

'And it'll look good in the workout studio back home. Make

sure you get one with a lot of blue.'

It was late in the evening when I put the finishing touches to the last of her trunks and cases. The job itself was super-unglamorous, but at least when Sigrid wasn't there I could do it with MTV on in the background, dancing my way around the suite. And hopefully I could make it sound more impressive when I told everyone about it next term.

With some help from the hotel concierge, the Matisse had been duly delivered by a local gallery a couple of hours earlier. It sat in the bedroom, waiting to be presented. A limited edition, numbered, seated nude. Iconic. Beautifully framed. And very blue. When you work for a celebrity who already has everything, it's amazing what people will do for you.

As I came out of the suite, I bumped into several people carrying bags and black silk bedding. One of them was Oliver. All of them looked stressed.

'What's happening?' I asked. 'Can I help?'

Oliver sighed. 'Yeah, thanks. We need to do this fast. Angus is moving suites.'

'Why?'

'Because he's decided the one we gave him is the one Princess Diana used before she died. Take this, will you?'

He handed me one of the guitar cases he was carrying as we half ran down the corridor.

'And is it?' I asked. 'Princess Diana's?'

'No, definitely not.'

'So why does he think it is?'

Oliver laughed. 'Rock-star psycho logic. You get used to it.

90

He says it gave him a "bad vibe" last night. The only other suite big enough that's available is on the floor above. Which, ironically, is closer to the real Princess Diana suite than this one, but he'll never know. We need to have the new one ready before he gets tired of the after-party.'

'No problem.'

It took a few trips to take everything upstairs, where hotel maids were busy making the new bed with Angus's favourite black silk sheets and spraying the room with his favourite scent of black orchids.

Angus had a favourite scent. How many bad boys of rock did that? There were so many things I wanted to tell Tammy, so we could laugh about them together. But after all the non-disclosure agreements I'd signed before I came out here, I didn't dare talk until we were face to face and I could absolutely swear her to secrecy. There was a lot of weird stuff the general public was never supposed to know.

Finally, Oliver looked around and decided the new suite was ready.

'Thank you, everyone,' he announced. 'You're free to go.'

By now it was getting late. He looked at his watch. 'Party time. Thank God. They're always good in Paris.'

'Have fun,' I said, calculating how to get back to my room from here.

He cocked his head to one side. 'Come up with me. You've earned it.'

'To the party?'

'To the party.'

'Am I allowed?'

He stared at me and sighed. 'You're on tour with a rock band, Nina. And you ask me that question. You have a lot to learn.'

12

Upstairs, a crowd of eager girls clustered round the entrance to the party room corridor, trying to assure tonight's security guards that they'd been sent by one or other of the boys to 'hook up with them later'. Oliver took my arm and helped to guide me through the throng.

'But Jamie told me to come 'ere,' a drop-dead-gorgeous model type complained to the nearest guard, in a French accent.

'No he didn't,' he told her cheerfully.

''Ow do you know?' she pouted.

She watched with a classic death-stare as the guard checked my pass and Oliver's, and let us through.

'How *did* he know?' I asked Oliver, as we slipped inside the door. 'They do that sometimes, don't they?'

'Because there's a code word,' he said with a knowing grin. 'Tonight it was "Nutella".'

I grinned back. This was another detail that Tammy would kill for.

Inside, the lighting was low and there was a DJ on decks in the corner. Beautiful bodies in beautiful clothes gyrated on the dance floor as the room throbbed with a heavy beat.

It was as if we'd stepped into an episode of *Backstage with Sigrid*, featuring The Point. Connor's bright white hair was easy to spot near the DJ, where he was talking to a girl in strappy heels, while another in thigh-high boots wrapped herself around his waist. Occasionally, his eyes flicked to a TV screen up high on the wall nearby, where the soundless news story showed the band arriving in France, and the bassist himself adjusting his dark glasses as he waved from the steps of the jet. This, I suspected, was about as close to Connor-heaven as you could get.

George was sitting at a pop-up bar, knocking back drinks and sharing jokes with the crowd around him. He spotted me and called me over, but I knew Sigrid wouldn't approve. And already he had a glazed look in his eye. Tomorrow, someone in the entourage would be picking up the pieces.

Oliver waved to someone across the room and headed in that direction. As we passed a group of candlelit tables, I spotted Angus deep in conversation. He certainly didn't seem bothered by the thought of the people who'd spent the last hour relocating his room. He was talking to a man whose long dreadlocks were topped by an oversize beret. His white silk shirt was as dazzling as his smile. I had never seen Angus look so eager and … respectful.

Oliver saw me watching. 'That's Nelson Reed,' he

explained, following my gaze. 'He's a living legend. One of the greatest guitarists there is. He joined them onstage tonight. It was epic.'

'And who's the short guy in the suit on his other side?' I asked, thinking he wouldn't know, because next to Angus and the living legend, he looked very boring indeed.

Oliver peered for a moment. 'The President of France,' he deadpanned. 'He asked if he could come tonight. And those *very* pretty girls next to him, staring over at Jamie? They're the daughters of one of France's top film directors. Big Point fans. Their dad's around somewhere. Actually, it's the dad that Jamie asked us to invite. I'll see if I can point him out to you.'

So. Jamie Maldon liked French films enough to ask to meet a director. That was unexpected. I considered this fact while Oliver scanned the room. Everyone was so glamorous. This was definitely the most amazing party I'd ever been to – and probably ever would – but I felt self-conscious in my work clothes and my flat shoes. I couldn't even remember the last time I'd brushed my hair. If I was going to stay here for a while, I didn't want to look too much like a wind-blown Shetland pony.

'Where's the Ladies?' I asked.

Oliver pointed to a distant door marked *Femmes*.

Femmes. Even the toilets sounded glamorous at the Ritz.

I made my way over there, moving in time to the beat of the dance track. There was a little lobby just inside the door, and I was about to pass through it when I stopped dead.

It was much quieter here, and a voice stood out against the silence. I recognized it instantly. It was my mother.

In Paris. How?

At least, it *sounded* like Mum. I was rooted to the spot, heart hammering. Was there an emergency at home? Why else would she come here? Why hadn't she called me?

'As soon as I heard the word "Croydon" I thought *Blimey almighty, this is my lah-cky day.* Those Lahn-don accents are hilarious, don't'cha think? I'm going to have to tone it dahn for the part.'

The accent and tone of voice were Mum's, but the words didn't make sense. Nothing made sense.

'I just 'ad to 'ave 'er. She's bluddy perfect. Jay-mee calls 'er Blanket Gir'.'

With a wave of nausea, I realized that it was Sigrid talking. About me. And it was my voice she was doing it in, not Mum's.

My body felt numb, but somehow my legs carried me silently across the floor. I peered around the lobby door. Sigrid was standing at a bank of mirrors with two glamazons beside her. They were touching up their make-up while Sigrid talked.

'The last one was a *disah-ster*. This one's not exactly *ugly*, but ... you know British dentists, righ'? Hahahahaha.'

She made a kind of rabbit face, with her upper teeth stuck over her bottom lip. I think she was trying to illustrate British dentistry. She couldn't do the tooth gap, but she was goggling her eyes, and puffing her cheeks, and doing her best at *not exactly ugly, but ...*

She lapsed into her own voice as she stared at herself in the mirror, letting her face return to its natural, modelesque lines. 'I mean, Kate rocks her bone structure, so we have that in common. And she married a rock guy. Omigod! Called Jamie! I just thought of that! ... But she's old now. And a different ethnicity. Like, I'm part Navajo, part Swedish, part Italian, you know? So I figure I'm going to need to swing this with the voice.'

'Well, you've got it in the bag,' one of the other women said. 'So funny!'

'Oh you think so? *Thank* you! Nina's a goldmine.'

My mind raced. I didn't understand it all, but I'd got the gist of it. Sigrid hadn't hired me for my fire-wrangling skills, or my cheap labour. She had chosen me because of a part she was going for, so she could copy me. I suppose it was easier than bringing a voice coach on tour.

I thought back, and it all made sense. The way she perked up when Ariel said where we were from. The intense way she listened when I talked. She'd started off with that strange Cockney accent on the jet, but she must have been mimicking me all this time behind my back, getting better and better. She had a real talent for it, it seemed. By now, she had nailed me perfectly, like a butterfly with a pin.

Did she do this to Jamie? *Those Lahn-don accents are hilarious.* The bunny-face. Did they laugh about me last night?

Humiliation coursed through me, so hot I burned. I needed to get out of here. All those chats about my home and family, when I thought she was interested, she'd been studying me.

Run, Nina. Run.

I was ready to turn and go when the strangest sense of déjà vu hit me.

Another party. Low lights and 'Eden' playing. Wandering around candlelit rooms, my tattoo fresh on my skin, looking for Jez, drunk with love, needing to talk about Aunt Cassie, needing him.

His hand in Ria's hair. The look he gave me. The sudden need to escape.

That night, I'd felt the same sense of shock and shame. The same sense of panic.

But that was love … and this was a job.

I calmed my breathing and told myself to get a grip. I was Nina 2.0. So Sigrid was copying my voice? She was an actress – that was *her* job. And she was good at it. This time, I wasn't going to crumble.

Shaking, I turned on my heel and walked back into the party room. Sigrid came out soon afterwards with her new friends and walked straight past me, without realizing I was there. I watched as she scanned the room for Jamie and saw him surrounded by beautiful, long-legged French girls, busy taking selfies.

She stiffened for a moment. For the first time, I saw what she usually hid so well: how exhausting it must be to know that most of the women in the world would steal your boyfriend in a heart-beat.

She stalked across the floor like a model on a catwalk, lured him away from the crowd and took him by the hand on to the dance floor. She'd come second on *Dancing With The Stars* last year, and now she shimmied like a professional, owning her man and showing off her moves.

Among a crowd of people, Jamie could be distracted and uncomfortable. He often looked as if he'd rather be somewhere else. But as soon as he hit the dance floor, he was at home. Every muscle relaxed and he moved as smoothly as she did, loose-hipped and self-assured. Soon the music took over and they drew together, eyes locked, twining and untwining, lost in the beat. Watching them was hypnotic. It took my mind off my burning cheeks.

'Good, isn't he?' said a voice from behind me.

I whipped round. It was Oliver again.

'What? Um … yeah. I … um … I was watching them both.'

'Course you were.' Oliver peered into my face and his wry smile slipped. 'Hey, you OK?'

'Yeah. Absolutely.'

'You don't look it,' he said. 'Come and talk to us.'

He led me over to a small group of people from the entourage, talking and laughing near an open window. One woman looked up as Oliver touched her on the arm. She gave me a friendly grin.

'This is Nina,' Oliver said to her. 'She's new. We need to be nice to her. And this is Cath. She's wardrobe.'

For a moment I pictured the furniture department at Ikea. 'You do the boys' clothes?' I asked. I realized that I recognized her from the first night in their dressing room.

Cath nodded. 'Their stage clothes mostly. But their day clothes too, on tour.'

'Oh, wow. That sounds fun.'

She wrinkled her brow. 'Not so much. It's mostly getting sweat out of delicate fabric. You wouldn't want to know.'

'Maybe not,' I smiled.

'Oh, and nowadays, it's trying to persuade Jamie not to go onstage in surf gear, or a loincloth, or whatever the Queen of Evil's latest plan is.'

99

'Who's the—?'

'*Cath!*' Oliver nudged his friend.

'What?'

'Did I mention that Nina's the new assistant for *Sigrid Santorini*?'

'Oh. Oh! Oh really? Right, well … *that* must be interesting,' Cath blustered, flashing me a rigid smile.

I sighed. 'She's the Queen of Evil, isn't she?'

'No, no!' Cath insisted. 'I was thinking about this other person who—'

But before she could continue with this *obvious* lie, the person standing next to her turned round to join in. It was Jess, the PR girl who'd helped me out with Sigrid's bag. She smiled at me.

'Hey, are we talking about Sigrid again? Is it the jet?' she asked.

'What jet?'

'Haven't you heard? She says that she and Jamie need to travel in their own private jet, so they have space to meditate between venues. When Angus heard, it made him want to punch something.'

'No! Seriously?' Cath said. 'That girl is such a yoko.'

'What's a yoko?' I asked. I was losing track of this conversation. Was Sigrid Queen of Evil *and* a yoko? Or was it some kind of acronym I should have heard of, like YOLO? (Or as Aunt Cassie would have said, *carpe diem*, which I seemed to be doing now.)

'Yoko Ono,' Jess explained.

'Oh, *that* Yoko. The one who married John Lennon?

She nodded. 'Everyone says she broke up the Beatles. I mean, they were fine until Yoko came along, and then suddenly they were arguing all the time. John and Paul stopped talking. The best band *ever* fell apart.'

'That wasn't Yoko's fault,' Oliver retorted. 'They were falling apart anyway. John was bored of the Beatles by then. He fell in love. He wrote some of his greatest songs for her. You can't blame her for that.'

'Of course I can.'

'Don't be stupid!'

'Hey! They broke up fifty years ago,' Cath laughed. 'I can't believe you guys care that much.'

'The Beatles wrote some of the best music in history!' Oliver protested. 'Of course I care.'

I loved how passionate they were about the music, but meanwhile the conversation had got me thinking.

'So, has Jamie written any songs for Sigrid yet?' I asked.

They paused and looked at me thoughtfully.

'Good point,' Cath said. 'Not that I've heard.'

'If he's done something, he's not saying,' Oliver agreed. 'The Point haven't recorded anything for a while.'

'Jamie's too busy meditating with her in that peace tent,' Jess muttered and Oliver laughed.

Cath, meanwhile, cocked her head and looked at me. 'So you're the new Pamela.'

I grinned. 'I guess.'

'You know what happened to the old Pamela, I suppose?'

I shook my head. Sigrid had called her a 'disah-ster' just now. I'd been wondering about her for a while, but hadn't dared ask.

Cath nodded in the direction of Connor's alien blond crop, as he moved towards the dance floor, a girl in each hand. 'They got together. Sigrid found out about it. You know what he's like. Be careful, OK?'

I laughed. If I'd been in any doubt before tonight about my irresistible allure – which I wasn't – Sigrid had confirmed it. It was kind advice, but Cath might as well have told me not to ski down a mountain naked. Never gonna happen anyway.

13

The evening had ended well eventually, thanks to Oliver, but the sound of Sigrid's voice pretending to be mine still echoed around my head. Every time I thought about it, my body started shaking. Back in my room, I turned on my laptop and googled: 'Kate' 'Croydon'.

All the results came up with Kate Moss.

Of course: Kate Moss and car parks – the two things Croydon is most famous for. And Kate certainly 'rocked her bone structure', and had married a rock guitarist called Jamie. But what did that have to do with Sigrid Santorini?

I added the word 'movie' to my search.

Hollywood studio set to make new biopic about Kate Moss, the stellar supermodel from Croydon, South London, who has dominated the fashion scene since the 1980s. Rumour has it that practically every major actress from Kate Winslet to Kate

Hudson is up for this role. But can an actress who doesn't share the model's first name crack this gem of a part? We list our top 10 favourites …

I clicked on the link. Sigrid wasn't in the top 10 list. But she obviously wanted to be.

'*I need to swing this with the voice.*'

From now on, I'd worry less about showing initiative, or getting every line on the spreadsheet right. To do my job perfectly, all I had to do was open my mouth.

In the days that followed, I added Zurich to the list of cities I didn't really see because the band was too busy, or hounded by crowds of chasing paparazzi, or because Sigrid needed me to do something critical, like chase down a rare vintage Rolex watch for Jamie, or wash her most delicate underwear by hand.

You know. The simple life.

I took my mind off it by focusing on my photography whenever I could. I took shots of sunsets out of plane and hotel windows for Sigrid's Instagram account. And, for myself, the havoc of a hotel suite after a pair of drones had raced around it, or a portable speaker after Jamie had taken a golf club to it because he didn't like the music that Angus was pumping through the Hotel California that day, or a pair of disappearing mega-famous haircuts, running down a service corridor towards a car. Everybody else showed the band sleek, styled and smiling. I was more interested in the chaos they left behind.

*

The flight to New York took private-jet flying to a whole new level. Up to now, we'd been on small planes, which to be perfectly honest, felt like travelling in a luxury car, but ten thousand feet in the sky. This one was the size of a passenger jet, with a curtained-off area for the band and other VIPs to relax at the front, and normal seating for several members of the crew at the back.

Soon, it sounded as though there was a party going on there. George went off to join it. I'd been looking forward to catching up with some of my new friends there as well, but my boss kept me busy up at the front.

By now, Sigrid had stopped trying to keep her new accent a secret from me. She opened her tote bag and took out the script they'd sent her for the biopic. 'You be Jamie,' she giggled, with a glance at her fiancé, 'and I'll be Kate.'

I didn't want to 'be Jamie'. Really not. But I had no choice. I looked over at the real Jamie. Luckily, he was busy talking to some senior record execs in suits, who were hitching a lift to the gig. Rory Windermere, the manager, was there too, in a panama hat, with a sky-blue scarf flung theatrically around his shoulders. They all seemed deep in conversation and Jamie didn't look happy. I heard the words 'new album' and 'next hit' a few times. At the hopeful mention of Digger V, he looked ready to hit the roof. But at least it kept his attention away from his fiancée and her script-reading companion, which was good for me, as Sigrid had chosen a love scene to rehearse, and it was excruciating.

When Jamie finished talking to the suits, he went over to a seat by himself, scribbled some words on a paper napkin, then picked up his guitar and started strumming fragments of a tune. It was a little bit sad and wistful, but he kept stopping it halfway through, as if he didn't know where it went from here. I knew the feeling. It reminded me of my life.

'You're so boring, baby!' Sigrid said with a forced laugh. 'I wish you'd read with me. Nina's trying, but she sucks at being a love interest.'

Jamie merely flicked his eyes up at us for a moment, then went back to his music.

'This part is so *tricky*,' Sigrid laughed, loudly. 'But I've got to get it right. Did I tell you I was auditioning with Leo, Nina? Leo DiCaprio? *Such* a darling friend.'

Each time she spoke, she glanced across at Angus, who was hunched in his seat, playing a game and radiating hostility. I sensed she was trying to impress him, and the harder she tried, the less impressed he seemed to be. I wondered if Angus knew she was known as the 'yoko'. I suspected he probably did.

After a couple of hours, George staggered through the curtains from the back of the plane.

'Best. Flight. Ever,' he managed, before heading quickly for the toilets at the front and staying there for a very long time.

Later, they turned the lights down and showed a rough cut of a new film that was being made about The Point. It was all about their charity work and the 'one in a million' friendship that bound the boys together.

Ariel would love it. As a total work of fiction, I admired it. George looked fresh as a daisy in every shot. Connor looked single. In their interviews, Angus and Jamie deserved an Oscar apiece for pretending their friendship still existed.

Sigrid sighed loudly throughout it.

'Of course, they filmed all this before I joined the band,' she whispered to me. As if she was the fifth member, not one of the reasons it was falling apart.

14

There is a booth at the London Aquarium where you can pay to stand inside and feel what it's like to be caught up in a tornado. Josh loves it: the sudden rush of air, the shock of the noise, the fear of being inside a force of nature that's out of control.

He would have loved to land in New York with The Point.

By now, I was beginning to know what to expect. There was a quiet moment before the plane door opened. They caught each other's eye and took a deep breath. Jamie put his head down. Connor put on his dark glasses. Angus put his arm around George's shoulder to steady him on the steps. And then … *wham*. The lights. The camera flashes. The screaming. It was as if the whole city had arrived at the airport and was ready to swallow them up.

Outside, the crowds of Pointer Sisters were denser and louder than ever. Even though we left the airport through a side entrance, the road was half blocked by a sea of waving hands.

The cars had to slow down in the crush and a few girls managed to rush forward, pressing their phones against the windows, and bashing the roof with their hands. Individually they were lovely, like my sister. Together, they seemed like an untamed monster. Tonight, it was scarier than ever. Like everyone except Connor, I hated this part.

Because of this, travelling with The Point meant running and hiding. Down underground corridors. Into basic service lifts. Waiting to emerge until Ian said the coast was clear. Then the safety of the Hotel California. Once we were there, we could breathe at last. This time the suite had floor-to-ceiling plate-glass windows and views across Manhattan. White orchids in bowls and scented candles in Sigrid's favourite fragrance. Beautiful blow-up photographs of headless, sculptural bodies adorned the walls.

Rory Windermere took the band and Sigrid out to dinner with some eager New York celebrities. Meanwhile, I ordered a club sandwich from room service and ate it while I supervised the building of the peace tent in a corner of the living room, close to the view. Then there was laundry and dry cleaning to arrange – with forms to fill out and a special plea to the hotel to do it fast, because we'd be out of here by tomorrow night. Constant travel meant constantly trying to fit in the boring practicalities of life, like getting clothes clean. I never ever thought I'd miss throwing things into the washing machine, but I was starting to.

It was late by the time I finished my chores and rang down to ask where my room was. A bellboy was quickly dispatched to show me.

It might have been a mistake. I didn't ask. But this time, he only led me a few metres down the corridor. Tonight, I wasn't in a cheap room on a distant floor, but had somehow been booked into the Hotel California. My room wasn't so different from the boys' suites – just smaller. There were orchids and electric curtains. The bed was big enough for my whole family (and if they'd been here, they'd all have jumped into it – even Mum and Dad – and actually, a part of me wished that would happen right now). From my window, the street below looked like a canyon of lights, twinkling in the darkness.

My English exam was coming up in a few days and I still had a lot of work to do, but I was too distracted to revise tonight. Instead, I turned on the TV and flicked between endless channels. I took a hundred pictures, and tried to sketch the city canyon. It would have been good to Skype Mum and Dad, but it was early in the morning UK time, and they wouldn't thank me. So I uploaded lots of photos on to my laptop and started playing around with editing features, making collages of each place we'd stayed.

Time ticked on, and I heard the boys return from their night out. I knew I should go to bed, but this was *New York*. Nobody sleeps in New York. I decided to run myself a bubble bath in my *marble bathroom*, but I was disturbed by the sound of a door slamming in the corridor, and the sound of running feet.

I opened the door cautiously and looked outside. A girl wrapped in a towel and clutching a jacket was busy shoving her bare feet into a pair of heels. One guard stood over her while another headed for Angus's room, a few doors further down from mine. The sound of Angus roaring in fury filled the air, followed by a crash and the tinkle of breaking glass.

Connor poked his head out of a door nearby to see what was happening, just as Steve Grange, the tour manager himself, raced towards the noise.

'Don't worry!' he panted, seeing me. 'We'll have this under control in a minute.'

But not before I'd caught sight of Angus's white face in the shadows of his doorway.

'She could have been anyone!' he shouted. 'Does nobody check *anything* round here? You're fired! All of you! Get out of here!'

Steve tried to calm Angus down, pointing out that they couldn't leave him if he was going to go around breaking hotel furniture. This succeeded in making him angrier still.

'I can break what I like! It's my money. I pay for everything round here with my music! You're all parasites, you hear that?'

Between them, Steve and the hotel staff succeeded in getting Angus back inside the room and closing the door, but you could still hear the shouting. Connor stayed where he was, and Jamie emerged too, in a T-shirt and boxers, looking furious.

'The usual?' he asked Connor.

Connor shook his head. 'Worse. They let a girl in without his permission. They're all fired. We're all parasites. Blah de blah de blah.'

'Yeah. Let him shout all night,' Jamie said, sarcastically. 'I mean, it's not as if tomorrow's an important gig or anything. Nobody needs to *sleep*.'

Sigrid appeared beside him. Her face was stretched and shiny. I realized she must be wearing a gel mask of some kind.

It made her look more plastic-doll-like than ever.

'Jus' nake hin shu' u'!' she fumed, her lips struggling to move as her facial muscles were held rigidly in place by the mask. 'Wha'e'er i' takes! Jus' do i'!'

'I can go, if you like,' I offered.

'You?' Jamie frowned.

'Yes. I'm used to flare-ups. We've had a lot of them in my family.'

He threw me a sceptical glance. 'Sure. Whatever. Knock yourself out.' He turned on his heel and Sigrid shut the door.

I grabbed my room key and headed down to Angus's room. Inside, Steve and two guys from security were standing in a semicircle with their backs to me. I couldn't see Angus, but I could sense that they were all facing him. The worst thing you can do to an angry person is crowd his space with other people. I knew that well enough from all Josh's episodes at home. My instinct was to give him room to breathe.

'Can I do anything?' I asked.

They spun around to face me. One of the guards had a cut hand and blood was dripping from it. The carpet was strewn with scattered pictures and broken glass.

Steve glanced at me sceptically. 'I don't think so. Go to bed, love.'

'No. Really. Give me a moment. I know what I'm doing.'

I stood my ground. Steve looked surprised. Then he surveyed the floor and the dripping blood. I could see him think-ing that the situation couldn't get much worse.

'Two minutes,' I said. I just needed the men to leave.

Steve hesitated for another moment. 'OK. If you say so,' he

agreed cautiously. 'We'll be right outside.' He hurried the other men out of the door and closed it behind them.

Angus was barefoot, crouched on the arm of a sofa like a brooding bird of prey, with his long arms wrapped around his chest. He looked at me with hooded eyes.

'Get out, Blanket Girl.'

I didn't.

His lip curled. 'I'm not in the mood for girls right now.'

'I saw that. If you were, I wouldn't be here.'

This surprised him. He peered at me suspiciously. 'So why are you here?'

To start with, I said nothing. I stepped carefully around the broken glass and went into his bathroom, emerging with a towel that I used to mop up the drops of blood from the carpet.

'That was an accident,' he muttered.

'I'm sure it was.'

He watched me, looking slightly sheepish. Even though he threw things at people that broke, he evidently didn't mean them to get hurt in the process.

When I'd finished mopping up, I went over to a nearby chair and sat down, tucking my feet under me. Two minutes had gone by, but Steve didn't return. I sensed him hovering outside, but he didn't interrupt us.

I said nothing. Angus threw me a hostile glance.

He sighed deeply, still angry.

'They come in and they lie and cheat and they think they're doing me a favour. If I want a girl I'll ask for one. I *don't. Want. People.* Why doesn't anybody listen to me?'

There were dark smudges under his eyes. That moody-boy

persona wasn't just an act.

'You look tired,' I said.

'I *am* tired.'

'But you can't sleep.'

'No. Exactly. That's what I've been trying to tell these bozos. I CAN'T SLEEP. I haven't been able to sleep for months. They keep telling me to take drugs to calm me down. Medications ... but I don't do that stuff.' He was pale and shaking.

'I know.' Ariel had mentioned a tough childhood. I wondered now what had happened, how he'd coped.

'Jamie used to talk, but ...' He trailed off sadly. In the silence that followed, he glanced out of the picture window. 'I hate this city. John Lennon was shot down the road, did you know that? Outside the Dakota Building, just a few blocks from here ...' He hunched forward, hugging his arms closer around him. 'That girl could've been ... Anyone can get a gun. They kill musicians here, you know?'

This sounded like Angus rock-star psycho logic. That girl was just a poor, hopeful groupie, more scared than he was. But he was right about John Lennon. I knew the story. Thinking of the Beatle's pointless death at the hands of a man who just wanted to be famous made me shiver, too.

We sat in silence for a moment.

'Have you heard of Durness beach?' I asked.

He looked at me, surprised, and shook his head.

'It's in the Scottish Highlands. It's beautiful.'

'And? So?'

'John Lennon used to play there as a child,' I said. 'I heard his granny lived there. I don't know if that's true, but there's a memorial garden to him by the sea. It's very simple. Peaceful, too. You should go there one day.'

Angus peered at me, hard, as if he was seeing me for the first time.

'How d'you know this stuff?'

I wrapped my arms around my knees, matching his body language without meaning to. This was not a place in my head that I normally liked to go.

'My aunt went swimming there, on holiday, two years ago. The beach is stunning, but it can be dangerous. There are riptides ...' My voice trailed off. I took another breath. 'Nobody could reach her in time. Mum went up there later, to see where it happened. She found the memorial garden to John. She said it helped her. Things growing. Nature never giving up. The lyrics to one of his songs are inscribed on stones there.'

'Which one?'

'*In My Life.*'

'Yeah. That's a good one,' he sighed.

It was a lovely, haunting song. Mum had played it over and over after Cassie died. I liked it, actually, that Angus focused on the music, not on what happened to Cassie. It showed his rock-star ego was fully intact, but it was easier that way.

He looked wistful. 'I wouldn't mind seeing that place.' In his mind, he was already there, I could tell. Blue sky mirrored on the rippling sands. Low plants clinging to the windswept shore. Lennon's soft, nostalgic music hanging in the breeze. He took a long, deep breath and something seemed to lift from his shoulders.

'Stay with me,' he said. 'Talk to me.'

'About what?'

'About death.'

Oh. Maybe not. Much as I wanted to help him, I wasn't going to spend my night feeding his dark obsession. It wouldn't do either of us any good.

'I could read to you,' I suggested. 'It might take your mind off things.'

'*Read* to me?' His lip began to curl into its familiar sneer.

'Yes.' I shrugged. 'I do it at home.' *To my little brothers and sisters*, I might have added, but I didn't.

Angus frowned. 'Read me what?'

This was tricky. With Josh and the twins, I read *The Gruffalo*, over and over. Ariel had loved a book called *Sisterhood of the Travelling Pants*. Neither of them sounded very Angus, and anyway, I doubted the hotel would have a copy of either. I thought of the two old and battered books in my room right now. One was an anthology of love poetry, which was hardly appropriate. The other was a possibility.

'Well, at the moment I'm reading *Far From the Madding Crowd*,' I said doubtfully. It was my revision book. 'It's about a girl called Bathsheba Everdene who—'

He held his hand up. 'I know it. Thomas Hardy. Read it a long time ago.'

'You did?'

'Don't look so surprised. After Jamie and I got kicked out of school, we read all the time. We competed: who could read Shakespeare the fastest ... Dickens ... Hardy too ... I like that one. Crazy story. Loads of people die.'

'Fictionally,' I pointed out, bearing in mind our earlier

conversation.

He laughed. 'Yeah. Fictionally. Whatever. It can't be worse than arguing with Steve about sleeping pills. I liked her in the film, too. Go and get Bathsheba Everdene.'

He motioned imperiously for me to do his bidding. I wondered whether he expected me to curtsey on the way out. They should bottle rock-star arrogance and sell it. But at least he wasn't breaking things.

Back outside, Steve was anxiously waiting.

'You're going to do *what*?' he asked.

'Read to him.'

'And he calmed down just like that? Are you magic?'

'Something like that,' I smiled. 'I come from a big family. I'm used to …'

'… brats?'

'Children. On a bad day.'

He grinned. 'In this business, we like to call them *artists*. Do you have your phone on you?'

I patted my pocket.

'Call me if there's a problem. And Paul's here if you need him.' He indicated the guard in position at the end of the corridor, who acknowledged me with a nod.

'Sure.'

'Do you want someone to help you? Me? Housekeeping?'

Strangely enough, I felt safe with Angus, and he seemed to feel safe with me.

'We'll be fine.'

*

I collected the novel from my room and took it back to the suite. I sat on an armchair and read aloud while Angus lay on the sofa and listened with his eyes closed. For chapter after chapter, we followed Bathsheba Everdene managing her sheep, falling for the wrong men and making them unhappy. Slowly, Angus's muscles relaxed. He stopped scowling. After almost an hour, he stretched and announced he was ready for bed.

I looked at my watch. It was two in the morning. I got up to go, but he frowned at me.

'You said you'd stay.'

'Yes, but ...'

'You were right. I don't feel so ... I might want you to read some more later.'

'But where would I ...?'

He looked around and indicated a spot on the floor of his sitting room, just beyond the bedroom door.

'If you're there, I can call you.'

Oh, nice. Just like some kind of medieval servant-girl. I looked at his face again. It was still taut around the edges. The dark smudges under his eyes stained his cheeks like purple bruises.

'OK,' I sighed. 'If it helps.'

'Yeah, well ... good.'

While he got ready for bed in the room next door, I raided the closets for every spare pillow and blanket I could find. I made a nest for myself out of these and some sofa cushions, near the door, as I'd promised. It reminded me of the nights I'd slept next to the twins after Mum took them in and they were taking a while to settle. Then I'd only had one of Dad's old, smelly sleeping bags from his Massive Kegs days. This was much better.

Wrapped in a hotel robe, Angus came over to inspect the nest.

'That looks pretty cosy.'

'Actually, it does.'

'Promise me you'll stay there?'

'I promise.'

About two hours later, I was asleep in my comfy blanket-nest when I thought I heard shouting. Indistinct words, loud and desperate. I called out to him:

'I'm here. It's Nina. Everything's OK.'

But the noise continued. Tentatively, I turned the bedroom door handle and pushed it open. There was a little light creeping in through the curtains from the city that never sleeps, and I could just make Angus out, sprawled under the duvet. I crept in further. He was lying on his back, in a cold sweat, eyes open but seeing nothing. Every now and then his body convulsed and he cried out something incomprehensible. He looked terrified. I wondered how often he spent his nights this way.

Carefully, I climbed on to the bed beside him, keeping the duvet between us, and put my arm around him. It was what I'd done for Josh a dozen times.

Instinctively, Angus's body turned towards me, as Josh's had. His breathing calmed a little. He put an arm around me too.

'It's OK,' I murmured. 'You're safe. I'll stay with you.'

Gradually the convulsions stopped. His panicked breaths

grew calmer. Soon he was sleeping deeply, but when I tried to slip away, his arm stayed wrapped around me. I stayed where I was and watched him sleep. Poor Angus. Girls threw themselves at him on a daily basis, and he was the loneliest person I knew.

15

I woke up early.

Sunlight was filtering through a gap in the curtains. The snake-circled, sculpted arm of the hottest rock guitarist in the world was still lying across my chest, making it hard to move. I lay there for a while, focusing on the surreal-ness of the moment. Rock stars snore. They also drool slightly. But they look adorable with their dark hair resting on the pillow, and their lips, for once, not curled into a sarcastic smile.

Angus stirred, opened his eyes, saw me lying next to him and looked surprised. His eyes drifted down to the duvet tucked chastely between us, then flickered with alarm.

'Um, so did we …? Did anything? Did I …?'

I gave him a 'You're not all *that*,' eye-roll.

He laughed. Dammit – if he wasn't a rock star, I could imagine being friends with this boy.

'We did nothing,' I assured him, getting up and slipping my

shoes back on. 'You called out. I kept you company. End of story.'

He yawned and stretched. 'That's the first good night's sleep I remember in I don't know how long.' Then he looked at me from under his thick, dark lashes. 'Don't tell anyone, though.'

'About Thomas Hardy?'

'About what we ... didn't ... um, you know. I have my reputation to consider.'

'And I have mine,' I retorted sharply. 'I'm not some cliché rock-star groupie.'

'True. Although, round here that's not considered such a bad thing.' He saw my stony face. 'But – sure. Whatever you say, Nina.'

He'd remembered my name, even. We were making progress.

My phone buzzed in my trouser pocket. I didn't need to check what it said. 'Sigrid needs me. Gotta go.'

'Good luck with that.'

He grinned and put his hands behind his head, which some-how emphasized his perfectly bulging biceps. *Focus on the face, Nina. On the face.*

'Goodbye, then.'

'Be good.'

I smiled. 'Aren't I always?'

I quickly put away all traces of my blanket nest from last night. Back in my room, I checked my face in the mirror to make sure I wiped off all traces of a smile from that too.

Sigrid gave my shaggier-than-usual hair and more-smudged-than-usual eyeliner a second glance.

'Did you sleep OK?' she asked, sharply.

'Perfectly,' I assured her.

'Good. Because we've got a busy day.'

She didn't refer to the night before again, and I didn't mention it either. It was probably easiest if she didn't know anything. There was enough bad blood between her and Angus already.

The rest of the day was, as usual, madness.

After hair and make-up in the hotel, the boys had an interview to do at the Rockefeller Center. The ride through the city streets to the TV studios required a police escort because of the vans of TV cameras and paparazzi trying to get pictures of them all. Getting out of the car required facing a wall of noise. Our view as we went inside was a row of security men's backsides as they kept the crowds at bay. Still jetlagged from the flight, and trying to function on not enough sleep, I had to remind myself more than once what we were supposed to be doing here.

Even though it involved copious amounts of lying, I was starting to admire the boys for coping as well as they did. Inside the studios, George managed not to look as hung-over as he had done half an hour ago, when he'd nearly thrown up in the limo. Connor distracted attention from him by saying seductive things about American girls and making the audience swoon. Angus didn't mention his nightmares, or broken furniture, or his list of famous people who'd been shot in this city. Jamie answered each old, familiar question about Sigrid and the wedding as if he'd never been asked it before. She waved at him coyly from the audience, while a camera zoomed in on her loved-up face.

*

Afterwards, there was a photoshoot in Central Park. I took pictures of Sigrid for her Instagram account, while the boys larked around on the official photographer's instructions. Crowds of paparazzi clustered round to take pictures of their own. The boys were surrounded by a cage of cameramen constantly shouting, vying for their attention. It made me think of the animals in the nearby zoo.

I was grateful when the time came to go to the waiting limos. At least there would be a little peace and privacy – once security had rushed us past the sea of waiting hands nearby, reaching out to try and touch the boys.

But in the rush to get to the venue for the sound check, Sigrid became separated from Jamie and by some hideous accident, we ended up in a car with Angus. She sat, rigid and uncomfortable, on the seat behind the driver, while Angus and I instinctively sat at the back, as far away from her as we could.

As we drove away, I stared at the yellow-taxi-speckled traffic, the grand glass-fronted shops and busy sidewalks, drinking it all in.

'First time in New York?' Angus asked.

'Yes,' I said, not looking round – not wanting to miss a moment.

'You should skip the sound check,' he said. 'Go up the Empire State Building. See the Statue of Liberty. I did it once with Jamie. Our first trip. We had about ten dollars in our pockets and played every bar that would take us. Best holiday we ever had.'

I turned to smile at him. 'New York's not all bad, then.'

124

'Nah. Actually, I miss it. Been back a few times on tour, but like the man said, these days it's a car and room and room and a car and a cheese sandwich.'

That wasn't *exactly* how I'd describe their life on tour, but I knew what he meant. It was relentless.

'Which man?' I asked. 'No, let me guess: John Lennon.'

Angus raised an eyebrow. 'Got it in one. But it doesn't have to be that way for you.'

'I'm afraid Nina's busy this afternoon,' Sigrid cut in icily. 'She's working. She doesn't have time to be a tourist. Phone.'

This last word was another instruction. I was getting better at spotting them. I reached into her bag and placed it in her waiting hand.

Angus watched me obey her every command with amused detachment. 'But you're coming to the show, right? Frankly, tonight we *are* what's happening in New York.' He gave me his arrogant grin. For some reason, it didn't annoy me as much as it used to.

'I – I don't think so.' I glanced at Sigrid, who was glowering.

'Oh? Why?' he smirked. 'Don't you like us?'

'There's more to life than a bunch of rock songs,' Sigrid said testily, tapping away at her phone with fingernails like talons. She was trying to look busy to impress him again, and it was almost sad. She didn't explain what I'd be doing instead tonight. Probably packing. She'd brought a lot of party outfits that were currently scattered all over her suite.

Angus didn't bother to reply. He wasn't going to waste his breath arguing with the Queen of Evil about her assistant. But when he stretched his arm along the back of the seat, and his fingertips happened to touch my hair, he didn't flinch and pull away. I could feel them resting near my shoulder.

He wasn't trying anything on – just getting comfortable. But I sensed that I'd been forgiven for who my boss was. Maybe things would start getting easier now.

16

New York was quickly turning into my favourite tour date. So good, in fact, that I even got an hour to myself after all, taking pictures of cafes and galleries in East Village while Sigrid had her face 'plumped to pillow freshness' at the best secret skin clinic in the city.

When everyone left the hotel to head to Madison Square Garden for the concert, I assumed that I'd have Sigrid and Jamie's suite to myself for a while. I was dancing around to the TV again when I was surprised by a knock at the door. Oliver walked in with a strange, conspiratorial smile on his face, accompanied by three hotel maids.

'I've brought you some help,' he said, introducing them.

'Thanks, but I'll be OK,' I assured him. 'I'm used to doing this by now. What are *you* doing here? Aren't you supposed to be at the venue?'

'I am,' he agreed, 'but I've come to get you.'

'I don't understand.'

'Angus asked around. He tells me you haven't seen a show yet. Is that true?'

I shrugged. 'Well, you know … Sigrid keeps me busy. She likes everything to be done the way she—'

'That's *insane*. Look, I know you work for her, but I work for the band, and in Rock, Paper, Scissors, Angus is the rock, and she's the scissors. Which means he wins. I'm taking you now. You're meeting her at the airport afterwards anyway, right? She'll never know.'

'But there's a spreadsheet …'

'Ignore the spreadsheet. Who unpacks for her?'

'I do.'

'So …? I promise we'll take care of everything.'

He held out his hand. I grinned and took it. I was *on tour with a rock band*. What else was I supposed to do?

An hour later, I was inside Madison Square Garden, near the VIP section, not too far from the stage. The place was huge, and bright, and loud. Thousands and thousands of fans sat in rows that seemed to stretch up as high as a skyscraper. The people at the top seemed so small and far away they were like pixels on a screen. Nearer, I spotted lots of faces painted blue and yellow (like Ariel with her hair, they were confused about Jamie's favourite colour), and others painted with the band's target logo. Some were happy and others were already crying.

The lights went down. A disembodied voice simply said, 'Ladies and gentlemen … The Point!' and the stadium was suddenly filled with a vivid red and blue laser display.

The crowd went WILD.

I could hardly even think over the sound of the screaming as everyone watched the empty stage. The thud, thud, thud of an electronic drumbeat over the sound system was so loud I could actually feel it in my ribcage. Lasers swept the stage and the crowd and the noise kept building until it was a full-bodied ROAR.

It was huge, and I was just a tiny part of it. So *this* was what I'd been missing.

When the band finally hit the stage, the screaming was already so loud it couldn't possibly get any louder – and yet somehow it did. George raised his drumsticks in acknowledgement. SCREAM. Connor slung his bass strap over his shoulder. SCREAM. Angus and Jamie walked on together, their arms around each other's shoulders.

I was thinking how good it was to see them not arguing for once. Under the lights you would never know their relationship was fractured. The crowd were clearly just thinking OH MY GOD ANGUS AND JAMIE – SCREAM SCREAM SCREAM SCREAM SCREAM. I wasn't sure I would ever be able to hear properly again.

Jamie walked up to the mic and instantly, they were into the first number. It was 'Kiss It Better' – one of Ariel's favourites. At least, I thought so. It was almost impossible to hear it over the sound of the crowd. Luckily, three vast LED screens lit up – one at the back and one each side of the stage – so we could see Jamie's face, blown up to the size of a building, and work out what he was singing from the way his lips were moving.

When the song was over, he walked to the front and

grinned into the crowd.

'Hello New York!'

AAH! AAH! AAAH! AAAAH! AAAAAAH! I gave in and screamed along.

'It's good to be back in the temple of rock and roll. This one's for you.'

Eventually the screaming died down to a manageable level, and you could hear what they were playing. Now it was 'Unlock Me', one of the songs I'd always liked from their first album. As Jamie reached the chorus, some of the girls around me grabbed each other and hugged.

I knew that feeling. Special memories. Captured moments. I wished Ariel could be beside me, because every note would be special for her. She'd be hugging me all the time. I took out my phone and videoed Jamie in close-up for her.

Two songs later, he strapped on an acoustic guitar and walked up to the mic to sing 'Eden'. This time I froze. That break-up song again.

I knew this moment would come eventually, and I thought I was prepared, but the punch to my stomach still felt as strong and hard as it ever did. Jez and Ria dancing. The look he gave me. The drink that fell from my hand.

Special memories. Just the wrong ones.

'Are you OK?'

A warm hand on my arm. The girl beside me, with blue hair just like Ariel's, looked worriedly into my eyes.

'Yeah, fine,' I said, numbing myself as best I could.

Things get better, I told myself. *It's just another song.*

It was true. After three minutes and twenty-seven seconds of heartbreak, Angus launched into the driving, happy riff of 'You Don't Know What You Just Did To Me'. With Connor rock-steady on bass, Jamie pranced, preened and flirted with the crowd. George sat at the back with a huge grin on his face, hitting everything in sight with the force of a hurricane, perfectly sober, perfectly in control.

Everyone around me threw their arms in the air and started dancing.

They knew all the words to every lyric, and thanks to my sister, so did I. I gradually forgot that I wasn't supposed to be here, and that I'd ever been humiliated to music. It didn't matter any more. Anyway, after 'Eden', this gig could only get better.

The music quickly became a physical thing, even for me. My chest and throat were soon tired from belting out the lines along with Jamie, but by now I couldn't stop.

Jamie danced across the stage. That boy could *move*. And that face. Those lips ... that Mona Lisa smile. He was having his usual effect and I gave up trying to fight it. Right here and now it was too powerful to ignore. It was as if we were all linked up to him by our own private wires, feeling his power, sharing ours, buzzing with something like love, but bigger. And he absorbed all our energy like some kind of silk-clad, mole-cheeked lightning conductor, and fed it back to us.

Yeah ... so ... Jamie Maldon. I got it now.

When he sang, especially the slow songs, his expression looked transported. As he and Angus had written most of them, it was obvious they had a special meaning for him. They did for the fans too. Meanwhile, Connor held the beat and Angus showed off on his favourite battered Fender Stratocaster. His solos were like fireworks. He was furious and intense, but clearly loving it, as shown by the close-up of the half-smile on his face. Half a smile from Angus was worth a thousand grins from anybody else.

But it was Jamie I kept coming back to. He was a showman and a songwriter, equally. How could a boy with lips like that, and hips like that, also have the soul of a poet? It wasn't fair.

Once or twice in each song he and Angus caught each other's eye and decided to do something together. You could tell that although they'd rehearsed, there were moments when they'd take a risk and go in a new direction. There was no sign of their off-stage animosity. Right now, they were just having fun. They radiated it into the crowd, and we radiated it back.

Jamie danced up and down the runway, throwing out towels and water bottles to the people nearby. The stage in front of him gradually became a colourful carpet, made out of paper flowers. It was a Pointer Sister tradition to throw them. Jamie picked a few up, kissed them and threw them back into the audience.

The crowd went WILD. AGAIN.

Angus was right: we *were* New York. There was nowhere else to be tonight.

Song after song went by ... and suddenly the lights went out and the boys quickly ran offstage.

Nooooooooooo! It couldn't be over! We screamed for them to come back. There was more roaring and stomping, and I realized I was roaring as loud as anyone. The crowd was a living, happy thing, and I just wanted to stay a part of it.

Luckily, they were kidding and were quickly back for an encore. After an ear-melting rock rendition of One Direction's

'What Makes You Beautiful', and a blasting re-creation of Oasis's 'Wonderwall', Jamie walked to the front of the stage and asked for quiet.

'This really is the last one, guys. I want you to sing with me. You know how it goes ...'

He stepped forward and sang the opening lines:

> *She moves like a miracle*
> *So I sold up my guitar*
> *Spent the money on a golden ring*
> *Don't get you very far*

We knew it instantly: the band's first single, 'Amethyst'. There was so much love and longing in this one that it wormed its way under your skin – even though the girl in question turns down the ring and he ends up writing the song for her knowing she'll turn that down too.

> *Amethyst for a heart of stone*
> *Amethyst you'll always be the one*

It seemed a strange song to end on. But when Jamie got to the first chorus, he stopped singing and held his mic out to the crowd. We all sang back to him. The sound was unearthly.

> *Amethyst for a girl that's gone*
> *I can't help my heart, you're the only one*

He closed his eyes, listening, and we heard our voices too – so many thousands, all singing together, gently, from the girls standing at the barriers near the stage to the people high up in the topmost seats, near the sky.

'That was beautiful, New York. One more time.'

He sang, we sang. He crouched down, we sang quietly. He rose up, we got louder. His voice cracked with emotion, we all shared his pain. Angus and Connor played almost imperceptibly in the background. George's brushes shimmered on the cymbals as the lights went down.

Jamie reached into his back pocket and pulled out his phone. He held the lit screen up to the crowd. We got the message and held our phones back to him. Thousands of tiny lit-up screens twinkled around the stadium like stars. Jamie's voice grew quieter and quieter, until there was almost silence.

In this massive space, the quiet of the crowd was like a living thing. We breathed together so softly that we could hear Jamie gently humming. Everyone in the front rows stretched out their arms with a look of anguish and wonder. He echoed their expression, sharing the moment.

Amethyst for a girl that's gone
I can't help my heart, you're the only one

He sang those last lines one more time and Angus played three melancholy final notes on the Stratocaster.

'Thank you, New York. You're magic. Goodnight!'

The stage went black.

Shock.

This time, it really was over.

And yes, it was magic, and the magic still hovered in the air.

I felt like something had been ripped away from me. How could four people *do* that? A whole stadium of fans, all connected, longing for it not to end.

Four people, yes, but a tiny part of me had to admit that one of them had moved me more than the rest – inspired me, and transported me, and filled me with emotions I thought I'd lost for ever, the way a desert flourishes after rain.

I was glad, for once, that he didn't usually bother to talk to me. How could I find the words to explain what he just made me feel?

17

The band were booked to play in Verona the next day and we all met up at the airport, ready to head back across the Atlantic less than thirty-six hours after we'd arrived.

Any sensible person would have used the flight to get some sleep. Sigrid certainly intended to. She turned her seat into a bed, got an attendant to cut some cucumber slices for her eyes, put on one of her meditation apps, and instructed me to tell everyone she shouldn't be disturbed.

But rock bands are not sensible people. And when you've just played Madison Square Garden, the last thing you want to do is sleep. Nobody else seemed tired at all. Guitars appeared from nowhere. Boys and roadies took it in turns to play. Connor grabbed the nearest air hostess and started dancing. Jamie shimmied hips with Cath from wardrobe. George tried to dance with me. Even Angus asked me, but I knew my boss and reluctantly said no. I ended up doing a salsa with the manager.

I was still living the gig in my head. The experience had explained a lot to me. Now I knew why Jamie was so distant much of the time, and why Angus was so rude. A part of them must still be onstage, sharing a moment with all those people reaching out to them.

And I understood the girls who lurked in hotel bars and corridors, hoping for any scrap of attention. Because if you thought you could re-create that experience in person, one-to-one … wouldn't you?

At one point during the flight, I noticed that Sigrid wasn't wearing her cucumber slices any more. Her body was motionless under a cashmere blanket, but her eyes were open and she was watching us dance. I thought she might call me over and give me some pointless job to do, but that didn't happen. She merely closed her eyes and turned her meditation app up louder.

The hotel in Verona was so historic and beautiful it was like living in a Shakespeare play, or a fairy tale. Thick, plush fabrics coated every surface. Everything was red or yellow, and most of it was silk. Beds were four-posters. Mirrors had massive gilt frames. Staff bowed politely in carpeted corridors, and mysteriously knew everyone's name – even mine.

We arrived at lunchtime, with two hours to crash before the band were due at the open-air arena for the sound check. The boys, as usual, ordered pizza and sushi on arrival, and headed for their rooms. At least pizza was, for once, a relevant national dish.

Once they had set off for the sound check, I supervised the

unpacking of Sigrid's cases. As Oliver had promised, every-thing had been beautifully packed in Paris. I didn't need to worry.

This time, the suite was red-swagged and tasselled, with a painted ceiling. If Renaissance princes had had TVs in their bathrooms, this is how they'd have lived. Through the open curtains, beyond the sea of girls holding candles dedicated to The Point, I could see people strolling past bright shop windows. The longing to explore this city was as strong as it had been in New York.

Sigrid had hardly said a word since we got off the plane. She barely looked at me now. I put it down to jetlag when she retired to bed with a migraine.

After what happened yesterday, I'd been hoping to see the band in the ancient stadium somehow. The atmosphere would be electric tonight – outside, in the warm Italian air, with the sense of history infusing Jamie's songs with even more magic ... but before she lay down in her darkened room, Sigrid insisted that I shouldn't be more than ten minutes away by phone.

'I might need you,' she said weakly. 'Stay close.'

Good reminder, Nina. You are not a fan with a ticket to every gig. You're working.

I had a bad feeling about this. I wasn't sure if the migraine had changed Sigrid's mood, or if the mood had caused the migraine. But something was different. It had been different since the taxi ride in New York. And it wasn't good.

Never straying too far from the hotel, I spent a couple of hours wandering the narrow streets of the city with my camera, taking

138

pictures of ancient buildings with crenellated roofs in the different styles of Montagues and Capulets, and of blue-and-yellow Pointer Sisters gathering in excited groups in squares and on street corners.

For Mum's sake, I risked a quick visit to the house with Juliet's so-called balcony (a sign explained it was added in the twentieth century) and discovered that the outside walls were covered in graffiti and were, indeed, incredibly disappointing.

At least – they were disappointing as history. As art, they were fascinating. Colourful names from around the world were scrawled in pairs on white plaster in every sort of pen imaginable. Big hearts and small hearts with names and initials inside, name upon name until they formed a thick tapestry of red, green, blue and black: *Marco e Anna; Kurt + Katia; Susie & Lola; Amy and J.D.* ...

There was so much love there. So much hope. The more I photographed and videoed the graffiti the more it appeared to me as an artwork – anonymous and chaotic, unpredictable, and ugly at first sight, but ultimately beautiful.

I couldn't wait to download my pictures and play with them. I hoped it would take my mind off whatever Sigrid was up to, and what I'd be missing in the arena tonight.

Back in my room, which was tucked away in the attics this time, I got out my laptop and lost myself in making scrapbook pages from the images. Cropping, enlarging, playing with the settings, and layering them on each other, I wanted the pictures themselves to give the same impression as the graffiti – confusing at first, but finely detailed when you zoomed in closer. I loved the shifting pattern of hearts; the endless names; all those love stories captured in a moment, but that we'd never really know.

They'd make a perfect backdrop for one of Jamie's lyrics, I thought. I experimented with layering some lines from 'Unlock Me' over the top, in thin gold lettering, to make his words stand out over the lovers' writing. Meanwhile, Italian pop songs floated through the open window from a radio on a nearby balcony. Listening to the music, not understanding the words, I lost track of time as I finished one design and started another, trying to capture the magnificence of the Medici princess suite.

Bang bang BANG!

There was a sudden, furious knocking at my door. I ran to answer it. Sigrid was standing there, barefoot, in a hotel robe. Her eyes blazed into me.

'What are you DOING? I've been calling you for HOURS.'

I was shocked. 'B-but … I had my phone on. It's been beside me all day. I …'

And then I remembered. I'd switched it to silent while I was closing Sigrid's curtains for her and tucking her up in bed this afternoon. For once, I didn't remember turning the ringer back on again.

'Is there a problem?'

'Of course there is,' she said, pushing past me into my room and standing in the middle of my floor with a hand to her head. 'I woke up and it was TOTALLY dark and TOTALLY silent. I couldn't remember what day it was, or where I was supposed to be. I was terrified. So I called for you and … nothing.'

Meanwhile, I was fishing my phone out of my bag and

140

checking it. Six missed calls and messages.

'I'm so sorry, Sigrid. But I'm right here. Can I do anything for …?'

But she wasn't listening to me. She was playing a new part this evening, and this one was Very Angry Boss. As usual, she was playing it with everything she had. She was a ball of dark fury and her eyes darted round my room, looking for trouble. Her glance fell on my open laptop.

'What's that?'

'Just something I've been working on.'

'But that's a picture of my room! What is it doing on your computer?'

Her voice was quiet, but deadly.

'It's just a private thing,' I assured her, desperately. 'I play around with my photos sometimes. I—'

'No pictures. Don't you know ANYTHING?' She stalked across to my laptop and stood over it, shaking. 'Show me!'

'I – I don't understand,' I stuttered. It was as if she'd come here deliberately to find fault with me.

'Show me everything. Everything you've been up to. Every picture you've taken.'

'I wasn't going to publish them. They're just personal. I—'

'SHOW ME!'

It was impossible to reason with her. She made me show her every collage, gasping at every picture she saw.

'There's Jamie, practising guitar! Does he know about this?'

'No. I don't know … He might have seen me with my camera.'

'You've been photographing us in secret? Omigod! There's my peace tent!'

141

'But Sigrid! You asked me to take pictures!'

I realized too late that this was the worst thing I could say. She turned to me with venom in her eyes.

'For ME! On MY phone! *I* decide what gets published. Jamie's passionate about his privacy. Didn't you sign the NDA?'

'That agreement? I did, but this is private. I was only going to show my family.'

'Oh yes?' She juddered with indignation. 'That's what you *say*. But I know girls like you. People would pay thah-sands for this stuff. Oh my God, there's Jamie's *handwriting on a pizza box*! Does he know you took it?'

'No. He threw it away. It looked like a song. I just—'

'What else have you stolen?'

Stolen? At the mention of the word, my heart plummeted.

'I haven't stolen anything!'

'YOU THINK?' Sigrid shouted, slamming the lid of my laptop down. 'I bring you here to do a specific job ... I give you the chance of a lifetime ... And all you are is a low-down flirt and a spy. You're just some cheap groupie from Sa-af London.'

By now my cheeks were burning. 'I'm not! I've never flirted! I haven't spied on any—'

She pointed at the computer with a shaking finger. 'Yes, you are. And the proof's all there. I'm taking it.'

'No!'

I tried to stop her, but she grabbed the laptop and hugged it to her tightly. At the doorway, she turned back theatrically for a moment.

'And just in case you were wondering, you're fired. You can

go back to your tacky family tomorrow. On a BUDGET FLIGHT.'

Then she broke down in sobs, as if *I'd* just done something horrific to *her*, and ran until she was out of sight.

18

Croydon seemed colder and greyer than ever after the warmth of the Italian sun.

Just as I'd started to enjoy myself, everything was spoilt. But it was good, I told myself. It had all worked out for the best.

True, I missed the end of the tour. I never got to see The Point perform in Poland or Budapest or Berlin, but I could focus on my last English AS level paper properly, and take it in the school gym, with everyone else. No more arranging karmic almonds, or jumping to attention when somebody said 'Phone'. I'd never again have to sit in a room and watch George drink himself into a stupor in one corner, while Sigrid draped herself all over Jamie in another.

Tammy was furious on my behalf, which helped.

Early the next morning, the band had gone on to an open-air festival in Gdynia, on the Polish coast. It was the first time Sigrid got the requested personal private jet for her and Jamie, and I'd been forced to share it with them. Only then could Oliver arrange my journey home.

It was, categorically, among the worst few hours of my life. The manager was there too. Sigrid had spent the whole flight showing them my artwork and telling them about my *spying* and *betrayal*. Her eyes dared me to interrupt her, and all the time her lips dripped poison.

Afterwards, as I waited for them to leave the plane, Jamie had turned to me, briefly, once. 'If you wanted something, you should have just asked for it,' he'd said quietly.

I hung my head in shame. A moment later the manager had asked for my laptop and Sigrid had handed it over triumphantly. He still hadn't given it back.

'They should call her the Empress of Evil,' Tammy muttered, over commiseration chicken at Nando's. 'She was jealous of you, it's obvious.'

'Not jealous – angry,' I corrected her. 'She must have found out what happened with Angus. I wasn't supposed to get close to her boyfriend's friends.'

Tammy liked to think she was a great psychologist, but as she got all her psychology from the E! channel and Perez Hilton, I wasn't too sure.

'Nuh-uh. Jealous,' she insisted. 'She wants them all to like her, and they don't. They liked you, obviously. She couldn't handle it. Evil, I'm telling you.'

'Well, whatever it was, it worked,' I said, picking at my chicken wings.

'You miss them, don't you?' She sounded surprised. I could feel myself blushing.

'Well, um … you know …'

'You said they were a bunch of spoilt millionaires.'

'Oh, they are. They absolutely are.'

'So?'

I tried to avoid the question by pretending my chicken was too spicy to let me talk. 'Phew! Hot!' I fanned my face.

She grinned, knowingly. 'See? Told you.'

'What? Oh, not *them*. I mean, they are, but …'

Everything was so simple in Tammy-land. Boys are hot. Girls like them. Nobody gets hurt. My world was practically the opposite.

'What?' she asked.

'They're messed up.' I looked across at her and tried to find the right words. 'But they're more interesting than I thought, when you get to know them.'

She laughed. 'Break the internet! The Point are *interesting when you get to know them*.'

'Haha. What I mean is, offstage they hardly know what day it is. They play Pizza-Frisbee in hotel corridors. Their lifestyle's insane. But when they play their songs, they have this incredible … Jamie's so …'

'Again,' Tammy grinned. 'Nina Baxter discovers the absolutely obvious. Anyway, back off – Jamie's mine!'

I made a face at her. 'You can have him.'

She put narrowed her eyes and gave me a searching look. 'Really?'

It made me uncomfortable. 'Really,' I assured her. 'Join the queue. They're interesting, that's all I'm saying. I wouldn't have minded staying with them a bit longer.'

'Oh, Nina,' Tammy sighed at me. 'What have they done to you?'

The next day, I was back at work at Mum's salon, earning some holiday cash. Two girls walked in to get their highlights done: Clementine and her best friend, Becca.

I swallowed. So, this was going to be fun.

'Can you get Rebecca ready for me?' Mum asked cheerily, seemingly oblivious to what was about to happen.

'Of course.'

With my heart beating like a drum-and-bass track, I sat Becca back in the chair by the basins, and started to wash her honey-blonde hair.

'So,' she said, examining her fingernails. 'You're back early.'

'Yes,' I agreed, quietly.

'I mean, Clemmie's off to Nepal next week, aren't you, Clemmie?'

From the basin next to her, Clementine smiled serenely. 'Mmm hmm.'

'And yet you're already home.'

Becca waited for me to fill the silence. I didn't.

'Anyone would think that Tammy was making it up,' she went on. 'All that stuff about you and The Point. Or maybe she was confused. We checked your Facebook status – nothing.'

She shook her head sadly at my stupid fantasy life.

'Oh, I joined them in Spain,' I said. 'I have …. pictures.' I ended lamely.

'Of you and them together?'

'Um … no.'

'What, then?'

'Their hotel rooms, and stuff.'

'That's where you worked?' Clementine asked. 'So you were, like, a maid?'

I nodded unhappily.

'Sorry?'

'Yes,' I whispered.

'And then – what? Did they fire you?'

The accuracy of her question hit me like a missile. My face said 'yes' – my voice didn't need to.

'Hahahahaha.'

Mum came over to wash Clementine's hair.

'Is Nina telling you about the tour?' she asked.

'Uh huh,' Becca said, screwing her face into a picture of awkwardness before shooting me a mock-pity glance.

Mum looked sad for me and sighed. 'Well, at least she's home safely.'

This was hardly the triumphant return Tammy had predicted for me.

Clementine turned to Becca. 'Did you hear, by the way?' she said, ignoring me now. 'Jamie secretly married Sigrid after this gig in Poland?'

'No!'

'There was, like, a shaman there or something, and they did this ceremony under some sort of peace tent thing in their hotel room. He's gone a bit …' She made her eyes go googly and circled a finger beside her head.

'That's not true!' I spluttered. 'They wouldn't!'

She turned round to sneer at me. 'Oh yeah? How would a *maid* know?'

A maid would know, I thought to myself. And she was right – that's pretty much what I had been. Like a maid, I knew what brand of boxer shorts Jamie wore, what time he got up and when he went to bed. I knew he liked Matisse and was allergic to strawberries. I knew he didn't even like Sigrid's stupid peace tent, and the most he could be persuaded to do under it was yoga. I knew he wasn't married yet, because Sigrid still hadn't decided which wedding planner to use, and no way was she walking up the aisle in her 'simple Valentino beach dress' until every last detail had been organized, down to the orthodontic appointment she needed to make because her back teeth weren't quite perfect.

I knew all this, and I couldn't tell Becca and Clementine – or at least, I wouldn't – because it was private. Not because I'd signed all those agreements, but because on tour the band spent most of their lives in a fishbowl, being stared at, and the one place they relaxed was in the Hotel California. It was the only place they felt safe. Despite anything that Sigrid said, I wasn't going to spill their secrets now.

When we'd wrapped the girls' hair in towels, Mum and I took them through to the main salon. They chattered on about Angus's 'secret girlfriend' (he didn't have one) and George's drug problem (actually drink, which was just as bad, I suppose). Mum was surprised I didn't correct them, but now my silence was my armour. I knew the truth – they didn't. I shared a connection with The Point, albeit a broken one, that these girls could never imagine.

All the time, I kept catching sight of my backstage passes from Barcelona, and the special one I used in the Hotel California. When she first saw them, Mum had treated them like ancient relics and asked to borrow them. She'd tucked them into the frame of the mirror at her salon station, where they blinked and shone at me now, like secret talismans.

19

At home, things were different. Every night, Mum and Dad asked me for real stories about the secret life of the band. I'd come back in such disgrace that they wanted to understand what had really happened. And the more I talked, the more they wanted to know.

I didn't notice the effect on Ariel at first. Nobody was that surprised about the Queen of Evil, but each time I mentioned George's drinking, or a fight between Angus and Jamie, or the way they treated me, her eager expression grew sadder and dimmer. Her idols were tarnished and it was my fault. Gradually, she stopped playing their songs. One by one, the posters came down. The Jamie Maldon duvet set was listed on eBay.

I went up to the bedroom she shared with the twins, as she was peeling the last of the stickers off her window, and tried to explain.

'I think they were just tired. Touring's crazy – you never stop.

I caught them at a bad time, Lellie.'

She didn't look round.

'Jamie was horrible to you.' Her voice was full of hurt.

'He was at first,' I admitted. 'He just wanted some privacy. I think Sigrid hired me without checking with him first.'

Looking back, Jamie was actually more normal than Sigrid a lot of the time. He was friendly with the entourage, and never directly mean to me. He just seemed to tune out when his fiancée was.

Ariel seemed to read my thoughts. She looked back at me now, and her eyes were blazing. The last time I'd seen them like this she had been fired by a fierce, protective love of Jamie. Now it was bitter disillusion. 'Why did he let her be so nasty to you anyway?'

She looked on the verge of tears. I tried to put an arm around her, but she shrugged me off.

'I don't know,' I sighed. 'I don't think he noticed me much. And he loves her.'

'That's no excuse,' Ariel muttered. 'Why can't he see what kind of person she is?'

'She's very, very beautiful. She's nice to *him*. And he's locked in this world where everything's perfect. Everything's done for him. I don't think he notices anything much any more.'

The more I tried to make it better, the worse it got.

After the twins' tea, when I went up to run the bath for them, I caught her in the bathroom with a pair of scissors, cutting off the bottom half of her hair.

'Ariel! Your blue!'

She looked at me dully in the mirror above the basin.

'I don't want it any more.'

The floor around her was scattered with thin blue strands, like a sea of fine needles.

'But … it was your glory.'

She surveyed the strands without emotion, then cut off another hank.

'I don't need it. I'm better like this.'

She was beautiful however she chose to cut her hair, but her sadness made me want to cry. If she hadn't been brandishing a very sharp pair of scissors, with a purposeful glint in her eye, I would have hugged her. Instead, I watched as she finished the job.

'There. Done. I'll go and get a brush.'

Jamie Maldon was out of her life, whatever his favourite colour was.

She walked past me without another word.

He wasn't out of mine, though. None of them were. And not just because their manager *still* hadn't given me back my laptop.

Yes, they turned out to be 'interesting when you got to know them', but I had to stop obsessing about them all, like a sad, crazy stalker, following every story about them on the internet. It wasn't my business if Jamie was busy ranch-hunting with Sigrid in Montana. *'My heart really lies in the mountains': Sigrid Santorini tells all about her life-long love of horses, and how she can't wait to settle down with her rock-star beau and raise a family of cowboys.* Or if Angus was due to feature on Digger V's latest album. Or if there were rumours that George had finally passed out onstage at a gig with some friends in LA and been taken to hospital in a coma, or that he and Connor were fed up with waiting for Jamie to write more songs, and were starting a breakaway band.

I found out all this information on my phone. The lack of a laptop was completely infuriating. I rang Rory Windermere's office every day to try and get it back. But each time I spoke to someone, they said he was busy.

A week went by, and then another. I found the office's address online and even went to Soho in central London to visit it in person. But they said he was away that day, visiting a sick aunt. The most pathetic lie I'd ever heard. Meanwhile, nobody knew where my precious computer was.

'Tomorrow I'm reporting it stolen,' I told the girl at the reception desk.

'Mmmmm hmmmmm.'

The wall behind her was lined with gold and platinum discs in Perspex frames. She didn't seem that interested in a schoolgirl's computer. I wanted to kick something, or cry. Instead, I wrote a message to Mr Windermere demanding the return of my property, and made her promise to leave it on his desk.

He rang me the next day, soon after breakfast.

'Miss Baxter! What wonderful timing! I gather you popped in. So sorry I missed you. Thank you for your note.'

He sounded friendly. Very. Not like a man who'd sat on my most precious possession for over a fortnight. Or who'd watched as my ex-boss ripped my reputation to shreds on a private jet in front of his biggest client. I'd half wondered if he'd kept the laptop in case Jamie wanted to sue me.

'Are you busy?' he asked.

'Um, no. Not exactly.'

I'd been googling Montana real estate. Pathetic.

'The thing is ...' he went on, 'I have a terrible favour to ask.'

'A *favour*?' I stared at the phone in my hand to see if the sound was working properly. 'I don't understand.'

'I'm so sorry about your laptop. I'd forgotten all about it. I'm having it couriered to you as we speak. But your note got me thinking ... Look, I know things ended badly before, and I'm sorry. But I can promise it will be different this time.'

This time? The tour was over. The last date had been a massive outdoor gig in Berlin. The Point had released a thousand silver balloons into the night sky and partied until dawn, then flown off in different directions and apparently not spoken to each other since.

'What time?' I asked.

'Well, as I'm sure you're aware, the boys are supposed to start writing their new album. It's long overdue. Someone's let me down and I think you could be the girl to help me.'

'O-kay,' I said, still confused. I was beginning to wonder if he wanted me to ranch-sit for Jamie and Sigrid or something. Which Wasn't. Ever. Happening.

'They need some time together to write songs and get some demos down. I'm sending them to a secret location for a few weeks. I was wondering if you could go too, if you're willing.'

'Me?'

'You, Nina. Absolutely. Your note was a timely reminder. I need someone who can cope with them, and whom I can trust completely to be discreet.'

'But … Sigrid …'

I couldn't bring myself to describe the way things had ended. But he'd been there on the hideous plane ride to Gdynia. Surely he remembered?

'Ah, yes,' he acknowledged, with a polite cough. 'While Miss Santorini is a joy to behold … one can't always rely on absolutely everything she says. She gave the impression that you were inclined to divulge private information. Whereas I happen to know that you don't.'

'Oh?'

'Well, for example, you spent the night with Angus and didn't tell a soul.'

What? He knew? He *knew* about that? I felt my face burning.

'Um … we didn't … there wasn't … I—'

'I know nothing happened,' he said with a smile in his voice. 'And don't be surprised – a manager hears *everything*. You were very helpful to Angus that night, and afterwards your lips were sealed. Believe me, that's rare. And your artwork was fascinating, by the way. You should do more of it. I rather liked it.'

Oh. My. Goodness. Everything I thought they thought was wrong. He didn't want my laptop so he could sue me after all. And he liked my pictures. Rock bands began to rise in my estimation.

'Thank you, Mr Windermere. But what about Jamie? Doesn't he …?'

'Don't worry about Jamie. I'm just making the final arrangements for the studio. Do say you'll come,' he went on smoothly. 'It will be an entirely more civilized affair, I promise. No

156

crowds. No girlfriends. *Categorically* no girlfriends. No hustle and bustle. They'll be staying somewhere private, near the sea. There wouldn't be a huge amount for you to do. Just a little light housekeeping and helping out. I had a woman lined up, you see, but she's twisted her knee. Most unfortunate, and at the last minute too. The deadline's very tight, I'm afraid. I need you to be ready in less than a week. I'll come and pick you up, if you agree. And do call me Windy. Everybody does.'

He didn't know it, but he had me at 'categorically no girl-friends'.

My brain, which had stalled around the 'Sigrid is unreliable' moment, suddenly went into overdrive. *'Your artwork was fascinating … You should do more of it …'* I pictured myself lounging round a pool on an island somewhere exotic, pausing to photograph the dappled light on the water while the boys jammed with local musicians and hung out with their friends. Maybe there would be movie directors and artists to talk to, if Jamie's tastes were anything to go by.

'A little light housekeeping … No hustle and bustle.'

Nobody's bags to carry, and nobody making bunny faces.

A total absence of supermodels and movie stars.

As if I hadn't got fired the last time. As if I hadn't been humiliated in public on a daily basis. As if Rory Windermere wasn't just a little bit crazy. And I wasn't just a little bit crazier for trusting him.

20

'**Y**ou want to do *what?*' Dad spluttered, when I found him in the shed doing some joinery for a project he was working on.

'Go and work for the band for a few weeks.'

'But they treated you like dirt! They sacked you!'

'*They* didn't – Sigrid did. I thought they all agreed with her, but it turns out they didn't. And ...'

'I thought you hated them.'

'I didn't. Not all the time. Sigrid was the problem really. And she won't be there.'

'C'mon,' Dad said. 'We need to consult the oracle.'

He went to join Mum in the garden, where she was hanging out the washing with the twins, which mostly involved stopping them from dressing up in it. I helped her peg out underwear while we talked.

'Where would you be going?' Mum asked.

This was tricky. I shrugged, rescuing a pair of Dad's underpants from Lara's giggling head. 'Windy said it was a secret, so I don't know, exactly.'

I had a clue, though. I'd done some extra searching online after we'd ended the call. According to the fan sites, lots of people assumed the band would go to Jamaica for the new recording sessions. Some favoured Mustique. Others talked about a studio on one of the Greek islands, where there was a gorgeous villa with top-class recording facilities, overlooking the sparkling sea.

This time, though, Mum didn't seem so keen.

'This secrecy thing sounds very fishy,' she mused.

'I know it seems odd,' I agreed. 'But you've got to understand. As soon as anyone says anything about the band, it's on the web in seconds. I'm sure Windy's just being careful. You'd like him, Dad. He's the man with the MGA, remember?'

'Ah, lovely motor,' Dad said. 'He can't be all bad … but just because a bloke has excellent taste in vintage sports cars, it doesn't mean he's reliable. He's the manager of a *rock band*. I mean, of course the man's unreliable.'

'What about your A levels?' Mum asked.

'Well, I probably wouldn't miss much school anyway. I could start the syllabus while I'm there. And there's always the internet. Everywhere's connected these days.' Rock bands were rubbing off on me, I realized. If you think big, you can make things happen. This wasn't a bad thing to learn.

Dad appealed to Mum. 'Make her see sense, will you?'

But that dreamy look was starting to creep back into Mum's eyes. She tried to frown so it wouldn't show, but I saw it anyway.

159

'You barely lasted a week last time,' she said. But I could tell her heart wasn't in it.

'Only because of Sigrid.'

'When you Skyped us, we could see how stressed you were.'

'Yes! But the things that stressed me wouldn't be happening this time.'

Me. And The Point, and their entourage – who I liked. In an exotic location. Without Sigrid Santorini to mess things up. I needed Tammy to be here to say, *Hello?*

Mum turned to Dad. 'What do you think? After everything they put her through, they owe her a decent holiday. If anything bad was going to happen, it would have happened by now, wouldn't it?'

Dad made harrumphing noises.

'One of them's a drunk.'

'But he's trying to give up, Dad.'

'One's a maniac.'

'Angus? Yeah, but when you get to know him ...' I realized I was starting to sound like Ariel used to.

'Ha! One of them's a skirt-chaser.'

'Connor'll have plenty of other skirts to chase, I'm sure. In the entourage.'

'And one's ...'

'What? Jamie's practically married.'

'He's dangerous, I'm telling you.'

It was true, but not for me. I'd seen how close he was to Sigrid, and I was still touched by what he'd tried to do for her in Paris.

'I'm not in danger of *anything* happening with Jamie Maldon. Trust me.'

It took me two days, but I wore them down in the end.

Ariel was devastated. Michael was pleased. He'd been itching for me to leave home so he could use my room, and this seemed like the first sign of it.

'I don't get you! You *told* me what they were like!'

'But that was on tour, Lellie. This is different.'

'You're so two-faced! I *hate* you!'

She ran off to her room and wouldn't talk to me.

Tammy had no problems with the new plan at all. She screamed so loudly when I told her that I worried I would never hear properly in my right ear again. She insisted on buying me three bikinis with her own money, because she said I looked amazing in all of them.

'And if anything happens while Jamie's away from Sigrid, the same rules apply as last time.'

'I've got to tell him that you'll be there to comfort him? Spiritually?'

'You bet. She's the Queen of Evil. He's bound to work it out eventually.'

'She has the most beautiful face in the world. I've seen it close up first thing in the morning. It's flawless.'

'OK, Angus, then. I could comfort Angus. I'm generous that way.'

'Fine.' I realized that I'd sort of done that myself already. Which was bizarre.

'Or Connor …'

'OK, OK! I get the picture!'

'Not George, though. I have my standards. And what am I telling everyone at school, if you're not back by the start of term and this secrecy thing is still happening?'

'Tell them …'

I'd just been reading a book by Malcolm Gladwell, called *The Tipping Point*. According to Oliver, this was the book Jamie was reading when he got the idea for the band's name. I knew almost as much as Ariel about him now. He'd left school at sixteen, but since then he'd devoured any book he could get his hands on. This one was all about how successful ideas spread in exactly the same way as a cold.

'Tell them I have a virus,' I said.

It seemed appropriate somehow.

21

By the time Windy arrived to pick me up and take me to the airport, the suitcase had been packed for twenty-four hours, and repacked four times in the process, just to squeeze in extra essentials. After a two-hour session in the salon, my new highlights shone in the sun. My skin was already smothered in tan lotion, just in case I forgot to apply any when I arrived. My new Jackie-O sunglasses were firmly on my head. The butterflies in my stomach felt as though they'd been on a seven-hour flight already. My wallet was full of cash, ready to be exchanged for whatever currency would be required when we got there.

Windy was as flamboyant as ever, in a striped linen jacket, a pink shirt and a blue tweed cap at a jaunty angle over one eyebrow. He looked at my case, and then at the boot of his car. So did I. So did Dad.

'Ah,' he said.

It was the same tomato-red MGA as last time. I'd sort of assumed that he'd turn up in an airport car to collect me this time. Or some kind of band-related limo. Just this once, that would have been useful.

But no.

The MGA is a stunning open-topped sports car with a long, sweeping bonnet over its twin-cam engine. There's room for a driver and passenger in the cockpit – no back seats. And behind them, as an afterthought, is a dinky little square boot – just about large enough for a picnic hamper.

'Ah,' Dad echoed eventually, spotting the problem and heading for the boot. 'Do you mind?'

'Not at all,' Windy agreed, gesturing for Dad to open it.

We all looked inside. It contained a spare wheel, a canvas holdall, a leather case and a large blue dog bed, covered in hairs. Altogether, they already took up three-quarters of the space. There was just about room left for a tote bag.

'I think we're going to have to juggle a little,' Windy admitted. 'Are there things in the, er ...' he indicated my cases, '... that you really need?'

'Yes. Everything.'

'Ah. Would you mind *terribly* repacking? I'm sorry. I didn't really think this through.'

Oh, really?

For the next twenty minutes I silently swore at Rory Windermere and his stupid taste in transport as I went back inside and repacked the absolute basic essentials – not much more than my computer, bikinis, underwear, wash things and some kaftans – into my tote bag, plus a couple of plastic supermarket bags that

Ariel rescued for me from the kitchen. She got me the mankiest ones, I noticed. She still hadn't begun to forgive me for going off with her new worst enemies.

Dad squeezed the bags into the boot as best he could and just managed to close it by pressing down on it hard.

'And this,' Windy said proudly, striding round to the front of the car, 'is Twiggy.'

'Who?'

In all the horror of the suitcase situation, I hadn't noticed the other occupant of the car. She was sitting in the passenger seat, shivering slightly, and looking up at me with big, brown eyes.

I should have realized. The dog bed ...

'Isn't she a darling?' Windy enthused. 'I'm inordinately fond of her. She's just what the boys need for company.'

'What is she? A greyhound?' Dad asked, peering at the narrow grey face uncertainly.

'A whippet. The most elegant dogs on earth, and she knows it, don't you, darling?' Windy bent down to ruffle behind her silky ear. 'You won't mind her on your lap, will you, Nina? Your brother kindly took her for a walk while you were packing, so she should be happy for a while.'

I was too confused to answer. Dad was right: the man was clearly insane. And I was heading who-knows-where with him and a whippet.

'Call me,' Dad said, squeezing me close to him. 'When you get there. Tell me you're safe.'

'Sure, Dad,' I agreed, with feeling.

The rest of the family came out to see me off: Mum with Pip and Lara attached to each leg, Michael with his hands in his pockets, Josh shooting Nerf bullets all over the front lawn, and Ariel standing in the shadow of the front door, glaring. I climbed into the car, and the whippet balanced her thin legs precariously on my thighs. Windy revved the sports car's engine and set off with a theatrical wave.

While he busily negotiated the traffic-clogged streets of South London, Twiggy and I tried to work out how we were going to manage her long, skinny legs, sharp claws and bony rump against my thighs and stomach. I assumed she'd get some sort of special dog seating area on the plane. How had Windy even got permission to take her with him? But … you know … rock band. The normal rules wouldn't apply.

Gradually the road grew wider and calmer, and Twiggy settled herself more or less comfortably on my lap with her head poking out of the window. I calmed down a bit too. Maybe the bag fiasco wasn't necessarily such a disaster. Surely there would be other girls I could borrow things from? Maybe even girls like Cath and Jess, who I knew from the tour.

'Who else will be there?' I asked.

'Hmm?' Windy said, distracted by the road ahead.

'At the studio. Who'll be there apart from the band?'

'Um … not many people. You know what I said about it being top secret? We're talking about a skeleton staff.'

'Oh. Right. How many other girls?'

'Well …' Windy seemed to consider for a moment. 'Actually, none.'

'What?'

'Not *girls*, exactly. Unless you count the chef. And as I was recently invited to her thirtieth birthday, I can't say I do.'

Oh-

kaaaaay then.

I was very quiet for a very long time, while my brain tried to process this information. Jamie Maldon, and Angus McLean ... and me. Just me. In my bikinis and kaftans, with my highlights glowing. There was a strange, flippy feeling in my stomach which wasn't entirely down to Twiggy digging her back legs into my flesh.

The Point, and me. Why had Windy chosen *me*?

It was one of Ariel's fanfic stories times a thousand. My heart raced, but my mind couldn't really go there. The weirdness was too immense.

'I'm not saying it'll be easy, sharing with a bunch of lads being forced to do something they don't entirely want to do,' Windy added, breaking the silence. 'We tried it in Jamaica last summer. Disaster. Then Miami at Christmas. That was actually worse. But you know what they say ... third time lucky ...'

His face twisted into a grim smile. This made me nervous. I thought back to the backstage tensions between Jamie and Angus, which I'd kind of forgotten about since leaving the tour. What I tended to remember was the music, and how I'd felt watching them.

'Don't they want to record?'

'Well, not exactly. I mean, they do, but not together. They keep talking about their solo projects. They take it for granted, this ... gift they have together. They don't how extraordinary it is. Most great bands don't, until it's too late. They let little things drive them apart, and before they know it, it's over. That's why I've had to be strict this time. No entourage. I need them to focus on each other, not hangers-on.'

This sounded bad.

'Are they OK with that?'

'Mmm ... you see, the thing is, they don't exactly ... know. There's quite a lot they don't know, actually. If I'd told them everything, they wouldn't ... but I'm sure they'll come round. Eventually.'

Oh dear. This sounded very bad.

'They ... they know about me, though, don't they?'

'Not yet, no.'

Oh.

The flippy feeling subsided into something more flappy – like a sea creature suddenly stranded on a beach. I'd assumed my invitation must mean that Jamie had forgiven me for the photographs. But it sounded as though he hadn't been consulted.

'What else don't they know?' I asked nervously.

'Well, I'll explain most of it tomorrow. But let's just say I've had to think radically. No distractions. No excursions. None of those devices they're addicted to. I need to force them together to write.'

This was sounding worse by the second. Less like a luxury holiday, and more like a luxury boot camp. It was not what I'd signed up for at all.

'And that's where you come in, Nina,' Windy said, reaching over and patting my hand. 'It's not just your housekeeping skills I'm after. The boys will need a friend. Someone else they can talk to at the beginning, when things are ... sticky. Someone about their age, who they can relax with, but who won't take sides. Another boy in the mix would only make things worse. All that testosterone …' He shuddered. 'So … I thought there should be a girl. But not a *girl* girl, obviously. Ha!' He chuckled to himself.

I glanced at him.

'What do you mean, "not a *girl* girl"?'

He grinned back at me, like it was obvious.

'Not a girlfriend sort of girl. Not someone they're going to fight over all the time. That would be *dreadful*. Just … you know …'

'A person.'

'Exactly.'

'Who none of them fancies.'

'Yes! Precisely! And just as importantly, someone who doesn't fancy any of them. I've seen the way you are with them. You're sensible. You're responsible. You know how to be friendly without flirting – and *that* would be a disaster, I hardly need to tell you. You've seen the effect that *girls* have on the band. Catastrophic. Utterly catastrophic. But you'll be perfect company for them all.'

He smiled at me happily.

Not a *girl* girl.

'And Twiggy, of course,' he added, turning his eyes back to the road. 'She's essential to the mix. I'll need you to look after her too.'

Yeah. Silly me. For glamour, they'd have the dog.

22

As London gradually gave way to intermittent patches of green and glimpses of countryside, we drove on in silence. My thoughts drifted. Not in good directions. Why had I ever imagined – even for a moment – that I could be *that girl*?

If anything, I had passed the audition to be the most reliable young female you could put in close proximity to The Point and be certain that nothing was going to happen. I'd proved it with each of them in turn. I'd even spent the night with one of them and nothing had happened. Well done, Windy.

By now, I'd stopped noticing where we were heading. It was only when I felt light raindrops on my face that I looked up and saw a sign saying 'M1 – The North'. Wait: this was not the way to any of the airports I knew. In fact, it was pretty much in the opposite direction.

'We're not going from Gatwick or Heathrow, then?'

'No,' he acknowledged, absently. He was looking up at the

looming grey clouds that had appeared from nowhere in the bright blue sky.

Oh, of course. We'd probably be taking a jet from a private airfield. That would explain how relaxed he was about travelling with a dog.

Soon we turned off the dual carriageway and on to a minor road. Twiggy shivered on my lap as the warm summer breeze gave way to a sharp, cold wind. Two minutes later, Windy pulled in at a lay-by and got out of the car.

'Would you mind?' he said, indicating that Twiggy and I should get out too. 'Won't be a moment.'

He pushed the seats forward and started to undo a series of metal fasteners on a canvas cover that was neatly tucked behind them. Soon he was unrolling an old-fashioned metal and canvas structure. It was like a little tent being constructed over the cockpit of the car. The hood! You'd never know it was stored there, in its secret compartment. And if we *hadn't* got near our destination yet, we were really going to need it. What had started as a gentle shower was turning into relentless drizzle.

Holding the whippet's lead in one hand, I helped Windy as best I could, fixing the frame in place on my side of the car, stretching the canvas over it and working the tricky fastenings into place. By the time we were done, we were both pretty wet. Twiggy, in her damp felt overcoat, looked utterly miserable.

Windy smiled at the car from under his dripping cap.

'This is more of a sunny weather vehicle,' he admitted ruefully, as we slid back into our seats. 'But I couldn't resist one last run up north in her.' He patted the car fondly on its wet wooden steering wheel.

'Um … "up north"?' I asked.

From London, hot places are south. Everybody knows that. You get in a plane and fly south.

'Yes,' he said. 'We're not quite halfway, but nearly. We should be there by nightfall.'

I was getting nervous now. 'Up north' was not a private airfield. It wasn't the Caribbean. It wasn't Mustique, or a Greek island, or LA. 'Up north' was not bikini country.

'I might as well tell you now,' Windy said, pulling back on to the road. 'We're going to Northumberland. Not far from the border. Stunning countryside.'

'The border with *Scotland*?'

'Mmm hmm.'

'You're going to shut us up in a house in *Scotland*?'

'Well, nearby, certainly. You'll love it. Very bracing. And it's less than twenty miles from the sea.'

'*Twenty miles*?'

'At most. Probably nineteen.'

'But you said no excursions, so we can't even go there.'

'True …' he ruminated, stroking his chin. 'But you won't need to. Lovely house. And very private. Lovely grounds. Exactly what the boys need. I only wish I could stay there with you.'

'You're not staying?' Everything he said made it worse.

'Too much to do,' he shrugged. 'And the boys don't need me for this bit. They need inspiration. Freedom. Peace.'

'They'll hate it,' I said, with feeling. As would I, sharing it with them. They wanted nightclubs, DJs, champagne on tap.

They wanted models and Matisses and ranches in Montana. Even I'd been banking on sunshine, not gloomy English weather. Almost *Scottish* weather, which was worse. Dad always joked that the Scots have more words for rain than the Inuit do for snow.

Windy went quiet for a moment. Then he said, 'They might hate it. But it'll be good for them.'

Oh, fabulous. I so looked forward to their reactions when he told them. Because we all knew how much rock stars liked doing things that were *good for them*. That wasn't going to be a problem at all.

23

On we drove, through a storm and a spectacular sunburst. Past grey concrete cities and hills that looked like mountains. With the hood up, the cabin steamed up with our hot breath and it fogged up the windscreen so that Windy kept having to wipe it with his cap. I thought about all the things I'd re-packed (kaftans and flip-flops), and all the things I left behind (jeans, long-sleeved shirts, my best angora jumper).

Then I thought what a girl like Sigrid Santorini would say if you told her she'd have to live in a freezing cold house in Northumberland for several weeks, with four angry boys and only a skinny dog and a plastic bag of bikinis for comfort. At least picturing her reaction gave me something to smile about.

At sunset we drove through a stately town with quiet, wide streets and slate-roofed houses, then out into what seemed like endless countryside. The hills ahead got higher and the roads got narrower. The road signs had more Scottish names than

English ones and we simply had to be there soon. There wasn't much of England left.

'It's somewhere … down … here …' Windy muttered.

He was looking at the hedgerows and scanning every road sign. After a mile or two he spotted a pair of small stone houses either side of some wonky wrought-iron gates. He stopped, tapped in a code to open the gates and swung the car between them.

We drove under an avenue of bushy trees whose branches seemed to reach across the space above us to blot out the sky. The drive curved through the rolling landscape, and the occasional sheep, caught in the bright beam of the MGA's headlamps, lifted its head to check our progress. Twiggy, sensing them, sat alert on my lap, her nose pressing against the window. Like me, she would be glad when this journey was over.

I just caught sight of a tall building through the gloom, but it was blocked from the light of the headlamps by a line of huge cedar trees. A couple of minutes later we pulled up outside some ramshackle buildings and Windy turned off the engine.

'Here at last!'

He slowly unfolded his long frame from the low-slung seat and stretched happily, breathing in the evening air. I let Twiggy out and cautiously followed her.

'Isn't it wonderful?' he beamed. 'I was so lucky to get it. Now, off you go inside.'

Picture a bright, sparkling villa in Mustique … and then change *absolutely everything about it*.

That was where he'd brought me.

A door in the dark mass of rambling buildings stood half open, letting a sliver of light fall on to the dirty cobbled court-yard where the car was parked. I hobbled across to it, still bent double after all that time in the cramped, tiny cockpit. Inside was a long, thin corridor that smelt of damp and mould, lit by a single light bulb.

I looked down at Twiggy, who was padding at my heels.

'Toto, I've a feeling we're not in Kansas any more.'

Despite her gracious lines and grand demeanour, the whip-pet didn't seem as bothered by it all as I was. She trotted quickly past me, her claws clattering on the flagstone floor. Windy appeared in the doorway behind us, his arms full of bags and dog beds.

'Carry on! Carry on! That's it. Turn right at the end. No, left. Excellent.'

I found myself in an enormous high-ceilinged kitchen, lit by a mixture of lamps and candles. It wasn't quite as cold as the corridor outside, and there was a vast red Aga range at the far end, where a pan was simmering away on one of the hotplates. Twiggy was already making herself at home next to it and I went over to join her. The oven's gentle warmth was a relief after so many hours in the cold, damp car.

The smell coming from the saucepan was delicious too. I lifted the lid to see what it was. A bright green liquid bubbled like something out of a witch's cauldron. Windy saw my face and laughed.

'It'll be fantastic, whatever it is. Orli's food always is. And talk of the devil!'

'I'm an *angel*, Windy, and you know it.'

A young-ish woman with short, blonde corkscrew curls walked in through a side door, wiping her hands on a dish-cloth. She had a round face and green eyes that seemed to sparkle with laughter. If she wanted to be an angel, she could be, I decided. I needed an angel right now.

'Orli, this is Nina, like I promised,' Windy announced. 'And Nina, this is Orli. She'll be looking after you and you're very lucky. She only cooks for the very best – I had to prise her out of the clutches of an Arab prince, didn't I, Orli?'

'Well, not exactly his clutches,' she giggled. 'Now, I expect you're starving, Nina. Windy thinks the world lives on crisps and prawn sandwiches. I've cooked you a chicken and a bit of soup. I wasn't sure when to expect you, but they can be ready in five minutes. Why don't you show Nina to her room, Windy? D'you need help with the luggage?'

'No, this is it,' Windy said, cheerfully indicating the sad little pile of bags in the corner.

'Oh, *Windy*!' Orli took in the size of my tote and the plastic bags beside it, put her hands on her hips and flashed him an exasperated look. 'What's the girl going to *wear*?'

'She packed the essentials. Didn't you?' Windy asked me, hopefully.

'What's in there?' Orli asked.

'Mostly bikinis,' I admitted, in a small voice. 'And my camera. And my laptop and charger.'

'Oh, *Windy*!' She threw up her hands in despair. 'You didn't tell her *anything*, did you? All this secrecy business … it's ridiculous! It'll be worse tomorrow, and you know it. Come on,' she added to me. 'You can't trust that man to do a *thing*. I'll take you to your room.'

I followed her out of the kitchen and down a different corridor, at right angles to the first, which was blocked at the far end by a heavy door backed with thick green fabric.

'Now, they keep me in the servants' quarters,' she said with a twinkle in her eye. 'But wait until you see this part.'

The green door opened on to a huge hallway, two storeys high, with a wide oak staircase that divided in the middle, leading to a gallery above. The floor was dusty chequered marble. Dark portraits in gilt frames adorned the walls, lit by a vast brass carriage lamp suspended on thick gilt chains.

This was *not* what I'd expected after the ramshackle courtyard and the kitchen. I caught my breath.

'I know. Pretty fancy,' Orli said. 'But watch your step on the stairs. Half of them are rotten. And don't use the far staircase *ever*. It's got a hole in it big enough for a hippo to fall through. This place is great, but it needs some attention, shall we say. Windy loves a cheap deal.'

The gallery ran from left to right at the top of the stairs. Several doors and two other corridors opened off it, leading towards the back of the house. This was a place where it would be easy to get lost. Orli turned right and I followed her. She stopped outside the farthest door on the main corridor, turned the handle and put her shoulder to it.

'Sticks a bit,' she said, grunting with the effort. 'Everything does. Anyway, just wiggle and push.'

She did both, and the door opened. The bedroom we entered was at least as big as one at the Ritz. How bizarre that

I should know that. It didn't look anything like the bedroom at the Ritz, though. In the dim light from the corridor, this one seemed brown and gloomy. Orli went up to a set of heavy curtains and pulled them apart. Instantly, moonlight streamed in through the many panes of a wide window, forming dramatic parallelograms on the floor. Outside, the sky was dark purple, and the moon hung like a perfect silver disc in the centre of the frame. I caught my breath again.

'This window's OK,' Orli said, tapping the glass with her knuckle. 'We've tried to put you all in the rooms with the fewest broken panes. Also, you're pretty much above the kitchen here, and I'm hoping the heat will rise so you won't freeze. If you need more blankets later, let me know. Now, soup'll be ready soon. Come down when you are. Don't forget – use the staircase on the left going down, or you'll die a horrible death. Oh, and that's the bathroom, in case you were wondering.' She pointed to a door in the far corner. 'See you in a mo.'

'Yes. Right. Thank you.'

I stayed where I was for a moment, taking it all in. The air smelt musty. Opposite the window sat a wide, brass bed with old-fashioned bedknobs at each corner, spread with a faded pink quilt. The carpet was a patchwork of rugs, all faded and worn. There was a dressing table, a small set of bookshelves, and, to the left of the door, a dark mahogany wardrobe so big you could get lost in it – and quite possibly travel to Narnia.

Along the wall from the wardrobe, it looked as though a cube had been carved out of the room. This contained the door to the bathroom Orli had mentioned. Stepping gently over the parallelograms of light, I headed towards it.

By now, I was expecting grand Victorian plumbing, with lots of chrome and copper piping, but this little room was a massive disappointment. Its thin, wonky walls contained a bubblegum-pink bathroom suite, cracked green tiles and a round mirror in a yellow plastic frame. Dad, who was a talented builder and prided himself on his craftsmanship, would be horrified by these people, whoever they were, and what they'd done to their house.

But at least they'd left the window. This one matched the one next door, and without any curtains, it let in even more light. I'd be able to lie in the bubblegum bathtub and look up at the moon. In fact, I couldn't wait to do exactly that, as soon as supper was over. A quick glance at my bedraggled hair and pale, puffy skin in the mirror told me I was doing a fair impression of a resident ghost.

I was sorry that Orli had to see me like this, but Windy deserved it. I scraped my hair out of my eyes and decided I was too tired to bother to reapply any make-up. Despite what Orli had said about the heat from the kitchen underneath, the room was cold, and I shivered.

I'd pictured myself lying by some pool in the sunshine by now, starting on my tan. When would I ever learn?

Supper consisted of fresh pea soup, homemade bread, roast chicken and a dish of steaming vegetables. We ate it around the kitchen table, while Twiggy watched us from her dog bed, hoping for scraps.

'It's just something I threw together when I heard you were on your way,' Orli said dismissively with a wave of her hand.

Yeah, right. It was a feast, and tasted glorious. Maybe I was going to spend the next few weeks in the freezing cold Northumberland 'summer', wearing nothing but blankets, but at least I wasn't going to starve.

The kitchen was interesting. Big but homely, with a rocking chair in the corner beside a tall, deep-set window, lots of mismatched painted cupboards, and a pine dresser full of crockery taking up nearly a whole wall.

'What *is* this place?' I asked, helping myself to vegetables.

'Ah. It's gorgeous, isn't it?' Windy said. 'I'm rather proud of finding it fully furnished. It belongs to the Otterburys. Old family. Had it for generations. All barmy, of course.'

'What, barmier than you?' Orli asked him, laughing.

'Oh, much barmier than me. I got the full story at the pub in the village. The Otterburys have been here since Victorian times, but the house is much older. They made all their money in diamond mines. Hunted, shot, fished and held the best parties south of the border.'

'So why aren't they here?' I asked.

'All those parties ...' Windy explained. 'Lots of social graces and no business sense. They should've hired me. Now the place is owned by Venetia Otterbury and her brother Percival. They don't have enough money to keep this place up, but they can't agree how to split the money if they sell it. They've been arguing about it for thirty years, apparently. They've tried to rent it out, but nobody's wanted it till now. I can't think why.'

I looked up at a large damp patch on the ceiling, and thought of the hole in the stairs, and my bubblegum-pink bathroom. I could think of a reason or two.

'Where are they now?' Orli asked, passing around seconds of vegetables.

'Venetia moved to London, and Percival lives in Tuscany. According to pub gossip, they had a nanny who never let them wear jumpers and they can't abide the cold up here. Madness! The place is glorious, but the best thing is, it's remote.'

I looked up from my almost-empty plate. 'Why does it being remote matter?'

'Because if even one Pointer Sister got one single inkling that Jamie and the others were here over the next few weeks, then the place would become surrounded. They'd camp in the woods. They'd hide in the shrubberies. They'd hide in the bedrooms, if they could get inside. The paparazzi would descend in a pack. The boys would do no work and I'd be back to square one.'

'How will you stop people finding out?'

'As long as the boys behave by the rules,' he said, 'we'll be fine. And that reminds me – don't call home tonight. I'll explain it all tomorrow, OK?'

Well, no. Not OK, Windy. Do you really think I'm going to spend several weeks away from home shacked up with a bunch of unstable rock stars and *not tell my family where I am*? Oh, and did I hear you mention the boys *behaving by the rules*? When was *that* ever going to happen?

I thought all of these things, but somehow I was too tired for the words to come out of my mouth. I'd say them tomorrow. Very firmly. Meanwhile, my mind wandered to the room upstairs, wondering if the bathwater would be hot, and if the bed was as comfortable as it looked.

'She's falling asleep, God bless her!' Orli laughed.

My head jerked up. 'No, no, I'm fine!' I forced my eyes to stay open.

'Come on!' she said. 'I'm taking you back upstairs while you can still stand. Poor creature.'

Back in the bedroom, she took off my shoes for me and helped me under the bedclothes. I started to protest that I needed to brush my teeth and make that phone call home. But the words wouldn't come. All I could think about was the soft, comfy pillow under my cheek. Before she'd even left the room, I was asleep.

24

In the morning, I woke up to endless leaden grey skies. Welcome to Northumberland.

I pulled the pink quilt around my shoulders and wandered over to check out the view from the window. After the brief glimpse of the cluttered courtyard where we'd parked last night, I'd half expected to see a farmyard, but instead, the room looked over a grassy slope leading down to a small lake, surrounded by trees. To my left, near the house, was a sunken garden, where straggly rose bushes bloomed between weed-strewn paths. Up ahead, beyond the lake, purple hills rose to distant hazy blue mountains, the colour of thunderclouds. I found myself staring at them for ages, lost in their ancient shapes and watercolour shades, until the quilt slipped from my shoulders and reminded me how chilly the air was.

While I ran the bath I so badly needed, I checked my face again in the tiny bathroom mirror. It was marginally less ghost-like than last night, but L'Oréal wouldn't be hiring me any time soon. However, I had a worse problem than my pale skin: what to wear? I'd travelled up in jeans, so there were those, and … basically nothing. The T-shirt I'd been wearing stank. No way was I traipsing round this place in a kaftan. In the end I was reduced to a moth-eaten (literally – there were more moth holes than actual fabric) woollen dressing gown I found hanging on the back of the bedroom door. I looked like Arthur Dent in *The Hitchhiker's Guide to the Galaxy*. The boys were *so* going to respect me in this.

Downstairs, Orli had obviously thought about my predicament too. There was a small pile of clothes laid out on a bench underneath the kitchen window.

'I found this whole cupboard of clothes the family left behind. I'm sure they won't notice if we borrow a thing or two.'

She'd dug out a flannel shirt and a pair of corduroy trousers that looked as though they'd been used for gardening. They smelt of mothballs and face powder, and somebody else's life.

'Thanks,' I said.

She saw the look on my face, though. 'I was in a hurry. I'm sure you'll find something better.'

While I changed into the shirt (the trousers were beyond hope, so I stuck with my jeans), she toasted some home-made bread for me and refused my offers of help with the washing-up.

'I've got this. Why don't you take Twiggy for a walk? She's looking restless.'

The slim whippet rose to her feet at the sound of her name and 'walk' in the same sentence, and looked up at me hopefully. I grabbed her lead from a counter by the door. The corridor outside was freezing, but it contained a cupboard full of old coats and boots in a vast range of sizes. I slipped on a man's tweed jacket, fraying at the elbows, and took the dog outside, retracing our steps from last night.

Windy's sports car was still parked in the courtyard. Beyond it was a range of outbuildings with broken windows and sagging doors. The house itself was a higgledy-piggledy mess of pale grey pebbledash and brick. It was big, though – much bigger than I'd realized last night, as if a child had drawn it and kept adding on new pieces.

A cobbled path ran between the side of the main building and a walled garden beyond, and I followed it curiously, past a patchwork of windows, while Twiggy sniffed the plants along the way. The path led through a brick archway framed with trailing ivy, on to a gravel drive. The sunken garden was beside us now. I recognized this as the view from my bedroom. Ahead, the rough lawn led down towards the lake, with its view of the thundercloud mountains.

The house faced this way, I realized, and I walked across the grass and turned to stare at back at the facade from a decent distance. From this direction, it looked like a totally different building. It was three storeys tall, built of moss-mottled stone, with rows of mullioned windows and a steep roof pierced by sharp gables shaped like inverted Vs. Above it, soaring, twisted chimneys stretched towards the sky. A paler stone structure, decorated with a coat of arms, formed a portico around the front door. It was almost covered by a wisteria tree that climbed up past every window, enveloping the house in its thick green fronds and making it look mysterious.

OK, so it wasn't Mustique. But it wasn't bad. It looked like the kind of place Queen Elizabeth I might have visited on her travels. If she ever came as far as Northumberland. Which I doubt she ever did.

The front door was partly open. Now that I saw how big the place was, I gave up on the walk idea and led Twiggy back inside. Her claws tapped on the marble floor as she trotted smartly across the hallway. You could almost fit our whole house into this single space, I thought.

The first room on the left was long and low, with deep-set windows, a moulded ceiling and a massive stone fireplace, big enough to stand inside. The main piece of furniture was a battered leather sofa draped in an ancient, king-size Union Jack. Twiggy could see that I wasn't going back outside for a while, so she gave me a reproachful look and curled herself up on it.

I walked slowly around the room, taking in the view from the windows overlooking the lake, the ornaments on every surface, the hangings on the walls. Like my bedroom and bathroom upstairs, the furniture was a mishmash of styles, from grand antique display cabinets to junk-shop bamboo tables. One of the armchairs had been hand-painted in colourful splodges over the fabric. Half the ceiling mouldings were broken or missing. The carpet had seen better days.

On the other side of the hall, another room, almost as big, contained a billiard table set with balls and cues under low brass overhead lights. I was just checking out the room next to it, which was packed with amps and instruments, when Windy

187

appeared behind me in the doorway.

'Good morning, Nina! I trust you slept well?'

'Yes, thanks. Better than I thought I would.'

'Ah, excellent. I'm not surprised. It's the air, you see. The air up here is magnificent. And what do you think of Heatherwick?'

I frowned at him. 'Heatherwick?' Was this someone I hadn't met yet?

He gestured grandly around us. 'Heatherwick Hall. It dates back to the Domesday Book. It used to be an Elizabethan manor house, but I'm sure you'd guessed that already. Bits got knocked down in the Civil War. The Georgians added a wing or two at the back. The history's quite fascinating. Percy Otterbury spent a very long time on the phone from Italy, telling me all about it. He hates *living* here, but he's fond of the old place.'

'It's … great. In a cold way.'

'It's summer!'

'It's still freezing inside,' I pointed out. It was mid-July, and I was glad of my jacket.

'There are fireplaces everywhere! You'll have a *ball*. The boys will like it, won't they?' A worried look flitted across his face, but he smiled determinedly. 'I mean, of course they will. It took me ages to find. It's perfect.'

'You'll find out soon enough,' Orli called out, striding down the kitchen corridor towards us. 'Sam's just called to say they're five minutes away.'

'Really? Quick!' Windy grabbed my elbow and pushed me unceremoniously across the hall to yet another doorway. 'Hide here. Listen out. I want you to be a surprise. See that door at the far end of the wall? It connects to the sitting room. That's where we'll be. Go through it when I call you.' He gave me a stuck-on smile. 'Trust me. It's all going to be good.'

25

It was *not* going to be good. For a start, I needed to do my make-up, brush my hair and change. I wasn't ready to see them again – not at all. I felt myself having a mini-Sigrid-Santorini moment and groaned.

Grow up, Nina. Deal with it. You're not here to be their girl-friend anyway.

I focused instead on the room Windy had shoved me into. This one was large, panelled with dark wood, and hung with the gloomy mounted heads of several dead stags whose staring glassy eyes seemed to blame me for what had become of them. A vast mahogany table sat in the middle, surrounded by a motley selection of chairs, only some of which looked safe enough to sit on.

Beyond them, a window decorated with stained glass looked out towards where the drive curved round and disappeared behind the row of cedars we'd driven past last night. I waited for a convoy of vehicles to repeat our arrival, but nothing came. Instead, there was a 'whoop, whoop, whoop' in the air, getting louder and louder, and I just caught sight of a helicopter's tail rotor as it came in to land on the lawn.

Of course. Rock band. Helicopter. Obviously.

I went back to the door to the hall, and opened it a crack so I could see what was happening. Windy was standing on the steps of the portico, holding his arms out wide.

'Welcome, everybody!' he called out with exaggerated jollity, as the noise of the blades died down. 'Welcome to Heatherwick Hall!'

'Hey, Windy! Good to see you, man!'

Jamie was the first to embrace him. He sounded more cheerful than I'd heard him in a long time.

He walked inside and stood in a shaft of sunlight. He seemed happy. Rested. The silk-shirt style he'd worn on tour had been replaced by a simple skinny T-shirt and jeans. His hair was longer now, curling around his collar. He'd been somewhere hot, with Sigrid, presumably. His skin had lost its pallor and was clear and golden. The three black moles stood out darkly against his cheek.

My eyes strayed to his hands, hanging loosely at his sides. No sign of a wedding ring. I knew there wouldn't be.

'Mr Windermere. Interesting place you've got here.'

Connor. More guarded. Understated. Too cool for school. I bet he'd keep his sunglasses on when he got inside. He did.

'What *is* this place? Some kind of messed-up *Night School*?'

Angus. Cynical. Downbeat. Rude. Dressed in black as always. I slipped further behind my half-closed door in the shadows as he stared around, taking in the grand portraits and the gaping hole in the stairs. He frowned and turned to where Windy was standing.

'And what's the story with Declan, man?' Why was he hitching a ride? Said you told him to—'

'Ah, *Declan*!' Windy exclaimed, ignoring the last question. 'Welcome, welcome!'

A tall boy with curly strawberry-blond hair walked in, ducking his head under the ancient wooden doorframe.

'Good to be here, man.'

Oh. Wow. He was gorgeous – if you like your boys athletic-looking and enthusiastic. Tight-fitting T-shirt, low-slung jeans, big smile. Tammy would have jumped on him without a moment's hesitation. I thought I was immune to gorgeousness by now, but as it turned out, no – whatever Windy might think. I could feel myself blushing just admiring him from a distance. His teeth were extra-white and perfect. His accent was American, from somewhere in the south. He looked like the kind of person who wins everything in the Olympics. The other boys all stared at him suspiciously.

'Well, shall we get started?' Windy asked, rubbing his hands together.

'When's George getting here?' Angus asked, letting the words hang in the musty air.

'Ah,' Windy said. 'We have a lot to talk about. First, let me show you the music room. I—'

'Don't care,' Angus said, walking through the nearest doorway, which happened to lead into the grand drawing room with the fireplace. 'Why didn't we just go straight to the hotel?

And, like I said, where's George?'

Connor muttered that he needed to make a call and wandered back outside. Keeping the boys in one place was like herding cats. I hoped it wouldn't be part of my job later.

'All right, then,' Windy said, following Angus with a sigh. 'Let's talk.'

Jamie and Declan joined them in the drawing room. I could hear Windy's voice rumbling disjointedly, but to start with I couldn't make out what he was saying. Then I remembered the interconnecting door on the far side of the room. I went across, opened it very, very slowly and peeked through.

Windy was standing in the middle of the room, still talking, while Angus lurked by the fireplace and Jamie prowled around, distractedly picking up ornaments and putting them down again. Already, things weren't going well.

'Rehab?' Angus spluttered. 'For sixteen weeks? Why didn't you tell us?'

'I'm telling you now.'

Jamie sighed. 'If he's in rehab, we wait. Without George, we can't play.'

What? No George? He wasn't coming?

'It's not just rehab,' Windy insisted. 'I really think another tour could kill him. He doesn't *want* to come back. You haven't spoken to him recently, I take it?'

'No,' Jamie admitted, sulkily.

'I didn't think so. We'll all miss him, but musically, this could be a good thing. You've played with Declan before. You know how good he is on drums. Or frankly, anything. And if you remember, George wasn't always *brilliant* in the studio. He used to drive you mad with those intros, Angus. You threatened to walk out on "Not Another Love Song" ...'

'Sure, but he's one of us,' Angus said flatly. 'No George, no deal.'

I didn't blame him. Annoying though he was when he was drunk, in some ways, George had always been my favourite, from his frizzy hair and Simpsons pyjamas to his little-boy-lost look the first day I met him. But Windy had a point – he was heading down a dark, dark road, and no one in the band seemed to be able to pull him back.

I admired the other boys' loyalty to their friend, but this must be hard on the new boy. I squeezed the door open a bit further and glanced across at Declan, who was watching them without a word from one of the window seats. He sat, backlit and silent, his face topped by those strawberry-blond curls, like a thoughtful, sad Greek statue.

'And why are we here anyway?' Jamie asked, checking out a collection of old photo frames. 'I mean, this is only a meeting place, right? Can't George join us wherever, when he's ready?'

'You're not going anywhere,' Windy said. 'Not till you're done. This is it.'

Silence.

'It's the perfect place for you to write,' he continued, gesturing around enthusiastically. 'It's secluded. It's secure. When you've got some songs down, you can record the demos here, and we can tidy them up in a studio later. I know it's a bit shabby in places, but it's got character. Think of those dives you stayed in when you started.'

Connor came crashing back into the room.

'Where's my phone?' he demanded. 'Beardy Man took them off us outside. I thought he was going to charge them, but now he's disappeared.'

'That was Sam. He's taken them,' Windy said calmly. 'At least, I assume he has.'

'He *stole* my *phone*?'

'Not stole. Confiscated. Temporarily. It wouldn't be any use to you anyway. The signal round here is terrible. That's another—'

'Wait. He *stole*. My *phone*?' Connor's angelic face was pale with fury. 'Verushka'll be expecting a call from me any minute.' He looked around the room with the hint of a smug smile. 'You've all seen Verushka, right?'

Angus and Jamie nodded, unimpressed. I'd seen her too, in one of those 'Model flaunts her curves in white bikini' stories. She was an Angel for Victoria's Secret. They'd met in Hawaii, and they'd been going out for about two weeks.

'She'll survive,' Windy said. 'If it's true love, she'll wait for you.'

The others sniggered at this, and in my hiding place, I found it hard not to smile. Even two weeks was good going for Connor.

'So I'll email her,' he said, clicking his fingers as if he expected a phone or computer to be delivered on a plate.

'Not exactly. No Wi-Fi.'

'No—?' Connor struggled to get his head around the concept.

'No broadband,' Windy continued. 'If you went on the internet, you'd be tracked down in moments. I chose this place because it has no communications except for a landline, which is for absolute emergencies only, and believe me, I'm not going to tell you where the phone is. I did say before you got here that it was going to be a top-secret location.'

So this was the plan he'd referred to so cagily last night. No wonder he was looking nervous this morning. Surrounded by glass-eyed animals, I felt suddenly scared, and very alone. Not talking to Mum and Dad was bad enough, but not being online *at all*? Being cut off from everything, turfed practically back to the last century? With only these four for company? Was he *mad*?

'Yes, but ...' Jamie was struggling with the concept.

'You can't ...' Angus could hardly get any words out.

'That's just ... How are we supposed to talk to anyone? How are we supposed to *do* anything?' Connor said.

'Talk to each other. Write songs.'

'But ... the fans ...'

'They'll cope without you for a few weeks. It'll be a struggle. They'll survive.'

'Our families ...'

'I'll tell them how you're doing. They can always go through me if they need to tell you anything. And you can write, via my office. Do you realize, in the olden days, we used to live like this? We wrote letters. We didn't live in each other's online pockets all the time. It used to be normal. Hard to imagine, I know.'

'It's not human,' Connor muttered, staring hollowly around him like some kind of apocalypse survivor.

'Come on, Windy,' Jamie entreated. 'Don't be ridiculous.'

Angus threw his hands up. 'You're not leaving us alone in this godforsaken hellhole! Look, Windy, you're a great guy, but this is the worst idea you've ever had. No George? No offence to Declan, but … some hired session musician? And you want to coop me up in here for God knows how long with lovesick Romeo over there? I mean, if you're setting up some kind of horror story, if you want to come back and retrieve the bodies later, this is genius. But otherwise …'

Windy glanced around the room, from the ancient fireplace to the plastered ceiling.

'I'd hardly call the place godforsaken. There's a room back there crammed with your favourite instruments. Go and check it out. A mobile studio's on the way. I've even lent you my own record collection, see?' He went over to a sideboard near the Union Jack sofa and took a couple of LPs out of a box. There were three more boxes like it, all crammed with records. 'Remember when all you wanted to do was listen to Muddy Waters and play like Jimmy Page?'

Jamie turned on him. 'That was a lifetime ago! Now look at us!' His fists were clenched and a muscle pumped in his neck. He tried to keep his cool. 'Look, Windy – I could do this. If I had to. While George gets better. But Connor will literally implode unless he'd fed fresh females every fifteen minutes. And there's no way Darth Vader over there could cope. Did you bring his black satin sheets?'

He scowled at Angus, who sneered back.

'This, from the man who travels with a *peace tent.*'

'Not my idea, mate.'

'No – your girlfriend's. Like the *second jet.* "Ooooh, I just want everything to be simple. Feed me caviar ..."' Angus cavorted round the room, doing a bad impression of Sigrid's voice. She'd have mimicked him much better.

'Hey, guys ...' Declan said, standing up, trying to be the peacemaker.

'Shut up, Declan,' the others chorused, without even looking at him.

With no warning, Windy suddenly roared at them with the force of one of Josh's tornado machines.

'Is that all you can do? Fight over women who aren't even here? Stop being so bloody irresponsible!'

He glared around in the sudden silence and the room seemed to hover, suspended in time. Even the motes of dust in the air seemed to stop falling. After an endless pause, he gathered himself and spoke in a low, angry growl.

'Global Records have paid millions for this album. If you leave now, you'll have to find a way of paying the money back, because I'm not getting you out of this hole again. This is it. My last hurrah.'

The three original band members stared at him, wide-eyed. Windy never spoke to them like this. For a moment, their idol-faces slipped and they looked faintly terrified. Even Declan looked surprised.

'And you won't be alone,' he went on, more calmly. 'I've got Orli Greenberg in to cook for you. You'll remember her epic meals from last year.'

They grudgingly agreed that Orli was 'a bit of a genius, food-wise'.

'Ed Masterson's coming with the studio,' Windy added. 'He

worked with us on the *Oyster* album. The best sound tech in the business. I mean it. The *best*.'

'OK, I remember Ed,' Angus acknowledged. 'He was minorly awesome.'

'And "Beardy Man", as Connor so accurately described him, 'is Sam Kitavi. He helped out on the Asia tour. Top-class security. Discreet. Implacable.'

'And that's *it*?' Connor demanded, with a flash of his old defiance. 'Like, *three people*? Are you *insane*?'

'Probably,' Windy said. 'For putting up with you lot for so long. But not three people, Connor, four. The last one has come all this way at very short notice to help you out. She's the *pièce de résistance*. My genius touch. Promise that you'll take care of her.'

There was another long silence. He coughed. I realized suddenly that this was my cue.

I was supposed to be it. The missing piece that would pull this whole terrible plan together. My heart started pounding so hard in my chest, I could swear I could see it through the flannel shirt.

Shaking, I opened the door properly and walked out in front of them. Their mouths opened as incredulity and confusion flashed across their faces. Nobody said anything.

For the first time, I was grateful for Windy's little anti-pep talk in the car: at least he hadn't expected me to wow them with my feminine charisma. I stood on the worn carpet and felt the whole room deflate around me, like a tired balloon.

Angus peered at me.

'Blanket Girl?' He turned to Windy. 'Your secret weapon is

Blanket Girl? Don't say Sigrid's coming. If she is, I'll walk home until my feet bleed.'

'I don't get it,' Jamie said faintly. 'Sisi's in Vancouver. I just spoke to her ...'

They hadn't even said hello.

'Sigrid certainly is in Canada,' Windy answered calmly. 'We said no girlfriends for the next few weeks. Nina's here to take care of some practical details. And to be perfectly honest, she's the only one of you I trust.'

'Hi Nina,' Declan said, waving to me from the window with a smile.

'Hi.' I waved back. I couldn't muster a smile, though, even for Greek God Boy.

The others just stared. I looked down at the carpet underneath my feet. Surely a house like this would have a basement that could swallow me now?

'Nice seeing you, Leena,' Angus muttered, moving towards the door. 'But I'm outta here. Get the chopper ready, Windy. Call me when you've got Mustique sorted, will you? And make sure Digger V's there. He'll come if he knows I'm asking.'

Windy's voice roared like a hurricane. 'JUST TRY IT!'

Angus stopped dead in his tracks, and Windy strode towards him.

'I'm not joking,' he said, moving swiftly on and heading for the door. 'If anyone leaves, that's it – you're on your own. You can forget keeping me as your manager. I'm done. You explain it to them, Nina. You live in the real world.'

With that, he stepped into the hall. The door slammed behind him with an impressive judder.

The boys continued to stare at me, glassy-eyed. As if wondering how a pasty-faced girl in an oversize jacket was going to fix this unholy mess.

I wondered that myself. The *pièce de résistance*. Blanket Girl.

So *this* was what it was like to be on my own with the hottest band in the world.

Really *really* uncomfortable.

26

Nobody said anything, but nobody walked out to the helicopter. Windy had scared the boys off that idea, for now at least. Instead, Orli came in and said hello. They tramped unwillingly up the stairs behind her as she showed them to their bedrooms. They clearly didn't want to stay, but for the moment they didn't dare go.

Windy disappeared for several hours to make phone calls from a nearby village where he could get a signal – apparently unaware of the supreme irony of what he was doing. Meanwhile, we ate an awkward lunch together in the dining room, hardly speaking, followed by an awkward supper. In between, Sam the security man handed the boys back their disabled phones, including the spares he'd found in their hand luggage. Connor offered him a thousand pounds to give him one of his SIM cards back. Sam laughed.

'Nice try.'

'Ten thousand.'

'You keep your money,' Sam grinned. 'Like the boss says, try writing a letter. It's a dying art. You're good at writing, aren't you?'

'*They* are,' Connor grunted, flicking a look at Angus and Jamie. 'I just do the dirty work.'

'Well, do that, then,' Sam suggested. 'Play your guitar. Take your mind off things.'

Connor glowered at him. He was used to staff like Oliver, obeying his every whim.

'It's a bass,' he muttered. 'There's a difference.'

Sam merely smiled in a 'whatever' kind of way. This didn't help Connor's mood.

Without Windy to be angry at, they drifted from room to room like unmoored boats on choppy seas, uncertain what to do. At least I had a job to focus on. It made sharing the house with them easier, after the drawing-room disaster. After the helicopter left, a Transit van had arrived, piled high with their belongings. I spent my time helping Sam carry flight cases and suitcases upstairs for them.

The full contents of my luggage would have fitted into one of Connor's carry-on bags. It was turning into a day for irony.

After supper, the boys disappeared to their bedrooms. Free at last of their glowering, angry looks, I went exploring through a maze of interconnecting rooms at the back of the house. First there was a library, packed with ancient copies of the classics, with gilt lettering on faded linen covers. Behind it, a smaller room was set with deep leather armchairs and a tall carved cabinet filled with crystal decanters. The smell of stale cigars still hung in the heavy velvet curtains. This was the place where George would have made himself at home, I thought.

Other rooms seemed half-decided. One was a mixture of filing cabinets topped with a collection of porcelain dogs. Another held an upright piano missing several keys, an old pram full of naked china dolls with bright blue, staring eyes, and a perfect wooden rocking horse. Its ceiling was marked with more patches of damp, and there was a hole where something had leaked and part of it had fallen in. Three of its walls were hung with pale yellow silk wallpaper, painted with flowers. Or at least, they had been once. Now the silk was peeling off the walls, revealing damp plaster underneath. The fourth wall was completely empty, apart from a collection of mottled stains. The room was in a slow process of decay, and it was weird, and sad, and beautiful.

That night, the weather closed in again. Dark clouds blotted out the moon. The wind howled in the trees. Raindrops spattered the windows.

I was in the middle of writing a letter to Tammy, but it was proving difficult to capture the sheer bizarreness of being here without giving too much away. There was a loud knock at my bedroom door. Sweeping the moth-eaten dressing gown around my shoulders, I tentatively opened the door to see who it was. All the boys except Declan were standing there.

'Can we come in?' Jamie asked.

I stared at them for a moment. Three of *Seventeen* magazine's 'Ten Hottest Humans' were asking to enter my bedroom. I stood aside to let them in. This was Planet Rock, after all – weird things happened every day. It was also Planet Me – nothing was going to happen at all.

Jamie marched across the room and draped himself on the chair under the window. Connor sat at my desk. Angus lay on the floor nearby, propping himself up on one elbow. They looked like they were posing for a magazine shoot, but their faces were tense and angry. With nowhere else to sit, I perched on the edge of my bed, facing them.

'You've to go to Windy,' Jamie commanded me. 'First thing tomorrow. Tell him this is absurd. We can't stay here.'

'He'll listen to you,' Angus chipped in. 'He said so.'

'He thinks we're being unreasonable. He thinks we're divas,' Connor pouted. 'But this is impossible. No George. No tech. No internet. How're we supposed to work?'

'He just wants to send us back in time,' Jamie grumbled. 'To when we were schoolboys. Well, I've moved on. I'm not that person any more.'

'No,' Angus sneered. 'You're not. You're the King of Holly-wood. You used to be a musician. Now you're a Kardashian.'

This was too much for Jamie, who leapt up, spoiling for a fight.

'Take that back!'

'Take what back?' Angus sneered. 'Didn't you spend the whole Easter break going on fake antique-spotting trips for *Backstab with Sigrid*?'

'*Backstage. Backstage*, you moron. And that was two days, that's all. She was just wrapping up the last series, then she's giving up the show. Give her a break, Angus. God!'

Angus glared at him.

'Yeah. Because Sisi's just a sweet little hometown girl who wants world peace and bunnies ... in the body of a RAGING LUNATIC. And you're Casanova. And the music ... the music's nothing to you any more.'

Angus whispered the last few words. His voice dripped with disdain.

'The music's everything to me,' Jamie growled back at him. 'And if you don't know that, then you don't get me and you never did.'

He flicked Angus a deadly look and stalked over to the window. Angus leered at his departing back and mimed stabbing actions at an imaginary body beside him. Whether it was Sigrid or Jamie he was impaling, it was hard to tell.

'So it's true,' I sighed, hunching my arms around my knees. I think they'd forgotten I was even there, but it was my room, and about time I said something.

Angus and Jamie weren't listening, but Connor looked up. 'What's true?'

'That you're breaking up.'

They were disintegrating in front of my eyes. It hurt me to think how Ariel would take it. Even though I'd spoilt the band for her, after so many years of loving them the news would still tear her apart.

'Who said we were?' Connor asked.

'Well, aren't you? Everyone on the tour was talking about it. Even Windy, on the way up here ...'

'What did he say?' Jamie asked, turning round.

'He was worried about you. He said bands like you don't

know what they've got till it's too late.'

Jamie frowned and Angus grunted, 'We're not breaking up. Just ...' He trailed off.

'Every band has its moments,' Connor shrugged. 'You know, we're just ...'

'Just what?'

'Just ...'

They looked from one to the other, each hoping someone else would explain. And I saw how, under the rock-god surface, they were just three boys who weren't sure what they were doing any more. They were scared and miserable, and they had been for some time.

'I'm sorry,' I sighed, thinking of New York, and my sister.

'What do you mean?' Jamie asked.

'I've seen you play together. It was the one time you seemed really happy. Couldn't you try and stay? Just for a while, anyway. Have you seen this place yet? Is it really so terrible?' I started to feel offended on behalf of the Hall, its lake and wisteria and faded grandeur. 'If you leave now, there isn't a plan B, by the way. This is already, like, plan Q. What are you going back to anyway?'

Angus and Jamie said nothing, but Connor piped up with a leer. 'I'm going back to Verushka, that's what I'm going back to.'

'Shut up, Connor,' Angus scowled, looking thoughtful.

The room descended into silence. I could see the danger they were in dawning on all three of them. *Were* they breaking up? If not, what was happening here?

Jamie looked back out of the window as the moon briefly

appeared through the scudding clouds, silhouetting his profile against the glass. He turned to Angus.

'I suppose we could try it for a while,' he said doubtfully. 'I write some songs, you write some ... It wouldn't kill us.'

'How long?'

'A few weeks?'

'A few *weeks*?' Angus retorted. 'You're kidding, right?'

'Maybe Windy's got a point. Maybe we need a change of scene. That last session in Miami was a waste of time.'

'That last session was *in Miami*. Beaches. Girls. Cutting-edge mixing boards. Remember?'

'I remember you spent most of the time with Digger V.'

'Oh, you noticed him there, did you? Amazing, as you were in your room with Sigrid the whole time.'

I winced at this. I tried not to. It was no business of mine what Jamie did or didn't do with his fiancée in hotel rooms in Miami, or anywhere.

'I was composing.'

'Oh, so *that's* what you call it. *Composing*.'

They stared at each other, breathing hard, already squaring up for another fight.

I gave up. I'd tried. What did Windy expect of me, anyway?

'Listen!' Connor held his hand up. 'What's that?'

We all sat in silence, straining our ears. The rain had died down, but the wind outside was still howling.

'What?'

'That! There it is again!'

I heard it this time. A strange, unearthly, rustling, flapping sound. The others heard it too. In fact, I'd heard it a couple of times while I was writing my letter to Tammy, and I'd assumed it was the wisteria tree rustling in the wind, or a nest of birds in the eaves. Now we all realized the noise was coming from inside. We looked towards the darkened corridor.

'It sounds like bats,' Jamie said.

'Oh, great. That's *exactly* what we need,' Connor groaned.

Angus smiled wickedly. 'They could be bloodsuckers. Coming for your beautiful white neck ...'

'Shut it, Angus!'

'You're such a wuss. You like to think you're so hard, but you don't even like bits in your orange juice.'

I sighed and got up, pulling the dressing gown tighter around me. While they sat and bickered, I headed into the corridor to see what the noise sound really was. I wouldn't be able to sleep if I kept picturing an army of bats nearby, assuming the fallen idols ever left me alone long enough to try.

The rustling was coming from somewhere down a corridor that ran towards the back of the house, opposite my room. I walked tentatively towards the sound, pausing in front of each closed door, listening. At the third door down, the noise was so intense it made me jump. This was the one. The fluttering came in rapid bursts and made me think not of bats, but of a thousand oversized butterflies trapped inside.

Was somebody breeding insects here? My head pounded and it was hard to breathe.

There were footsteps behind me, and an embarrassed cough. Angus and Jamie stood there, watching me.

'We're right behind you,' Angus said.

Gee, thanks. My hero.

I put my hand on the handle, and the boys walked closer.

'Go on,' Angus whispered. 'Open it.'

Sure. Because he was only a poor little well-muscled rock star. And I was … staff. I threw him a look. But after a deep breath, I opened the door all the same.

At first I thought I was hallucinating. The room seemed empty, but alive. We stood there watching as the walls seemed to ripple and cold air whipped our faces. Then it stopped.

The only light came from the bulb in the corridor behind us, and it was hard to see what was happening. All I could make out was a plain iron bedstead and some old, dark furniture arranged neatly around the walls. Everything looked normal. Then the wind blew again and I saw what the rippling was.

Paper.

Hundreds of sheets of yellowing paper were stuck to the walls like tiles. Each time the wind gusted through a hole in the window it caused them to flap furiously.

I looked around and saw that Jamie disappeared. I assumed he'd run away. Angus and I stayed close to each other, laughing nervously. If he'd put his arms around me to comfort me, I wouldn't have minded. Instead, he wrapped them around himself. For a bad boy obsessed with skulls and assassination, he was a remarkable scaredy-cat when you got to know him.

A minute later Jamie was back, armed with a smartphone. I stared at it and he laughed.

'Don't worry, I'm not going to use it to reveal our co-ordinates. I just need this.'

He switched on the in-built torch and put its beam of light up against some pages near the window. We watched as he stood there, examining them.

'What?' Angus asked.

'I don't believe it,' Jamie murmured, grinning. 'This is so messed up.'

'What d'you mean?'

'Look.'

We moved in closer. The fine print was verses.

'I know some of these,' I said reaching out a hand to touch the words. 'Wordsworth. Eliot. Yeats. Oh wow. Lots of Yeats.'

Each page had been carefully cut from an anthology. The Fluttering Room was lined with poetry.

Jamie grinned at Angus. 'Admit it. Windy's outdone himself this time.'

Angus nodded slowly. 'OK. This is weird. He always promised us weird.'

'He's never done anything by the book. It's why we liked him, remember?'

'We liked him because he found us gigs. He kept us out of YOIs.'

'What are those?' I asked.

'Young Offender Institutions,' Angus said, with mock formality. 'We were always doing stuff that nearly got us nicked. He promised us cheap motel rooms and years on the road if we worked hard, and that sounded better than being banged up.'

'He promised us girls,' Jamie said, with a wicked, nostalgic grin.

'Yeah. Shame none of that ever happened.'

'He said he'd look after us,' Jamie mused. He looked at me, then turned to Angus. 'He's trying, mate. In his own inimitable style. Give him a chance? Just for a little while? Look, if she can handle it, you can.'

He indicated me, shivering in my dressing gown, staring at the walls around me.

Angus nodded, reluctantly. 'I would've preferred bats.'

Yeah, right. I thought. I was getting the measure of Angus McLean now, and if he met an actual bat he'd run a mile.

But it was his way of agreeing. They weren't going anywhere yet.

27

Windy left early the next morning, without saying good-bye. Through my open window, I heard the roar of the MGA as he headed down the drive.

'He said he won't be back for a while,' Orli told me, as she made me pancakes for breakfast. 'But he can arrange for you to leave any time you need to. I think he's feeling a bit guilty about leaving you here with this lot in one of their moods.'

'I'll be OK.'

'But if you're not … well, don't forget about that landline. Just tell me and I'll call him.'

'Sure.'

'Promise me, Nina.'

'I promise. But … I kind of like it here.'

Besides, she didn't know that I had lasted precisely a week the last time I worked for the band. I was determined to do better this time.

Though a thin drizzle was falling, I took Twiggy outside for a proper walk. I felt I owed it to her after abandoning her yesterday. Shrugging on the old tweed jacket, I followed her through a side entrance in the cobbled yard, to an empty stable building with space for six horses. Vintage leather tack, mouldy with damp and age, hung from high hooks on the walls. I pictured the horses, their breath steaming in the cold morning air. In Croydon, you don't see many horses – unless they're police horses and there's some kind of demo going on. Out here, though I'd never even sat on a pony, I had a sudden urge to ride.

Twiggy urged me on, past an abandoned tennis court and behind the sunken garden, down the hill towards the lake. By the water's edge I spotted a rowing boat tied to a post. It was a little wooden craft with peeling green and white paintwork, and the name *Aurora* painted loopily on the side. I hoped for a moment that I could use it to get to the island in the middle. I'd seen a stone building there, hidden in the trees, that I wanted to explore. But like everything else, the boat was rotten and broken. It could still float, but only just. I wouldn't trust it to carry me as far as I could skim a pebble.

When the boys finally surfaced, Declan went for a run. The others spent time with Orli in the kitchen, eating more of her pancakes and catching up on her news. They didn't talk to each other, though. The rift between Angus and Jamie still hung in the air like a dissonant chord, making even Orli uncomfortable.

I left them to it and went on the hunt for something warm to wear that didn't smell of mothballs. The boys had a vanload of designer luggage and all I had, so far, was a moth-eaten dressing gown.

The attics were a disappointment, containing mostly broken furniture and boxes of out-of-date baked beans and cornflakes. However, a delicate wrought-iron spiral staircase rose up from one of the rooms, disappearing into the roof. I followed it up, feeling like I was in *Jack and the Beanstalk*. At the top, I found myself not in the clouds, but in a little tower, whose grubby windows looked past the chimneystacks to panoramic views of fields and mountains. If it had been mine, I would have painted here. It would have made the perfect hideaway. Instead, it was packed with garment rails. Given my quest today, this was a promising start.

The clothes on the rails were all neatly protected in garment bags, and underneath the plastic were silk dresses and fur coats. I needed warmth, certainly, but this was a bit extreme. Did the Otterburys do nothing except garden and go to balls? Then I spotted two large black bin liners in the corner marked 'CHARITY' and 'CHUCK'.

I opened the 'CHUCK' one and looked inside. The first thing I saw was a baggy, bright-turquoise, loopily hand-knitted jumper. I pulled it out to examine it and found a hole in the front the size of a saucer. Other than that, it was perfectly wearable, clean and smelt faintly of fabric conditioner. After hesitating for a millisecond, I put it on.

Underneath were several other equally useful-looking items and some party clothes. Nothing seemed to date from after about 1990, and whoever they once belonged to was about three sizes bigger than me, but that didn't matter.

The 'CHARITY' bag was similar. It was full of men's clothes, all neatly pressed and folded: stiff-fronted dress shirts, leather-buttoned cardigans, patched army jumpers. I didn't think it would make much difference to the universe if I borrowed some of them and put them back later. They weren't exactly what I'd have chosen on a shopping trip with Tammy, but they were a lot more practical than a kaftan. And nobody, except possibly Orli, would notice what I was wearing anyway.

My official tasks weren't difficult: helping to keep the place clean and tidy, and organizing the laundry, which was collected and delivered by a service in the nearest town. According to Orli, the Hall had an ancient, deaf housekeeper who was supposed to do all of this, but she was the person who'd twisted her knee and that's when Windy had got the idea to call me.

I was replacing a seventy-nine-year-old, infirm widow. Thanks, Windy.

Anyway, the job left plenty of time for other things. I found some tins of house paint in one of the tumbledown courtyard workshops, and decided to paint a mural on the bare wall in the Silk Room. It would cover up some of the stains there, and give me the chance to capture some of Heatherwick's eccentricity with my art.

I didn't usually go in for painting other people's houses without permission, but someone had already decorated a room upstairs with psychedelic swirls, and there were the mismatched kitchen cupboards, and the painted armchair in the drawing room. It seemed to be an Otterbury tradition. Besides, I was living with boys who played Pizza-Frisbee in hotel corridors and moved suites at midnight. I was learning how to break the rules.

I'd stopped caring what the boys thought about me, but after my brave stand against the walls of fluttering paper, they treated me with a certain respect. I began to like them, as I'd suspected I would. However, as the days passed, and an uneasy truce persisted, I began to wonder if Windy had brought them here too late. Angus and Jamie weren't ready to break up the band yet, but The Point was like the Hall itself – grand, glamorous, and falling apart.

Armed with his guitar, Jamie found quiet, cut-off places to work on his ideas for new material. Once, he disturbed me in the Fluttering Room, while I was trying to read some of the poetry. Another time, he somehow found a way on to the tower above the front door and sat with his legs dangling out of the window. When he saw me, he switched to 'Greensleeves'. Henry VIII in a T-shirt and jeans. It made me laugh, but he cut a solitary figure – one boy, alone, against the facade of a crumbling country house.

Angus, meanwhile, locked himself in his room with his computer, two guitars and a keyboard he'd swiped from the music room. I'd hear odd riffs and snatches of melody emerging occasionally, but nothing he seemed happy with: generally they were followed by silence and grunts of frustration.

A week went by, and the number of songs they'd written was precisely zero. With no new material to work on, Connor played endless, lonely games of snooker against himself in the billiard room. Ignored by the others, Declan spent most of his time in the music room, trying out drums, keyboards, saxophone and whatever other instruments he could find – even a mandolin. He was quite obviously genius-level good on all of them, and particularly dazzling on bass guitar. This only seemed to make Connor more annoyed.

28

It was Twiggy who found the path to the island, on one of our regular walks. One minute she was beside me, the next she was looking at me from across the lake, before disappearing into the bushes. I followed the water's edge until I got to a clump of weeping willow trees, whose fronds cascaded like an extravagant green waterfall. Behind them was a rickety wooden bridge. I ran along it, and soon I reached the steps of the building I'd seen before, almost hidden by the thick vegetation.

It was a folly, built of mossy grey stone like the house, and shaped like an ancient temple. Coming from inside, I made out the sounds of a guitar. They were the familiar chords of a piece Jamie had been working on during the tour. When I got inside, he was sitting with his back to the folly wall, wearing an ancient T-shirt and worn-in jeans, his guitar on his lap. Twiggy was sitting beside him, looking pleased with herself.

He looked up and smiled.

That Mona Lisa smile. It was bad enough normally, but its effect was magnified by a thousand whenever he was holding a guitar.

'I was hoping you'd find this place,' he said.

'Why? Do you need something?'

'No.' He looked surprised. Then he seemed to remember that almost every other time he'd spoken to me, it was to give me instructions. He looked slightly ashamed. 'Look, I don't expect you to fetch and carry for us here. It's kind of ridiculous.'

'OK.'

There was an awkward silence, in which we both remembered that I used to stand to attention while he looked on as his girlfriend gave me instructions for washing her underwear.

'Anyway,' he coughed. 'I thought you might like to see the windows.'

'Er, sure.'

He placed his guitar down and went over to the nearest one. The panes were old and dirty and covered in scratches, but when I looked closer I saw that the marks were names and initials etched in the glass. Couples' initials. Some of them were surrounded by hearts. This must have been a lovers' meeting place.

'It reminds me of one of your collages,' Jamie said. 'The one you made of Verona.'

I was amazed. 'You remember that?' I could hardly believe he'd noticed.

'Yeah. Those pictures were at the Juliet house, weren't they?'

I nodded again. While he'd looked at them on the plane to Gdynia, Sigrid had been whispering in his ear the whole time about what a thief and a flirt I was. Had he really been focusing on the pictures?

'Anyway, that piece was the best. I liked the others too, though. There was one that was full of mostly hair products. And Connor, blurry in the background, checking himself out. That was a classic.'

I smiled, remembering it. 'You didn't mind, then? That I took them?'

'No,' he said, shrugging. 'You didn't stick a camera in my face. You didn't try and catch me with my pants down. Or steal my hair.'

'Sigrid seemed to think I would,' I sighed.

'I know she did,' he said gently. 'People do that in her world.'

'I don't.'

There was another silence, until Jamie laughed. 'Have we run out of conversation so quickly?'

I shrugged. 'I was trying to think of a question I could ask you that I don't already know the answer to.'

He looked surprised. 'You know me so well?'

'You have one of the longest pages on Wikipedia. There are websites about your favourite breakfast cereal.'

He groaned. 'I'm sick to death of Wheetios. I mentioned them once and they sent me, like, a million boxes. If I never see one again, it'll be too soon. Don't tell anyone, or it'll be another headline: JAMIE MALDON HATES WHEETIOS. COMPANY GOES BUST. Or gets firebombed, or something. I can't open my mouth without … It doesn't matter. What about you?'

'What about me?'

He considered the question. 'OK – what's your favourite cereal?'

'Really?'

He grinned. 'You know mine.'

'Fine ... I think I might have to set up a shrine to Orli's pancakes, as far as breakfasts go,' I said. 'She puts homemade jam on them. They're just ...' I made a face to try and explain the ecstasy of eating them.

He laughed. 'Go on ...'

'What else? I come from a big family ...'

'Oh yeah! I knew that!' He looked proud of himself. 'Loads of brothers and sisters and cousins, all living in Sa'af London.'

I couldn't believe it. He was slipping into the Croydon accent, like it was a joke. I pictured his fiancée making fun of me behind my back, and I had to fight the urge to throw something. He saw the glowering look on my face.

'I'm sorry! Sisi made it sound great. She was an only kid, like me. Her dad was a workaholic, and her mum was this freak-out gym bunny, always moving houses. She was mostly on her own.'

I tried to form an expression that would look like sympathy for Sigrid Santorini. Before she got her break with Disney. And went out with Jamie Maldon.

Even thinking about Sigrid seemed designed to put me in a bad mood. I didn't want to spoil things, because I'd started to enjoy myself, but when I thought back to my family, my strongest memory was of Ariel cutting her hair before I left.

'Do you remember my sister?' I asked.

He shook his head.

'She was with me the day I first met you. When I used the *blanket*. She used to be one of your biggest fans.'

He cocked his head. 'Used to be?'

'Yeah. She slept with her face resting against yours on the pillow. She dyed her hair to match your favourite colour.'

'Which one?'

'Blue. And yellow.'

He sighed. 'You see? I don't *have* a favourite colour. They keep asking me and I just say the first thing that comes into my head. And then it gets all this … *meaning*.'

'Well, it doesn't matter,' I said. 'She cut the blue off, anyway.'

'Why?'

'Because of me. Because I told her you weren't the boy she thought she knew from the love songs. You were a rock star, living on your own special planet.'

He nodded. 'I was. Touring does that to you. It's bad for the soul. It gives you the biggest highs in the world, but …' He trailed off, embarrassed, I thought, at the person he'd become. 'Ariel's a lovely name,' he added thoughtfully. 'I'm sorry about the hair.'

'Me too.'

There was a scratching noise at the door. Twiggy was itching to go back outside and carry on with the walk. I joined her in the doorway, and Jamie sat back down with his guitar. I left him there, strumming a series of minor chords that hung in the cool, quiet air.

29

According to Wikipedia (I'd looked them up before I came), Angus and Jamie had written *Oyster* together in a frenzy of creativity during their first year of touring. Whatever had driven them apart later on, a big country house wasn't going to fix it. Not if they carried on like this. If anything, it just seemed to give them more space to avoid each other.

Another day rolled slowly by, and then another, while the boys circulated around the house and grounds, like magnets set to repel. I was used to a place crammed full of laughter and noise, and little ones constantly demanding my attention. Here, the only sounds were slamming doors, abandoned chord progressions, the clicking of snooker balls, and Declan's endless solitary drumming in the music room.

At least meals were sociable times for Orli, me and Sam. The security man was quiet, but friendly. There was a keen intelligence behind his dark eyes. I sensed he wouldn't have thrown himself on me if he'd found me wrapping a Hollywood star in a tablecloth. He was the one person who was allowed out of the grounds, and drove out each morning in a battered estate car to get provisions from the farm shop in the nearby village. Orli cooked something delicious with whatever he brought back, and we ate it together around the kitchen table.

Sam managed to rig up a radio that could only get two stations: Classic FM and a local pirate station. So we listened to snippets of Mozart and Rachmaninov, or grime and dubstep, depending on which signal was better. It turned out that Orli and Sam were big fans of Dizzee Rascal. And each other. They'd met through the band before, and gave each other long, lingering looks across the table. I sensed a lot of history from previous tours and recording sessions.

The boys avoided the kitchen at these times. They'd appear at random hours of the day, demanding instant food and disappearing with it to eat, separately and alone, in whatever sad little nook they were inhabiting that day. Orli disapproved, but said nothing.

'I'm their chef, not their mum,' she sighed. 'My job is to make their job easier.'

'But they're not *doing* their job,' I pointed out.

'Not yet,' she agreed, looking dubious. 'Not yet.'

Upstairs, in the big, quiet room I'd always dreamt of, there were times I missed my family so much it made my bones ache. I sat on my bed with the quilt wrapped around me, reading and re-reading a short, hurried letter from Mum telling me 'everyone was fine' and wondering about all the things she hadn't said.

What new phrases would the twins have learnt by now? What were they drawing? Was Josh crawling into my bed at night, like he used to do when I was home late, snuggling up to my ancient teddy bear? Or had Michael already commandeered my bedroom? Did it smell of old trainers and fresh Lynx yet?

And Ariel – had she forgiven me? If she could see how things really were in this crumbling place, would that make things better, or worse?

Ten days after our arrival, I woke up from a nightmare. I couldn't remember what it was about, but my muscles were tensed, as if I'd been running for my life. My heart was beating fast. I sat up against the pillows and looked out through the crack in the curtains, at the moonlit clouds scudding past as if they were frightened too.

Another storm was brewing and rain spattered the windows like gravel against the glass. The wind whistled and cooed as it rose and fell. Inside, Heatherwick Hall was an orchestra of rattles and groans that sounded like a mob of zombies breaking in and taking over the house. I had to tell myself that the cracks and rumblings were water pipes creaking in the cold air. The thumps, which sounded *exactly* like a heavy-footed swamp creature walking up the stairs, were floorboards contracting. The scratching noise was a branch brushing against the eaves. Not armies of insects eating their way through the ceiling beams to get me. Probably.

There was no way I was getting back to sleep. I grabbed the old woollen dressing gown and swung it round my shoulders, shoving my feet into the ankle-length wellies I'd adopted as a pair of slippers.

What am I doing in this place?

I paused in the corridor. Angus's room was four doors down from mine, but I knew he had fears of his own. Nothing could possibly be cheesier than to knock on Connor's door, or Jamie's, and say I needed company. It must have happened to them a thousand times on tour. They'd never believe me that 'company' meant *company*. Declan still felt like someone I hardly knew. By now I was getting used to all the noises anyway. I decided I could brave the rest of the house on my own.

Downstairs, there was no sign of life. Various lamps had been left on – which I was grateful for – but the rooms were empty. The sounds weren't so bad here. In fact, down here it was possible to believe the house wasn't being broken into, or eaten alive.

I wandered through the maze of rooms, picking things up and putting them down. One of them was a book of stories by Edgar Allan Poe. Dark, historical horror. It was perfect for a night like this, but I couldn't concentrate on the words, so I abandoned it on a table in the library.

Soon, I thought, Windy would have to end this experiment. It clearly hadn't worked. There must be somewhere else the boys could safely go, where they didn't just slowly drive themselves crazy. I missed Tammy. I missed my family, and what was the point? You couldn't just *make* someone make an album. Even if you paid them millions, you couldn't draw music from them. If the experiment had proved anything, it had proved that.

Restless, I moved on through the dining room, past the looming stags' heads on the walls. Lit only by the cloud-shrouded moon, it looked suitably strange with the wind howling and whistling in the trees outside.

I wandered into the drawing room to see if there were still any embers alight in the fireplace. The fire was dead for the night, but that's when I noticed the wooden box containing the old-fashioned record player that Windy had left for the boys. Beside it were the boxes of vinyl records he'd pointed out, in their original album covers. Jamie had practically exploded when he'd mentioned them. What made him so particularly furious, I wondered?

Idly, I flicked through the selection. Swirly names in psychedelic writing overlaid badly lit photographs of long-haired men. There were some really sexist pictures of nearly-naked women in overdone make-up. Some covers were just symbols against a black background. There were torn and peeling covers. Nothing I would personally choose.

Then I lifted up the glass lid and looked at the record player itself. Dad had fixed one like this once. I remember his excitement as he got it working, the glow of satisfaction on his face when the last piece of wiring was sorted and he got it to play. He showed me how to set the little dial in the corner to 45 for the little singles, and 33 for the larger albums. He said that once upon a time there was another setting of 78 for the really old stuff, but nobody used that any more.

Still picturing Dad, I switched this one on, made sure it was set it to 33, picked up the first album that came to hand and dropped it into place. I wasn't interested in the records so much, but the machine was a beautiful retro piece of engineering. When I lifted the needle arm and moved it across the record, the turntable started to move automatically. I placed the needle carefully on the edge of the black vinyl and waited.

A crackle. A kind of hiss. A click. A moment later, the air around me filled with the twanging sound of Indian instruments. Actually, I liked it. I turned up the volume. You get a different sound from vinyl records: it's scratchier, but more alive some- how, as if you're in the room with the players. And this music was like a river, shimmering and mysterious. Then a rhythmic drumbeat joined in, and the sound of a sitar.

I checked the album cover, which was a collage of famous faces with the Beatles in shiny satin coats at the front. I'd picked up *Sgt. Pepper's Lonely Hearts Club Band*, and this track was 'Within You Without You', by George Harrison. Dad had the LP at home, inherited from one of his uncles. He always said it was one of the most iconic records of all time – the one he'd save from a fire if he had to.

Now that I looked more closely, there were a few other singers and bands I recognized. The collection covered rock and pop, blues and jazz. I pulled out the ones I liked the look of, and all the time the air still vibrated to the gentle sound of George Harrison's sitar.

When that track was over, I changed the beat entirely to the insistent bass of Blondie's 'Rapture', and pranced around the room in a bad imitation of Debbie Harry, pretending to be cool. The sublime distorted guitar of a solo by Jimi Hendrix required a mix of headbanging and ballet to do it full justice, I thought.

Outside, the wind still howled, but I hardly noticed it. I put on track after track, each one totally different from the last. Sometimes I chose them deliberately, and other times I just let the needle land at random. It glided along the grooves in the record, and I danced and spun around the room as the mood took me. Whipping my hair to the Rolling Stones, strutting along to The Cure. For David Bowie, I invented new dance moves incorporating a sort of crawl across the Union Jack sofa – half yoga, half jazz. Thank God no one was watching.

I changed tracks all the time, admiring my own DJ skills, until I was so tired the storm didn't matter, and I decided it was maybe time to go back upstairs.

Just one more song. Maybe two. Something I didn't know. OK, this one. It had a picture of tall, narrow houses on the front, looking as though they might be New York tenements. No band or album name. It opened up like a book, and I realized it was a double album, so I slid out the first disc from its sleeve and put it on the player. I picked the last track, which was the longest, judging by the amount of space it took up on the vinyl. As I dropped the needle, I was already regretting my decision. Long tracks are usually terrible.

But as it started, I vaguely recognized the riff. It was heavy guitar: DA-da-da, da-da-da, DA-da-da, da-da-da, gradually climbing in a steady scale. The rhythm of guitar against drums was complicated and I didn't quite get it. Like the Beatles track, it had some sort of Eastern influence, but this one I couldn't place. It was magnificent and mysterious – the kind of over-the-top heavy rock that I'd instantly turn off if it came on the radio. But here, in this darkened room, with the wind whirling in the trees outside and one lamp flickering, it grabbed me. I left the needle where it was and sat in the nearest chair, listening.

This was how I felt when Jamie asked the crowd to sing in New York. The other tracks I liked, but I *got* this one. I didn't know why, exactly. I shivered. It was something to do with the unwavering guitar riff, and the lyrics about stars and desert streams … The music moved through me but for once, it didn't make me want to dance: it made me want to *be*.

When it finished, I played it again. It was a yearning song, painting pictures of adventures in distant lands, and making mystical discoveries. The wailing voice was strangely romantic and unafraid. I thought of Aunt Cassie. It was how I wanted to be, but never could be. After the third play, it didn't even feel like music – it just felt like the longing inside me, swirling around the room.

There was a noise out in the hallway. I looked up and there was Angus, standing very still at the foot of the stairs, staring at me. I realized that my cheeks were wet with tears. As the track came to an end, and the needle returned to position, I quickly used my dressing-gown sleeve to wipe my face.

'Sorry, did I wake you?' I mumbled. My voice was unsteady. I was really lost. I was in a desert somewhere, wandering … I must have looked an idiot, but for the moment I didn't care. The desert felt more real than this room. My mind was unsteady, too.

'Yes, you did,' Angus said, walking in. 'Do you have any idea what time it is?'

I laughed. The Bad Boy of rock, sounding like my dad.

'Not really.'

'It's three forty-five. Why are you down here?'

'I couldn't sleep.'

'I know the feeling. Are you OK?'

'Yeah, sure,' I said, sniffing and wiping my nose with my other sleeve. 'Why?'

'You looked … emotional.'

'Oh, right. Well. That song …'

He walked over to the record player and picked up the album cover. 'So you're a Led Zep fan?'

'A what?'

'You like Led Zeppelin? I wouldn't've had you down as the type.'

'Oh. That's them? I didn't know.'

He looked astonished. 'You were listening to "Kashmir", with tears streaming down your face, and you didn't know it was Led Zeppelin?'

Well, thanks for reminding me about the tears, Angus. But yes. I shrugged.

'You're creepy, you know that?' he laughed.

'Great. Thanks a lot.' I glared at him and got up to go.

'No! Wait!' he said. 'I'm sorry. I didn't mean it that way. It's just … this is how Jamie and I got together. Liking Led Zeppelin when we were twelve. No one else getting it. Trying to play like Jimmy Page …' He was still looking at the album cover and smiling.

'So that's why Windy brought this stuff down here?' I asked.

He nodded. 'And why Jamie was such a jerk about it. He doesn't want to be told to be twelve again. But I'd forgotten, until I saw you just now …'

He trailed off. There was silence.

'Forgotten what?'

'What it felt like. That first time. Wanting to climb inside that record and breathe it out.'

He smiled, and for once there wasn't any trace of irony.

'I should go,' I said. 'It's late. I was getting tired anyway.'

I wasn't sure if I wanted to stay or not, but I was pretty certain my face must be red and blotchy after all those tears. I wasn't dressed or made up for big conversations. Not with Angus. Not now. And he might have seen me dancing. Nobody was supposed to see that.

I bent my head so my hair fell across my face, and headed for the stairs. He waited until I was nearly there until he spoke again.

'Jamie did that too, you know?'

'Did what?'

'Cried when he heard "Kashmir". Went all blotchy, just like you did. Goodnight, Blotchy.' He turned away from me and back to the album cover, laughing to himself.

'Goodnight.'

Summoning what dignity I had left, I walked back up the broken stairs to bed. Behind me, Angus put the record on again, and the music swirled around me as I went.

30

I woke up late. The skies were still grey and the wind gusted against the window. Raindrops battered the glass. I bet the weather wasn't like this in Mustique.

With rock and pop songs ringing in my head, I went back to the tower room and rummaged through the 'Charity' and 'Chuck' bags again in search of something to keep out the worst of the cold. I picked out a pair of combat trousers and a baggy jumper with a comedy reindeer face on it and danced down the back stairs to my own internal version of 'Rapture'.

Downstairs, I could hear Orli singing as she made the mixture for a rich, dark pudding for later on, and the kitchen smelt of orange and chocolate. The sound of the blues was filtering through to the kitchen corridor from the main part of the house. I assumed that someone else had decided to try the record player, but then the tune stopped and started again. There was laughter. When I reached the hall, I realized the music was live. In the music room, Angus was perched on a stool with his guitar slung over his shoulder. Declan was sitting at the drum kit.

I paused in the doorway to watch. Declan saw me and grinned. Angus looked up from the guitar pedal he was adjusting.

'Hi, Nina. Go away, will you?' he said casually. 'This is not for human consumption.' He frowned, but his voice was friendly.

I did go, but was back ten minutes later to listen.

Angus looked up. 'Shoo! What did I tell you?'

'Sure. I was just … you sound good.'

'No we don't. I'm rusty. Declan's in some pact with Satan – he never misses a beat. But I'm a mess here.'

I shrugged. 'If you say so.'

He played a few more chords as I turned to go. I couldn't help pausing in the doorway still listening. Whatever he said, the music was great.

'This isn't … anything,' he insisted. 'Don't go imagining anything.'

'OK.'

'We're just having a jam.'

'Fine.'

'Talking of which, we could do with some sandwiches.'

I groaned. 'For that, you don't deserve any.'

He batted his eyelashes. 'Pretty please.'

I promised I'd ask Orli to see what she could do.

While they played on, I took Twiggy for a long walk in the rain. I was back in the house, up a ladder in the Silk Room working on a sky section of my mural, when Orli popped her head round the door.

'The post van's come. There's a parcel for you. He's really sorry but it got mis-delivered. It's been in the sorting office for a week.'

I took the bulky package up to my room, intrigued by its size and squishiness. Inside were clothes: not the selection I'd requested from home, via Windy, but some smart designer numbers, accompanied by a note:

Apologies for somewhat dumping you in it.
I'm sure you'll rise to the challenge.
Meanwhile, I hope the enclosed goes some way
towards making your stay at the Hall
more bearable.
    Yours, Windy

WITH COMPLIMENTS
· RW ·

Each item was encased in layers of tissue paper. I took them out and unwrapped them carefully, laying them out on my bed. It was exactly like unpacking for Sigrid, and some of the labels were the same: Isabel Marant, Miu Miu, Chloé … There were little trousers and little tops, a little cardigan and a jacket, two little dresses …

And that was the thing: they were all *little*. Somehow Windy had got hold of sample sizes. They would probably have swamped Sigrid, but then, I didn't live under a peace tent, feasting on green tea and almonds. It was very sweet of him to think that I would ever fit inside these things, but that was never, ever going to happen. I grew out of clothes this size when I was about eleven.

So I hung them around my room as decoration. When it came to practical, you know, *wearing* things, I'd stick with Charity and Chuck.

As I was heading downstairs to see how the jam session was going, I bumped into Jamie on the landing, looking tired.

'Hey! I'm glad I saw you,' he said. 'I wanted to apologize for Angus last night.'

'Angus?'

'He must have kept you awake for hours. He was playing Led Zeppelin until God knows what time. He kept us all up. He doesn't think.'

My hand flew to my mouth. 'Oh God, I'm sorry. That was me.'

'You?'

'Yes.'

'Playing "Kashmir"?'

I nodded. 'I had no idea it was that loud.'

Jamie didn't seem angry – just confused. 'You like "Kashmir"?'

'I do now. I didn't think I would, but that voice ...' I caught Jamie's eye and flushed. 'I just ... It felt as though he was singing the inside of my head.'

He stared at me curiously. 'Yeah. I get that.'

'Angus said it was one of the first songs you two listened to together.'

Jamie looked nostalgic for a moment. 'It was. So he was down there? With you?'

I was about to explain, but there was a flash of something in

Jamie's eyes that stopped me. It almost looked like ... jealousy. The idea was so bizarre that I had to laugh. *Me and Angus?* That was just funny. His last girlfriend was a dancer at the San Francisco Ballet. The one before that was a princess.

'That's right,' I said, jutting my chin out. 'We listened to it together. It was beautiful.'

Jamie stared at me again, hard, taking in my baggy trousers and my reindeer jumper, my hair still damp from walking in the rain.

'Oh. Right. Well, yeah, it is.' He frowned. 'Girls don't usually like that stuff.'

I shrugged. So this was what it was like not to be a *girl* girl. Liberating, actually.

That night, Orli cooked a Moroccan tagine for supper. It was something the boys had enjoyed in the old days, she said, as the smell of apricots and spices drifted through the house. This time, as we sat down to eat it, Angus and Declan arrived together, as if they showed up for meals all the time. Without a word, Orli quickly laid two extra places for them. We lit candles and passed around dishes, serving ourselves and each other as the conversation grew louder, punctuated by clinking glasses and clattering knives and forks.

Orli commented on the songs they'd been playing, saying which ones she'd enjoyed and which she'd heard Angus play much better in the past.

'You know Angus's playing?' Declan asked, surprised.

'Of course!' Orli laughed. 'I'm an expert. I cooked for every-one when they recorded *Oyster*. Saw them play at the Viper

Lounge and a few other places. Do you remember, Angus, when Dave Grohl dropped by?' Angus nodded reverentially. 'You guys jammed for hours. Oh, and the time you met David Bowie …'

'Don't mention that!' Angus warned her.

She grinned. 'He was so in awe he couldn't think of a single thing to say.'

I tried to picture Angus in awe of anyone. Then I remembered the way he'd looked at Nelson Reed in Paris. Next to a music legend, his ego seemed to reduce to something near normal size.

'I played with Bowie once,' Declan remarked quietly, helping himself to more tagine. 'Actually, twice. Awesome both times.'

He didn't look up from his food. He was just making conversation, but everyone turned to look at him.

'You played with *Bowie*?' I asked, thinking of all the fun I'd had strutting to 'Fame' last night, and hoping Angus hadn't seen that part.

'Um, yeah. You know … some tracks he was working on … It was cool.'

'You should see Nina do her Bowie dance,' Angus grinned from across the table.

Oh God, he *had* seen. My cheeks burned.

'Very … original.'

I glanced across at him through my fringe, to see how much evil was in his face. But tonight his grin looked innocent. Even so, I was keen to change the subject.

'So,' I said, turning back to Declan, 'who else have you

played with?'

'Well ...' he mused, thinking for a moment. I could tell he was distracted by the idea of my Bowie dance. But once he got talking, it quickly became clear that he had worked as a session musician with almost everyone, even though he was still only twenty-two. He was in the middle of a story about the time he *didn't* get to record with Madonna (she asked; he was busy), when he stopped mid-sentence. He was staring at the doorway. We all stared too, and there was Connor, standing just on the edge of the warm glow cast by the lamps and candles, watching us all.

Everyone went quiet. Then Orli quickly leapt to her feet and asked if he wanted to join us.

He shook his head.

'Oh, come and sit down. We've hardly started,' she said brightly, if not entirely truthfully.

Connor shook his head again. 'I'll have soup or something later.' But he didn't move.

'Don't be silly,' Orli admonished him. 'There's plenty right now, and I promise you it's good. But it'll be gone soon. Make space, Sam and Angus. Connor, pull up a chair.'

We all shuffled our chairs to make room. Connor hesitated for a long time. But the smell of the tagine, the light from the flickering candles and the lively conversation grew too much for him. He scooted into place, allowed Orli to pile his plate with food and sat quietly while Declan finished his story.

The talk was more stilted after that. We tried to regain the easy rhythm we'd had before, but Connor's silence and pale, tense face made it difficult. We finished the tagine and cleared the plates. By now, Jamie was the only person who was missing. His absence was tangible, and I wondered where he was.

'So,' Angus said, leaning back in his chair and turning to Declan. 'Same again tomorrow? His Royal Highness will be off writing love songs to his Hollywood laydee, but I've been working on some new material.'

'Love to hear it,' Declan agreed. 'And look, I'm sorry about George ...'

'Yeah, we all are,' Angus sighed. 'But it was going to happen. We couldn't stop him. We tried.'

'He can join you later, right?'

'If he wants to. But I don't think he will. To be honest, he didn't like the same stuff we did anyway. He was always more into heavy metal. Your style ... it's OK.'

Declan flushed with pride, and said nothing.

Connor watched them sulkily from across the table.

'And now ... pudding time!' Orli announced. 'He may be a bit rusty, but in honour of Angus's *attempts* to play the guitar again today, I got a bit inspired.'

While we cleared the table, she disappeared into the small room next door that served as a larder and reappeared with the chocolate pudding, as well as a chopping board on which sat a large meringue, filled with cream and chopped hazelnuts.

'Angus once told me this was his favourite,' she said. 'But the rest of you don't have to have any if you don't want to.'

Soon we were all digging in. Meringue crumbs stuck to our chins. Chocolate sauce went everywhere. There wasn't much talking, but this time the air was full of grateful moans of happiness. For a brief, unguarded moment, I saw Orli's face cloud over and I sensed that, like me, she was distracted by thinking about Jamie. It made me sad to think of him alone, wherever he was hiding.

After a particularly large mouthful of pudding perfection, Connor looked across the table and said to Declan, 'It sounded good today. Really good.'

'Thanks. Yeah. Right. Glad you liked it. Means a lot, man.'

Connor stared at him suspiciously, as if to check if he was being sarcastic. 'Yeah, well ... you know ... you've played with the greats. I just ...'

'You just what?'

'I just ... you know ... I just ... play whatever,' Connor finished lamely.

Declan grinned, assuming Connor was joking, but I remembered Ariel telling me that according to the fans, he was sensitive about his playing.

'It's not "whatever",' I said, dragging my thoughts back from Jamie and leaning in to make myself heard. 'When I saw you in New York, I thought you were incredible.'

Connor looked at me, surprised, and grateful, and uncertain, and not his usual cocky self at all.

'Yeah right. Thanks.'

For the first time, Declan noticed his lack of confidence.

'You're not serious?' he said. 'Your riffs are iconic, man. If I could come up with just one of those, I'd be ...' He trailed off, looking wistful in the flickering candlelight.

'But you can play every one,' Connor protested. 'I've heard you. You can play mine, you can play Flea's ... you can play better than practically any bassist I know.'

'Yeah, I can *play*. I can play pretty much anything you show me – it's just a weird thing I've got.' Declan batted his hand in the air, like his talent was some kind of freakish mistake. 'But I can't *create* them. Not like you do. I can improvise, sure, but it's all pretty obvious. What you do ... what you did on "Amethyst", you know? That shift down to G minor on the bridge and those triplets in six-eight time?'

Connor made a face, like he didn't really know what six-eight time was. Declan laughed. 'You just *found* it, man. It's genius. You know that, right?'

Connor's cheeks coloured as he ran a hand unconsciously through his hair. 'Nah. I don't ... I mean ... I just do what I do.'

'Look, I've read everything I can find about the band. These guys auditioned for a bassist for – what? – six months?' Declan glanced at Angus for confirmation, who nodded. 'And they hired you. Six weeks later, they had their first hit. Coincidence?'

He appealed again to Angus. This time, Angus held up his hand.

'OK, OK! So it wouldn't work without him. For God's sake, don't make me stroke his ego every day.'

Connor turned to him. 'You know, occasionally would be nice.'

Angus groaned.

'What. Ever.'

Connor smiled. The flush in his cheeks was still there, but the rock-god glimmer was back in his eyes. He was more insanely beautiful than ever. I pitied any girlfriend he might have – that sensitive ego would take a lot of stroking – but it would have its compensations. Just looking at him would be a start.

31

We played records late into the night. The next day, Connor was the first to head into the music room and strap on his bass guitar. The others joined him and soon they were racing through their repertoire of rock songs. Playing the blues. Rearranging old Point songs. Shifting amps and instruments around to get the sound they liked. Declan's drum kit sounded best in the hall, with its spectacular echo that made the whole house seem to rattle and hum.

Later, Orli and I listened from the kitchen while they played around with a couple of new songs. Not complete numbers, but ideas that Angus had been working on. This time, it wasn't pretty. Short phrases suddenly stopped, followed by a question. Repeat. Try again. Change a bar. Change of mind. It sounded nothing like the polished pieces they'd played before. Songwriting was obviously difficult. No wonder the boys had put it off for so long.

*

We ate together again that evening, sitting around the table and sharing stories. Afterwards Sam lit a fire he'd prepared for us in the drawing room and went back for a game of cards with Orli in the kitchen. The boys went into the billiard room for a game. I found the Edgar Allan Poe stories I'd abandoned earlier and went back into the drawing room to read them. The fire was already glowing invitingly.

I put some background music on, working my way through the record collection to find new tracks I liked. Meanwhile, the fire cracked and hissed, and filled the room with the olive-scented smell of its smoke.

Declan was the first to join me.

'Man, that snooker game is crazy. It makes no sense *at all*.'

He lay flat on his back on a window seat, looking at the moon rising above the cedar trees.

I decided Declan was a blues boy, and put on some Muddy Waters. I was getting to know the collection now. We spent our time in companionable silence, thinking our own thoughts and listening to the deep, slow vocals and blues guitar.

Angus came in next, holding a guitar and a mini amp, which he plugged in. He sat on the big sofa and played along to a couple of tracks, improvising as he went. Declan joined him, playing on a table with a couple of pencils for drumsticks. Connor arrived and stretched out on the floor near me, mesmerized by the fire.

The record stopped but Angus and Declan carried on, playing variations on what we'd just heard, picking up the tempo a little. Angus's guitar playing became more intricate. God, he

245

was good. A boy that good-looking had no right to be that good.

Soon he switched rhythm to something different – not mellow any more, but steady, insistent, complicated. I recognized the riff pretty quickly: DA-da-da, da-da-da, DA-da-da, da-da-da, in a rising scale. He was playing 'Kashmir'. And Declan, laughing, joined in, recapturing the complicated beat on a chair leg, a couple of photograph frames and the bucket containing the poker and the other fire irons.

It was slow and gentle, but enthralling, and I knew from the satisfied smirk on Angus's face that he was doing it to impress me. It was working, but I was determined not to let it show. He easily had a high enough opinion of himself already.

I put my arms around my knees and closed my eyes, dreaming. Soon I was back in that desert landscape. Then I sensed a shadow behind me in the real world, cutting my back off from the warmth of the fire. I looked round and Jamie was standing there, holding his battered Taylor in one hand.

He shrugged at Angus. 'Mind if I join you?'

A slow grin played across Angus's face as he gestured to the painted chair. 'Sure. You know how it goes.'

He started again, still smiling his secret smile. Jamie sat down with his guitar on his knee and played along. Together they created the same tune as before, but it was richer, more layered, even more beautiful. They'd done this many, many times in the past, I could tell. With no practice, they fitted together with not a note out of place, electric and acoustic, searching out new harmonies. They couldn't help catching each other's eye and nodding as the song progressed. It was as if they'd never been apart.

Connor, lying on his back with his eyes closed, grinned like the Cheshire Cat. Declan's expression was calm and focused, but I thought I detected an extra millimetre in the stretch of his smile.

What nobody was doing was what I was tempted to do, which was to get up and scream 'OH MY GOD. ANGUS IS PLAYING WITH JAMIE. WHAT JUST HAPPENED HERE?'

Instead, when they finished with 'Kashmir', Jamie suggested picking up the beat with a bit of Nirvana, and suddenly they were into 'Smells Like Teen Spirit'. Declan grabbed a snare drum from the music room and the sweet, soulful sound of Jamie's vocals carried over his percussion and the sound of the guitars.

From nowhere, they were a band again. It was the old magic – magnified by the flickering firelight and the darkness beyond the windows. Jamie was the missing ingredient. Nobody could match his voice. His touch on guitar might not be as flashy as anything Angus could do, but it melted me.

I let the music wash over me and round me and through me, as the firelight cast ever-changing patterns on my skin. I could hardly believe I was really here. It was like a mini-concert, just for me. Well, strictly speaking, for Connor and me. But when I looked over at Connor, he was grinning at me with the same knowing grin that Angus gave Jamie when he first came in. What did it mean? It was as if they all knew something I didn't.

I scooted backwards until my face was close to Connor's.

'What's going on between those two?' I whispered.

'Don't you get it?'

'No. Not at all.'

Connor looked at me and laughed. 'You really don't, do you?'

'No. Really. Explain it to me.'

He sighed. 'Why does any boy learn guitar?'

'To play like Jimmy Page?' I said, remembering what Angus told me.

'No, you idiot.'

They were playing 'Unlock Me', from The Point's second album. As always, it sent shivers through me.

'It's you.' Connor leant up on one elbow to whisper in my ear.

'What's me?'

He stared at me, confused by my stupidity – whatever I was being stupid about. When I finally got it, a flush spread through me that made my face glow hotter than the firelight.

They are playing guitar together to show off to a girl, pure and simple.

I feel dizzy with the strangeness of it.

Despite whatever Windy said, I am what just happened here.

32

Connor brought in his bass and another amp, and they played together until long after the fire was dead. But I'd been up late a lot recently, and walking in the rain again for much of the afternoon. At three in the morning I dragged myself up to bed.

I slept late, but when I woke up the house was still quiet. Orli had made coffee and left pancake batter ready beside the Aga. She'd left a note to say she'd popped into the village with Sam. This was perfect. With the kitchen to myself I made my own pancakes, the way I'd seen her do it. I walked Twiggy and did my chores and stayed busy and spoke to no one. I tried not to think about last night, or remember any details, because the weirdness was too immense.

When I'd run out of chores, I worked on my mural in the Silk Room. My face and hands were spattered with shades of green. I was painting trees today – beeches and oaks and great cedars of Lebanon. All I knew for certain was that I was happy. Because the band had got back together. That must explain the dizzy feeling that still hadn't entirely disappeared.

The boys emerged mid-afternoon for a late-lunch English breakfast, rock-star style. Afterwards they disappeared into the music room together and stayed there, talking, laughing and trying out the instruments. I lingered in the drawing room, listening to them across the hall for a while, then caught snatches of their playing while I painted.

They played together for a couple of hours, then things went quiet for a while. Taking Twiggy for another walk, I found Declan and Connor playing football on the overgrown lawn in front of the house with an ancient, bust leather ball.

'Where are the others?' I asked.

'Still inside. Talking,' Connor said. He shrugged. 'They've got some catching up to do.'

As I walked back inside, it felt as though a curse had been lifted from the house, or an evil resident ghost was gone.

I was heading up to my room when Angus looked up and saw me through the music-room door.

'Can you get Jamie's phone, babe?' he called out. 'He left it upstairs. He wants to show me something.'

'What did your last slave die of?' I asked, raising an eyebrow.

Angus shrugged, half-apologetically. 'We'd go ... but ...'

He indicated the guitars slung over their shoulders, the leads everywhere. More to the point, they were obviously in the middle of creating something and didn't want to get too distracted. I knew the feeling. Plus, it was technically kind of my job.

'OK. Fine.'

I went up to Jamie's room, which was bigger and statelier than mine, and found the phone lying amongst the general chaos of his unmade four-poster bed. He made me look relatively tidy by comparison. I tried to block out what Tammy would be saying if she could picture me in here, and focus on what I'd come for. *Not a girl girl, Nina, never forget.*

Back downstairs, as I handed the phone over, both boys grinned at me gratefully. 'Love you, babe' Angus said, with a distracted nod. This was my favourite Angus, hair in a mop, mind buzzing, caught in a creative haze.

'Love you too,' Jamie echoed as I passed him the phone, flashing me The Smile and catching my gaze for a second longer than he needed to.

Whoa. That smile.

I nodded and said, 'Yeah, course you do,' and walked away.

Because he was being a rock star, and that's what they say. *Don't get carried away, Nina. Just because he played guitar to impress you last night.*

I was calm and in control, but twenty minutes later, I was coming downstairs with the laundry basket when I heard the results of the new song they'd been working on. Angus strummed the chords and Jamie's voice sang out the verse and chorus, loud and clear.

I let you down
You cut your hair
All the blue
Gone

All the blue
Wrong

And now you're flying through the air
Like a bird, like an angel
Across the golden sky

Ariel
Take me there
Ariel
Take me anywhere

I stopped in my tracks and almost dropped the basket.
Jamie Maldon had just written a song about my sister.
Windy never prepared me for this.

'So, Nina,' Angus said over Orli's roast dinner that night. (We all ate together in the evenings now and Angus was sitting next to me.) 'Who's your favourite? Which one of the Point are you into? The bad boy?' He lowered his head and gave me his devil's smile. 'Or the angel?' He gestured at Connor, whose white-blond hair glowed paler than ever in the candlelight.

'Don't be a moron,' I muttered. Meanwhile I noticed that Connor's darker blond roots were showing. He was becoming less rock-god to me now, and more someone who needed some serious hair-dye attention.

But Angus wouldn't give up. 'Maybe the new boy?' He grinned at Declan, sitting opposite, who gave me a gentle-manly nod. 'No? Surely not ... surely not ... *Jamie Maldon*?'

Whoosh. My cheeks were on fire. I hated Angus and shot him a look but he didn't care. 'What girl could possibly fall for that hideous facial expression? He gets zits, you know. His, erm, gaseous emissions, if you'll pardon me, can be measured from space.'

'Gaseous emissions?' Jamie echoed in mock horror from across the table.

'You fart like a cow, man. It's not humanly possible to fart as much as you do. How can any girl like you?'

'You fart way more than I do! You hold the world record for "gaseous emissions". Don't put that on me.'

I thought I'd got away with maintaining a dignified silence, but Jamie gave me The Smile, and asked me, confidently, 'So ...?'

'I'm not *into* anyone,' I said hotly. 'The world isn't just a beauty contest between you guys.'

'Oh yeah?' Angus asked, with a lazy grin.

'And if you think it is, then what are you going to do when your hair starts falling out? And you get pot bellies? And the fans have moved on to people who weren't even born when you started?'

The grin on Angus's face faded. He looked offended. 'What about Mick Jagger?' he asked. 'He's still got it.'

'Mick Jagger's old enough to be my grandfather. I can categorically assure you that I don't fancy him.'

I was quite proud of myself – I'd managed to turn the conversation from me on to Mick Jagger. But Declan was grinning at me. Declan – who I trusted. It turned out that he was just one of the boys when he wanted to be.

'She colours. Look at her,' he said. He hadn't taken his eyes off me from the start. 'She colours beautifully.'

'What?' Angus asked. 'Like colouring in? She does pictures?'

'No. Her face. She can't help it.'

'Oh, she *blushes*,' Angus said. 'I know. Watch this. *Jamie Jamie Jamie Jamie.*'

It came so suddenly, I had nowhere to hide. The blush, which had started to fade, was back with a vengeance. I could feel my cheeks flaming.

'Aha!' Declan crowed. 'I knew it!'

They all laughed. Even Orli and Sam were smiling.

'It's not true!' I protested. 'How can you even say that?'

'And look!' Angus announced gleefully, leaning over and pulling the neck of my jumper down. His fingers were gentle as they brushed across the skin on my collarbone. Noticing his touch made my cheeks flush further, which infuriated me given how much I hated him right now. 'She even has his initial on her neck, see? Proof. The rest of us don't stand a chance, Sam.' He put his arm around the security man sitting on his other side, and pretended to weep on his shoulder.

'Haha, very funny,' I snapped.

'Wow,' Jamie murmured, looking surprised at my tattoo. 'You do.'

'It's not for you,' I said crossly, flashing him a defiant glance as I pulled my collar back into place. 'I had it done when I was fifteen. For some idiot who deserved it even less than you do.'

'Oh my,' Angus said beside me, whipping round to look at me with a wicked glint in his eye. 'What a romantic gesture.

You have secret depths, Nina Baxter.' He took my hand in his and pretended to adjust invisible spectacles on his nose. 'Tell Doctor Angus all about it.'

'Shut up, Angus. There's nothing to tell. I just ... There was a boy. I made a mistake. End of story.' I pulled my hand away. My eyes blazed into his. What happened with Jez wasn't dinner-party conversation, or teasing material for a bunch of boys unwinding after a songwriting session.

'Hey,' Angus murmured, switching suddenly from theatrics to gentleness. He reached out and stroked my collarbone again with a feather-light touch. 'It's nothing to be ashamed of. You feel things. I get that. It's beautiful.'

My skin tingled. Angus might be annoying, but I wasn't nearly as immune to him as I made out, and especially that gentle touch. I was more of a *girl* girl than they suspected. More even than I'd suspected, too.

For a moment, I imagined how it would have felt if it had been Jamie's fingers stroking my collarbone, not Angus's. The tingle almost floored me.

Jamie Jamie Jamie Jamie.

Angus was right. And I was a fool.

33

Rory Hippolytus Windermere (that's the full name on his Wikipedia entry) is an idiot and a buffoon. I should have known this from the start.

Let's see – what did he do here? He took a seventeen-year-old girl and put her among a group of nineteen-year-old boys and expected nothing to happen.

And it won't. Because I refuse to get my heart broken by some stupid rock star.

BUT IT COULD HAVE DONE, WINDY. OF COURSE IT COULD HAVE DONE. YOU MORON.

Because it turns out that even Nina Baxter, whose heart was declared dead at the scene by Jez Rockingham two years ago, is capable of finding the official Sexiest Boy In The World attractive, especially when he writes songs inspired by her family.

On top of which, Jamie had noticed that I – even I – was female. And single. And even though he wasn't (single, that is, he was definitely not female; life would be so much easier for me right now if he was), he seemed to operate by rock-star love-life logic, which meant that he was allowed to like me, regardless of the whole, you know, *fiancée thing*. And he did.

He just did. I'd tried pretending to myself that he didn't, but he hadn't tried pretending at all. He'd been giving me The Smile ever since the moment he joined Angus playing 'Kashmir'. And before that, too, now I thought about it.

Jamie Maldon liked me. And somehow, that made him want to play music with his band again. Which was why we were all here after all, so even though it was as weird and confused and as *wrong* as I could begin to imagine … it was also useful. At least, that's what I told myself.

The next time I took Twiggy out walking, he offered to accompany me.

First of all, he laughed at my outfit. For once it was quite warm for Northumberland, so I was wearing the old tweed jacket over a stiff-fronted evening shirt and a taffeta puffball skirt from 'Charity'. Jamie led me towards a spot beyond the copse of trees behind the lake that I'd never visited before.

The land rose here, with clear views across the purple moor to the mountains. If we looked back, the Hall glistened among its backdrop of cedar trees, where a rare patch of sunlight caught its mullioned windows. Connor was sunbathing (in a heavy jumper) in a deckchair on the lawn, but there was nobody else around for miles and miles. The only sounds were sheep and birdsong, a jet flying far overhead above the clouds, and Twiggy whiffling her nose into a nearby rabbit hole.

We sat on a grassy hillock and Jamie asked if I'd brought my camera. I always have my camera. I fished it out of the pocket of my jacket.

'Why?'

'I want to take a picture of you. I want to learn how you do it.'

I tried to help him, but didn't get very far. Guitar, he could do; photography, not so much. It was endearing how he didn't really have a clue. He crouched down, taking several shots of me squinting into the sunlight.

'They'll look terrible,' I assured him.

'They won't. Trust me.'

I laughed. Yeah, sure.

As he fiddled with the focus, I glanced down at my bare legs and battered trainers, then across the lake to the tall house with its twisted chimneys. 'I must look so out of place here,' I muttered.

'You don't at all,' he said. 'You look perfectly at home. That's the thing. You suit the place's strangeness.'

'Oh, *thank you*.'

'No, I mean it. It's a good thing. On tour, you were always in Sisi's shadow. But in the light, you're …'

'Strange.'

'Unusual. Unpredictable. It's a good thing.'

The steadiness of his gaze made me embarrassed.

'How?' I asked.

'Well, I wouldn't have guessed you have a tattoo. I like it.'

I smiled wryly. 'You would.'

'Not just because of the initial,' he grinned. 'Because of why you did it. I'm sorry the guy wasn't worth it.'

I squinted down at a wild flower in the grass. 'Don't worry about it.'

'I don't,' he said, evenly. 'You'll find a better guy.'

He gave me that confident smile again. I pretended to ignore it.

'Sisi got a tattoo when she sold her first million DVDs,' he added. 'A dollar sign, on her ankle.'

Was I supposed to be impressed by this? Surely not? Anyway, I wasn't. But ... Sigrid. Good reminder. Sigrid: the fiancée. I wondered if he was going to talk about her some more, but he didn't. Instead, he gazed out at the scenery, and back at me. I had a sudden urge to reach out and touch those three moles on his cheek. I got the impression that if I did, he'd like it.

Think about Sigrid. Talk about Sigrid. Say stuff about Sigrid and move on.

'Why do you ...?'

I stopped. *Why do you even like her?* I wanted to know. But then I pictured her. The answer was obvious – it was on the cover of a dozen magazines. And she loved him. In her own self-centred way, she did.

'Why do you want to settle down?' I asked instead. 'I mean, my mum got married when she was your age. She doesn't regret it, exactly, but she keeps on telling me to seize the day.'

'I've seized the day, believe me,' he said, with feeling. 'I've seized a thousand days. I seized so many they just began to bleed into each other. It's Monday? You must be playing the

O$_2$. Tuesday? There's an awards ceremony in Rio. Wednesday? You're meeting the President. Can't remember which country? Doesn't matter. Can't find a clean pair of socks? Don't worry, we'll get you new ones. Want a dog? Can't have one – because you don't have a home. I've got three homes, by the way. One I haven't seen yet; the other two are very nice. My mum lives in my house in London. But I've never stayed in them for longer than a week. I meet these people – famous people – and sometimes all they talk about is where their dogs are, which is usually on the other side of the world. Or their kids – same story. I was sick of it all. I just wanted it to stop.'

'And now?'

He looked straight at me. 'You played "Kashmir". You reminded us why we started. Now I know I can't lose the music. Everything else …' He shrugged. 'I'm working on it. Being here helps. Windy's not as stupid as he looks.'

Not about some things, I thought. Not about Heatherwick. About some others, maybe.

Jamie put the camera down and looked thoughtful. 'I've been wondering since we got here … why did *you* come here, Nina? After …'

'… what happened on the plane?' I suggested.

He nodded. It was his tacit admission that his fiancée wasn't the ideal boss. I was glad he'd noticed, because it was another sign he was human.

I laughed. 'My sister asked pretty much the same question.'

'And …?'

'Well, Windy promised me Sigrid wouldn't be here,' I admitted.

It was his turn to laugh.

'I wanted to get away,' I went on. 'I wanted to explore. I always have. I thought I'd get the chance on tour, but that didn't happen.' I paused for a moment. 'I had this aunt who travelled a lot and I want to see all the exotic things she saw. But actually, I think she'd have loved it here too. The lake … the mountains … those weird dolls in the Silk Room … I wouldn't change anything. Well, maybe I'd fill the stable with horses. I'd put chickens in the walled garden, and fix the broken bits, but that's all.'

He held out his hand to accompany me back to the house. 'Like I said, you look at home here. When I saw you in the room with the flapping pages that first night, and you weren't scared … you were *fascinated* … That's when I wanted to stay.'

I held my breath. He wasn't supposed to say that, or look at me that way. Or make me feel like this when he wrapped his fingers around mine. I was supposed to be invisible.

I knew I'd have to be careful from now on, or something precious was likely to get broken.

34

When we got back, he dropped my hand and I was relieved. Things were happening at the Hall. A large, blue truck had drawn up in the courtyard, driven by a short, well-built man with a grey-speckled beard. Ed the Engineer had finally arrived with the recording equipment.

'Should have been here two days ago,' he said, as we joined the others gathered round the truck. 'But she had a breakdown near Birmingham.' He tapped the side of the truck. 'Got to be careful. She's a grand old lady now. And what's inside ...' He sucked his teeth. 'Special. Ve-e-ry special. I don't know how the boss got hold of this. Practically museum material. As far as I knew, it *was* in a museum.'

'Can we see it, then?' Angus asked.

'*Avec plaisir*,' Ed announced, with a bad French accent and a flourish.

He opened up the back to show us the contents of his special truck. I wasn't sure what I'd been expecting, but when he said 'museum', I supposed I'd pictured something like the old radios Dad worked on sometimes – all grand wooden cabinets and delicate glass valves.

'Is that it?' I asked.

All I could see were a couple of rows of grey plastic decks, covered with hundreds of knobs and faders. They looked used and grubby, covered in peeling stickers and bits of tape. The floor was a nest of cables and wires.

'That, my dear,' Ed said proudly, 'is the equipment the Stones used to record *Exile on Main Street*. At least, some of it is. It's what Led Zep used for *IV*. *Capish?*'

I understood. A lot of old bands recorded famous music on this equipment a long time ago. Great bands who were now – if they were still making records – presumably using newer, better kit.

Remembering how the boys reacted to Windy's ideas about 'going back in time', I thought they'd go berserk when they saw it. But I was wrong. They looked as if all their birthdays had come at once. Like the rock geeks they were, they wanted to know about every band who'd ever used it, and every track ever recorded on its equipment. Angus was soon in the back with Ed, checking out the decks. Jamie was keen to set up the electrics and get plugged in. Before long we were hauling cables around and helping Ed to set the generator up. Then they wanted to practise, to see what it could do.

They chose the hall again, because it was the easiest place to lay cables to. This suited me perfectly, because I could listen to them down the library corridor as I sketched out a new mural in the Silk Room. I'd been working on a lake scene, but I'd changed my mind and now it was going to be about music. Four boys with iconic haircuts playing together, sharing the energy, almost like a dance. Ironically, my inspiration came from Sigrid's favourite French artist 'after Picasso' – Matisse.

A couple of days later, I was working on the mural again when I heard Angus and Jamie mucking around with a fragment of a melody that Jamie had been developing on tour. It always ended suddenly, with Jamie abandoning his guitar in frustration. This time, Angus suggested something. I couldn't hear the words exactly from their mutterings in the hall, but then Jamie laughed and played a set of chords, adapting them until he was happy with them. They formed the bridge between the first and second parts of the song. Jamie sang along indistinctly. Angus's voice again, suggesting something new.

I put my charcoal down and listened to the song, as Jamie's voice floated down the corridor.

> *She wears his name upon her skin*
> *But now the love is wearing thin*
> *I'll be there*
> *I'll find you*
> *My pilgrim soul will guide you*
>
> *She dreams of far-off desert lands*
> *I'll write her name upon the sands*
> *I'll be there*
> *Beside you*
> *My pilgrim soul will take you home*

My heart pounded out a routine like one of Declan's complicated drum solos. This was worse than the song for Ariel. It wasn't just my sister who was inspiring him – my life was leaking into his songs. The 'skin' was mine. The 'pilgrim soul' came from a poem by Yeats that I'd pointed out to Jamie in the Fluttering Room. The 'desert sands' were 'Kashmir'.

I wandered down the corridor to the hall. Jamie saw the look on my face. This time he didn't give me the confident rock-god grin. In fact, he looked almost embarrassed.

'It's not finished yet. Is it OK?'

I didn't know what to say. As a song, it was more than OK. My heart was still pounding. I got the sense that he was asking my permission to use it, though. And that felt wrong. Good, but wrong. Windy would kill me.

But Jamie was writing songs. That was what Windy wanted. I was so confused.

'I … It's good.'

Angus nodded, happy with my answer, but Jamie wanted more.

'Do you like it? I mean … can I …?'

Jamie Maldon, lost for words, like me. We stared at each other. Embarrassed smile met embarrassed smile.

In the end, it was art that gave me my answer – and then it was obvious. I was painting him on the wall in the Silk Room, and I knew I'd take as many pictures and make as many sketches of him and the others as they'd let me. What they were doing here was absorbing. I wanted to explore it on paper, and in paint, because … I had to. My fingers itched to describe what my eyes could see. Jamie did it with words and music. He did it with what inspired him. If, sometimes, that was me ... well ...

'Sure. Of course you can. As long as I can paint you.'

This time, his smile was totally different. Relieved. Happy.

'You can paint me any time. I love to watch you paint.' He was cocky, and irresistible, and he knew it.

'Yeah. Well ... thanks.'

I walked back to the Silk Room as steadily as I could, trying to pretend that I was immune to the Jamie Effect, and that it didn't matter he'd just written a song about me, and that I could hardly feel the floor underneath my feet.

35

Jamie liked me. Oh yes. And I liked him more than I wanted to, or could admit. But I would be just a fling for him, and my heart didn't work that way. So from a sense of self-preservation, I kept my distance. I treated him the same way I treated them all – like idiotic, occasionally adorable overgrown schoolboys. And maybe he didn't care that much, or he had more self-control than I ever gave rock stars credit for, because he flirted, like the rest of them, but he didn't try anything serious. Besides, he was busy: he was writing and arranging songs for the new album. Now he was back together with his best friend, they couldn't come fast enough.

Our days quickly fell into a pattern. The boys surfaced late, rarely emerging before midday. First, Jamie and Angus spent some time together, writing. Between them, they had so much material built up from the time on tour – scraps of melodies, riffs they'd been thinking about, rhymes and rhythms captured in late-night ramblings on their phones – that it flowed from them like a river of songs.

Listening to them write together, I could understand why Windy was so frustrated when they wouldn't even talk to each other. Jamie generally provided the lyrics, but Angus gave them new meaning with subtle melodies and pounding guitar riffs. If either got stuck, the other was ready with an idea. The joy on their faces when something worked was like sparks ascending to the sky. Nobody must ever stop them doing this, I thought. It was what they were made for.

When they had something they were happy with, Connor and Declan joined them and they would all wander off to wherever they'd decided to try the acoustics today. They worked on the arrangements together, while Ed followed them with a sea of cables to connect to the monitors, amps and instruments. When they were ready, Connor anchored each track with his steady bass. Declan gave them shimmering intensity with a range of backing instruments, and a dazzling display on drums.

While they worked, so did I – helping with the equipment, taking pictures, sketching them or painting my mural of them on the Silk Room wall. I walked Twiggy, tended to the tomato plants that Sam had got for me to grow in the walled garden, and got Ed to help me fix the ride-on mower I'd discovered in one of the outhouses. There were always new jobs to do at the Hall, and I couldn't get enough of them.

Sometimes, the boys took a break from music. If it was dry, we played football on the freshly-mown pitch in front of the house, or tennis (which only Connor and Declan could actually play) on the rough, netless tennis court. If it was wet, we watched kids' TV on the set that hardly worked, or raced each other round the house on skateboards and BMXs, in a dangerous game that Angus always won.

Sometimes … often … this would involve crashing into Jamie and collapsing in a heap. The electricity was just as powerful every time we touched, but I hoped it would subside eventually.

At four o'clock, we stopped for tea. Orli brought a tray into the sitting room, laden with tea and sandwiches. I didn't know that it was possible to be rock-star about sandwiches, but it is if you try. Angus announced one day that he wanted his cut diagonally, to make triangles. Jamie instantly ordered parallelograms, with a snarky glance at his friend. Connor insisted on pyramids and Declan panicked for a moment, until Orli raised one eyebrow and suggested, 'Circles?' I thought she'd be snippy with them for being so difficult, but she disappeared without a word.

When she returned, each plate of sandwiches was shaped as required. Even the pyramids. There was quiet triumph in her eyes. I'd underestimated how much she loved their silliness. It was a challenge for her – an easy one to meet – and she never forgot or got it wrong.

We all had our favourite mugs for tea and coffee, chosen from a large assortment on the big kitchen dresser next to the Aga. Every single one was chipped or cracked, but that didn't matter. Gradually we came to have our favourite chip, our special crack. Angus's mug was Mr Happy, and nobody appreciated the irony more than he did. Declan's had a picture of

Alnwick Castle. He couldn't get his head around the fact that the castle used as Hogwarts in the *Harry Potter* films was only a few miles down the coast and was already making plans to visit as soon as our isolation here was over.

Afterwards, there were freshly made local griddle cakes called singin' hinnies, laced with currants and topped with melted butter. Once, as I was handing them round, watching Jamie look at me, and smile, and graze my fingertips with his, I realized that I would never be this happy, or this unhappy, again.

During the times when Angus and Jamie were busy working on new songs, Connor and I developed his next hairstyle. We decided the world was ready again for a Mohican. Declan alternated between shooting hoops on a luxury basketball system he got Sam to install, and taking cooking lessons from Orli, so he could impress his mum when he got home.

Declan was perfect. He was charming, sweet and gentlemanly, single, and now he knew how to roast a chicken. He wasn't super-famous and had the most beautiful set of muscles I'd ever seen on a human. I wished it was him I fancied, not the romantically complicated, skinny-chested poet who burnt toast on the rare occasions he tried to make it, and who made my heart turn over every single time he looked at me.

But love is chemistry, and my chemicals had chosen Jamie's chemicals. I was every cliché in the world, but there was nothing I could do about it.

36

I was on my way up to the Charity and Chuck room to find some fresh shirts to wear one day, when I heard a noise above me in the tower.

Thud.

By now, I knew all the sounds in the house. Every creak and groan of the old pipes and the wooden floors, but not that one. What was it? I paused on the spiral stairs.

Thud thud thud.

Footsteps. They were definitely footsteps. The door at the top of the staircase was open. I was certain I'd closed it the last time I came up here.

Thud thud thud thud.

Now my heart was joining in.

Fans. Paparazzi. Oh God, we'd been discovered. My first thought was dismay that it was all suddenly over. Then my fear intensified. What if it was a stalker? I should call for Sam.

271

Except he'd gone into town this afternoon.

It was too late anyway. A tall, shadowy figure stood at the top of the spiral stairs, looking down on me. My heart beat so fast I thought it might explode.

'Hello? Can I help you?' a girl's voice called out. My pulse subsided slightly. 'Who are you? I say, are you a member of the crew?' She sounded confused, not homicidal.

'The what?'

'The film crew. I assume they're filming, aren't they? Auntie Ven didn't tell me, but I saw all the wires and everything. I suppose they need the money. Is it some kind of period piece?'

'Er, no. It's …' I squinted up at her. 'Who are *you*? How did you get here?'

By now, my eyes were adjusting to the darkness of the stairwell. She was nearly six foot tall, and maybe a couple of years older than me.

'I drove up yesterday,' she said. 'Stayed with some friends outside Newcastle. Except everyone had gone off to some festival or other, so it was just the oldies. *Such* a bore.'

Gracefully, she descended the stairs. In the light of the room, I took in her fine features, very pale blue eyes and fair hair caught up in a rough bun behind her head with chopsticks. She stood like a dancer, wearing cut-off dungarees over a dirty pink leotard. Her arms were adorned from wrist to elbow with bangles, bracelets, watches and festival tags of every kind.

'I mean, how did you get through the gates?' I asked.

'Oh, Auntie Ven hasn't changed the code in years. Didn't she say I was coming? I need an outfit and Auntie Ven has all the best clothes – if they haven't been eaten by rats or moths.

Honestly, this place is a wreck. I don't know how you bear it.'

'We love it,' I said simply. 'It's the most beautiful place I know.'

She put a hand on my arm delightedly. 'I know what you mean, really. I came here every summer until I was eleven. Christmases too. Then Mummy fell out with Auntie Ven over the whole fiasco of selling this place. They don't talk now. It's a nightmare. If the house was just looked after a little, it could be … *incantevole*.'

I sensed a proper Italian accent in the way she said the last word and it reminded me of something Windy had said.

'Are you … Percival's daughter?'

'Granddaughter, darling. Isabella Otterbury.' She held out her hand with mock formality. 'Call me Issy. Auntie Ven's my great-aunt, really, but if I called her Great-Auntie Ven she'd have a fit. And you?'

'Nina Baxter. I'm here with the band.'

'Oh, it's a *band*! Fantastic! You must introduce me. We can do clothes later. Come on!'

Why did I say that? I was too caught up marvelling at this tall, thin, exotic person standing in front of me. She must not, must absolutely not, see the boys and give away their location. That's what I was thinking as she took my hand and rushed me down three flights of stairs, but she didn't give me much choice. Following the sound of the music, she dragged me into the Silk Room – the chosen recording room for the day – where all four boys sat listening to the playback on Ed's monitors, oblivious to the world.

She paused in the doorway, watching.

273

'Holy Moly! They're *hot*!'

Well, yes ... yes, they were. I'd kind of forgotten. I mean, obviously I felt way too strongly about one of them, and the others were all amazing eye-candy, but I thought of them as friends now. Friends with bad morning breath, a shared Led Zep obsession, and a surprising fear of bats. They were, however, officially for the record, just as much as ever, eye-smoulderingly, ab-crunchingly hot.

'Mmm,' I mumbled. It was getting slightly weird to think of them all that way.

'Which one's yours?'

I was about to explain very clearly that I didn't 'have' one, I just worked here ... but at that moment Jamie looked up, caught sight of me, and gave me the full-on smile. Before I could say anything, she nudged me and nodded.

'Lucky you. They're terribly familiar. Do I know them?'

'Um, seriously?'

'Yes. I'm sure I've seen them somewhere.'

'They're The Point,' I said, assuming she was making a joke I didn't quite get.

'Oh! I've heard of them! Didn't they do "Amethyst"? Hey, cool! Isn't your one Jamie? I like the black-haired one, though.'

I turn to stare at her. She'd *heard of* them? *Didn't they do 'Amethyst'?* She wasn't joking. I had just discovered The Girl Who Wasn't That Interested In The Point.

When they finished the song, I introduced her to three of the most famous faces on the planet, and another that was about to join them as a global superstar. Issy kissed them on both cheeks, like she was being introduced at a posh party, and told

274

them she was 'more into reggae, really', but 'you guys sound great for a guitar band'.

At first they just stared at her, Angus most of all. They were completely not used to this. I could see them wondering if she was real. But Issy didn't seem to notice. She was more curious to know how they liked the Hall.

'It's a nightmare at first, I know, but it grows on you, doesn't it? I've always been fond of the old place. Nina says she loves it, don't you, darling? Do tell me you've all fallen for it too.'

'I find it absolutely enchanting,' Angus announced, imitating her voice with the wicked glint firmly back in his eye.

'I'm so glad! That's exactly what I said to Nina. *Incantevole*, no?'

Angus looked slightly stunned. The wicked glint flickered uncertainly. He wasn't sure if she was making fun of *him*. I was impressed. Not many girls could throw Angus McLean off his stride.

Ed appeared in the doorway, looking worried.

'I just saw a new car outside. Does anyone know—?' He saw us chatting to the new girl, and froze in shock.

'This is Issy,' Angus said, recovering and giving a mock bow as he introduced her. 'She grew up here.'

'But ... but ... no one's supposed to know ...' Ed ran a panicked hand distractedly through what was left of his hair.

Issy grinned. 'Ooh! Is it a secret? How exciting! Don't worry about me, darling. One of my great uncles was a spy in the war. The Otterburys are *terribly* good at keeping secrets.' She smiled at all of us. 'I promise I won't tell a soul.'

'How long are you staying?' Angus asked her.

'Oh, no time at all. This place is *creepy* in the darkness. Anyway, I'm off to Edinburgh for a party. I was just going to grab a couple of things to wear on the way.'

'I promise it won't be creepy,' Angus said. 'Please stay.'

She smiled and they locked eyes. 'I can't, darling. It's going to be a *gorgeous* party. But I suppose I could come back this way ...'

Ed groaned. But it was too late. She knew the secret now. And none of the boys seemed to care. The more she treated them like regular, hot guys, the more they seemed to like her.

I did, too. Her buzzing friendliness made it hard not to. She could see us all for what we were – a strange, secret gang.

Isn't your one Jamie?

She saw what I didn't dare even think about. Having her here made it somehow seem more real.

'Promise you'll come back?' Angus asked. He was trying to sound cool and casual, but he was practically begging.

She toyed with him for a while, enjoying herself, but eventually agreed to visit the Hall on her way back down from Scotland in a few days' time.

I'd never seen him look that way about anyone before. Perhaps, in a few days, bracelets and dungarees and '*incantevole*' would make it into a love song too.

37

We had been in the house for a month. August was about to give way to September. Outside, gathering swallows circled in the sky. Tucked under a hedge near the drive, Ed's generator chugged away like a tractor. Inside, the ground floor was a mass of cables and wires, snaking in and out of doorways and windows, depending on where the boys wanted to play that day.

My letters from home were full of news about the twins and questions from Mum about whether I'd make it back for the start of school. I replied to the bits about Pip and Lara, but ignored the school part, for now at least. What was happening here felt like all that mattered. The holidays weren't quite over yet. It was difficult to look out at the purple heather on the moors and worry about term dates. Or to sit with Twiggy by the fire, listening to the band, and want to be anywhere else.

A couple of mornings after Issy's visit, the paper was lying on the kitchen table when Angus came down for his usual late-lunch English breakfast. Sam always brought one back from his village trips. With no internet, he and Orli relied on its crossword for something to do.

Today, a particular piece caught Angus's eye. I was in the kitchen, rubbing Twiggy down after a walk, and saw his face flicker with mixed emotions as he read it.

'What is it?' I asked.

'Oh, nothing,' he said, looking thoughtful.

As he drank his coffee, his expression gradually lightened until he looked positively cheerful – by Angus standards. He folded the paper so one particular corner was on top.

'Leave that here like this, would you?' he asked, as he went off to tune his guitar.

I looked at the article at the top of the folded page. One particular name caught my eye.

⋆⋆CELEB⋆CORNER⋆⋆

BACKSTAGE is back! Despite rumours that she was giving it all up to become a quiet married lady, a spokesman for Sigrid Santorini has confirmed that she's signed up for a third series of *Backstage with Sigrid*. Fans of Pete the chihuahua will be relieved to know that they can keep up with his canine antics in full next season, while Sigrid puts in the final preparations for her wedding to Jamie Maldon. Will the ceremony itself be on the show? We'd like to think so. Sigrid hinted as much on the red carpet for the Hollywood Awards last week when she said that her fans wanted all the details of her big day, and they wouldn't be disappointed. Will Pete be a ring-bearer, in his own cute little chihuahua costume? Guess we'll have to wait for Series 3 to find out.

My heart contracted. Since we'd been locked away here the thought of Sigrid had been gradually fading, like an old sepia photograph. Now there she was, in full colour next to the article, smiling into the camera as she nuzzled up to Pete. Her left hand was just visible in the shot, holding the little dog's face in place next to hers. The Malteser ring still sparkled.

Why had Angus looked so cheerful as he'd left the room? Normally any mention of Sigrid was enough to make him throw things.

I needed air. All I could picture was Jamie with TV cameras stuck in his face. Jamie retreating into his own little world again. He really meant it when he said he wanted to escape from that life. Couldn't he see how she'd lied to him?

I walked quickly through the heavy morning drizzle, without much idea of where I was heading. By the time I got near the lake, the rain was falling harder. I took shelter in the folly, looking back at the Hall through the misted-up windows.

Behind me, I heard the sound of running footsteps. Jamie appeared in the doorway. Rainwater ran in rivulets down his face.

'Angus told me about the article ...' he said. 'He saw you go off in this direction.'

I made a new discovery. The only thing in this world hotter

than Jamie Maldon playing guitar and smiling at me was Jamie Maldon soaked with rain and slightly out of breath, looking concerned about me. This was the last thing I needed to know.

'You're not upset, are you?'

'No,' I lied. 'Why would I be?'

'That stuff about Sigrid—'

I knew I was going to regret this.

'She'll never change,' I blurted out, talking quickly, because I wanted to get it over with. 'She needs fame like a drug. She wouldn't know the simple life if you served it on a plate. With eleven almonds.'

'I know,' he said.

I thought he'd jump down my throat. Instead, he was smiling.

'Oh. You know?' I faltered. 'Well, there's another thing – Angus hates her, and you two ... you're more important than ... She just ...'

I ground to a halt in my misery. His smile didn't waver, though.

'Yes, Nina, I know that too. And Angus was right – you haven't got it.'

'Got what?'

'It's over.'

'What is?'

He came closer.

'I should have told you before,' he said. 'About Sisi. It was a mistake. I saw how she was. With you. With him. With everybody. What it did to the band. I'm not blind.'

'B-but ... the article ... the wedding ...'

He came closer still. 'It's wrong. I was wrong. I wanted to escape and I thought she was the girl to do it with. She played that part for a while, but then she got bored. She morphed from the barefoot, boho chick I met into ... well you saw. She literally made us take a bath in champagne once. It's sticky and ...' He saw me picturing him in a bath of champagne and how it was frying my brain, and he paused and half-smiled. 'Anyway, it took a while, but I woke up and smelt the coffee. I was going to end it after the tour, but we went on holiday. She'd planned it for ages and I didn't have the guts to tell her ... I needed some space to work out how to do it. Then as soon as I got back, Windy brought me here. And there was you.' His lips curled into that smile – not Mona-Lisa any more, but aimed right at me – and my heart missed several beats. 'I haven't told anyone yet. She deserves to know first. But Angus worked it out weeks ago. I thought you had, too.'

He reached out a hand to brush my hair from my eyes. The skin on his fingertips was rough and hard, but I liked it. Musician's hands. I'd been thinking about his fingertips for a long time. His head bent towards mine.

It was perfect. Too perfect. Half of me wanted to meld with him. The other half flinched away.

'Look, I don't play around,' he said gently. 'I know you think I do, but I'm not Connor. Not even close.' His fingers rested against my skin. His lips drew closer. 'I'll tell her soon. It's not fair on her to let her keep thinking we're still happening, when ...'

That 'when' was infinite. His fingertips were sending a constant stream of electricity down to my ankles. I wasn't sure how long I could take it.

And all the time, his lips were getting closer.

I pulled away. He looked surprised.

'What's the problem?'

Life is so easy when you're a rock star. One minute the papers were talking about his *wedding* to Sigrid. The next, he was here, with me. There were so many problems I hardly knew where to start.

'You hardly know me,' I said.

'I do. Test me.'

'OK. When's my birthday?'

He sighed, frustrated. *Nul points*, rock star. Then he took my face in his hands. 'I know you have a curious sense of style. You hate the limelight and you get that it's just a distraction. You can grow tomatoes, and fix an engine, which is more sexy than you know, and quote from my favourite books, and sing from my favourite tracks. You treat Angus like a naughty schoolboy ...'

'He can be very annoying.'

'He can indeed. You're best friends with a whippet. I think you love me. You're the opposite of Sigrid. She's all show. I watch you all the time and I'm still just starting to get you.'

'Stop!' I murmured, putting my hands on his chest to push him away.

I had no idea he felt this way. It was easier when I thought he was just idly flirting. But this wasn't flirting. This was ... more. Too much was going on inside me. Too much.

'What's the problem?' he asked, for a second time.

I dropped my hands (with difficulty – it felt so good to touch him, even to push him away), and tried again. 'Look,' I said, indicating the empty grounds beyond the rain-washed folly window.

He did. 'I don't see anything.'

'Exactly. Right now, I'm practically the only person here. But when we leave, you'll be surrounded by women, throwing themselves at you. I'll be a passing line in your biography. But me ... when I fall for someone, it's like falling off a precipice.'

He frowned at me.

'You think I have passing lines in my biography?'

'Yes,' I muttered. I'd have thought this was obvious. Didn't he?

'You think *I* don't fall off a precipice?' He looked hurt. 'Why do girls always think boys' hearts don't get broken? Don't we write enough love songs?'

'*You* do,' I admitted. I thought back to that night in New York. 'But in a month you won't even remember my name, I promise. And that's OK. As long as I don't ... this.'

Whatever it was he wanted right now. The thing that would break my heart one day. And from a greater height, and with more damage than Jez could ever have dreamt of.

'Just making sure here ...' he said, frowning. 'You think I just fell for you because you're the last girl in the world. Effectively.'

I nodded. 'Yes.' Finally, he'd understood.

'You think so little of me?' He looked positively wounded.

I was about to tell him that no, it was *me* I thought so little of, but then I realized that wasn't true. I knew I could be a great girlfriend for someone – passionate, fascinating, loyal. I just didn't think a boy like him would ever really notice.

But maybe he had. His eyes caught mine and wouldn't let

me look away.

'So you admit that this is happening, at least?'

I nodded dumbly. He didn't exactly have to ask.

He took two steps towards me again, and the backs of his fingers hovered over my tattoo, almost touching it but not quite. 'I wish you'd trust me. I could make you feel so happy, Nina, if you'd let me. Can I kiss you? Because my kisses are pretty persuasive, I'm told.'

I suppressed a shiver.

'I'm sure they are. That's not the problem. That's so not the problem.'

'So what do we do?' He was close, but no part of our skin was touching, and I was acutely aware of this. I knew the heat of it, the smell of it. My skin was obsessed with his skin.

'Stand on the edge of the precipice, I guess.'

'Until …?'

I tried to think. 'Until you're not super-famous. And engaged. For a start.'

'OK. I think I'm stuck with the fame part, but I'll see what I can do about the rest,' he said gently, stroking my hair and staring deep into my eyes. 'Meanwhile, if you change your mind, let me know.'

I swallowed. He took it as a 'yes'.

'Good.' He dipped his head again, teasing me with how close his lips were, then turned away.

The urge to change my mind right there was almost irresistible. But I knew what it was like when my heart smashed on the rocks, and it wasn't pretty. Avoiding that was worth giving up the feeling I'd get if he met my lips with his this minute.

Possibly.

I watch as he saunters back towards the house.

I have just turned down a kiss with Jamie Maldon.

My body thinks I'm crazy. I need to go to a darkened room and lie down.

38

Jamie's next song was called 'Falling Over the Edge'. There was even a line in it about a girl being 'a footnote in your bio'. This album was turning into a diary. It made me wonder how I'd feel when they came to share it with the world. It was so private to me, so personal. Just like the figures that I was trying to capture on my mural – the combination of concentration and joy that made them more fascinating, to me, than their fans would ever know.

In the four days that followed, they finished four new songs. Ed agreed that they were ready. They invited Windy up to the Hall to hear how they were getting on.

Meanwhile, what was happening with me and Jamie was twisted and bittersweet. It was out in the open now. Not passion, but close. Not falling, but nearly. Teasing, joking. Watching him borrow my jackets and wear them. The scent of his body on them when he gave them back. Pretending not to notice the longing in his voice as he whispered goodnight and traced his initial on my skin with his toughened fingertips.

We talked about stupid things. We made up a fantasy life, where we owned Heatherwick Hall and restored it to its former glory. I became a famous painter and he made cheese. Declan married us in a chapel in Las Vegas. Angus was godfather to our twelve adorable children. We were the only real people, and everyone else was an avatar.

We didn't touch. We didn't touch. We wanted to.

It was a mutual obsession and I cursed Rory Windermere because of it. But at least there was the music. Making songs was Jamie's distraction. Listening to them while I painted was mine.

Issy returned from Scotland the day after Ed made the call to Windy. Angus's delight on seeing her was infectious.

'A party!' he suddenly announced. 'We must celebrate your arrival properly. Another feast. We're good at them.'

'Oh, good, so am I!' she grinned. 'I'm a veggie, though. Will that be a problem?'

'Not at all,' he said, heading for the kitchen with the others in tow.

Issy and I stood in the doorway and laughed as the boys serenaded Orli in four-part harmony, begging her to create a vegetarian masterpiece.

She looked at the clock on the kitchen wall.

'It's just gone two. In – what? – six hours, you want me to summon up my finest cooking, with no notice, no decent shops for miles, no help to speak of. On a Saturday? In *Northumberland*?'

She tried to look annoyed, but it was obvious she was enjoying herself. When the boys asked for cheese on toast for lunch, she always looked depressed. This was much more her style.

'Well, scram, in that case, all of you. You too, Nina. I'm sure you've got things to do. Dinner will be at eight. Now leave me alone so I can get on with it.'

Angus spent the afternoon teaching Issy how to play chords on his guitar. This involved him sitting very close behind her, moving her fingers up and down the frets. Neither of them was put off by the rest of us laughing. It was clear proper songwriting was over for the day, so we set about getting the house ready for the party.

'We're dressing for dinner, I assume?' Issy asked, as she watched Jamie and me put the finishing touches to the dining room, hanging fairy lights around the stag's head antlers, to make up for the fact that most of the wall lights were broken.

'Of course,' Angus said, as if we'd all stepped from a storyline in *Downton Abbey*.

We all went our separate ways to get ready. The plumbing at Heatherwick Hall couldn't begin to cope with six people bathing at the same time (the Otterburys didn't seem to have heard of showers), so we went back and forth with kettles of hot water, cursing loudly to each other as we passed.

Later, Issy took me up to the Charity and Chuck room, and begged me to choose something from the rack of expensive-looking clothes that I'd ignored up to now.

'You've *got* to dress up properly,' she insisted. 'Auntie Ven would be so disappointed if you didn't. Honestly, she's a stickler for correct procedure.'

I tried on a dark green vintage satin dress, with a deep V neck and spaghetti straps that crossed over my back. I'd never shown this much cleavage before. My tattoo was fully on display.

'You look stunning,' Issy said. 'This is the dress for you, Nina. I won't let you wear anything else.'

Later, we both stared at my reflection in the long cheval mirror in the master bedroom with its four-poster bed and tattered silk hangings, which she had commandeered for the purpose of getting ready. The dress puddled on the floor because I was wearing it with bare feet. None of Auntie Ven's shoes would fit me, and I didn't think wellies, slippers or trainers would do for a night like this. Even so, I looked amazing. At least, I thought so. Smoky eyes – as trained by Tammy. Clear skin, from all the good food and fresh air. A general aura of happiness.

Issy played with my hair. 'You should wear it up, I think. Like this.' She twisted it into a loose knot at the nape of my neck and fixed it expertly with a pencil. 'Don't worry – I'll find a clip in a minute.' Then she teased out tendrils to frame my face.

For herself, she'd picked a red silk Chinese cheong-sam that hugged her whippet-thin dancer's body.

'Angus likes me, don't you think?' she asked, adding a matching slick of red lipstick from her handbag, and checking herself out in the mirror too.

'Yeah,' I said with a laugh. 'I think he likes you.'

'Good.' She nodded quietly to herself, satisfied. 'I'd hate for you and Jamie to have *all* the fun.'

I didn't correct her. I didn't want to. She was the only person, apart from Orli, Ed and Sam, who would ever see us this way.

When we were ready, we descended the stairs carefully, me in my too-long dress, her in her tight cheongsam. The boys were waiting in the drawing room. They'd clearly spent longer on their hair than we had on ours. They wore elegant evening trousers, T-shirts, and a variety of military waistcoats and jackets that they'd found around the house. They looked like exotic creatures from another age. Punk rockers dressed up for a ball.

Holy Moly, as Issy would say.

Four pairs of eyes turned to us. The effect was almost comic. Four pairs of eyes were saying *Holy Moly* back.

OK. So this felt good. It wasn't my normal style, but I must remember to do the spaghetti-strap thing again.

Angus took charge of the record player and we danced to The Cure and Velvet Underground, Talking Heads and David Bowie. We were all serious movers, getting into the rhythm, not caring what anyone else saw or thought. Issy was perhaps the best of us all, throwing her body into weird and twisted shapes, totally unselfconscious. She closed her eyes as she waved her arms above her head, undulating like a swimmer descending through the waves. Angus was transfixed by her. But whenever I looked at Jamie, he was watching me.

After half a dozen songs, Orli announced that dinner was ready. The dining room was already aglow with candlelight and paper lanterns. She brought in dish after dish. Soup, risotto, a tomato tart that looked unbelievably simple and was the most delicious, flavour-packed thing I'd ever eaten, and plates of glossy, jewel-like chargrilled vegetables. A mushroom and spinach concoction had Issy literally dancing on the table in appreciation – and climbing up there in a skin-tight dress wasn't easy, although the boys all seemed to enjoy watching her try.

Later Issy told us about the house. How the Fluttering Room (she called it 'Aunt Charlotte's room') was created by a long-dead cousin who was sent to the Hall for its fresh air while she recovered from tuberculosis.

'She got well enough to have an affair with one of the gardeners,' Issy said, 'but when it was discovered, he was sacked. They found him later, drowned in the lake. She locked herself in the bedroom for years, and papered it with love poetry. Can you imagine?'

'Yeah,' Angus murmured. This was exactly his kind of story.

'Nobody dared go in the room after she died,' Issy went on, her voice deep with drama. 'They felt too guilty about what happened. But as I say, my family is mad. It has dark secrets. We're good at keeping them.'

She told us about the priest hole, too, created in Elizabethan times at the back of a bedroom fireplace.

'Two priests were hidden there after the Gunpowder Plot. Both found. Both tortured to death on the rack. I say, I'm telling you the most *awful* stories. Tell me about you.'

She rested her chin on her hands and stared into Angus's eyes. So the boys told stories about touring. Not the late, crazy days, but the first tour, when The Point went around America in two vans and nobody could sleep because Angus farted through the night, and in one town only five people showed up to watch them play because the flyers all gave the wrong date, and how they nearly died on hair-raising roads, driving through snow and ice to make a gig in Seattle.

Their eyes glittered in the candlelight. They told her about the first time Windy got their song played on local radio in Chicago, and how the next day they couldn't fit the crowd inside the club they were playing. That was the first time there was nearly a riot.

Jamie's face lit up when he talked about his old life. It had got out of control, with all the endless interviews and paparazzi chasing them like a pack, but the music, the fans, the connection … it was what made him who he was. He needed the gigs, but he would have died in Hollywood. Sigrid would have made him so unhappy.

He was sitting opposite me at the table. Underneath it, his shoe brushed against my bare foot. As he talked, his gaze descended to my spaghetti straps, paused on my tattoo, and raised itself again to catch my eye. Each time, that smile caught mine.

'Weren't you engaged to someone?' Issy asked at one point, as if a dim memory had just resurfaced. 'An actress?'

'I was,' he said, without taking his eyes off me. 'Once.'

Then he changed the subject and went back to talking about the band.

39

After the meal, we went back to the drawing room, where the fire burned with a steady glow and Orli had thoughtfully laid out coffee on a silver tray.

As they'd so often done before, the boys drifted in with guitars. They played a couple of songs, but unlike me, Issy wasn't the kind of girl to sit back and listen to other people. She soon challenged anyone who was interested to a game of snooker across the hall.

Angus and Connor got up to join her. Declan seemed undecided. Then he looked at Jamie and me sitting close to the fire, Jamie with his guitar resting on his lap, me with Twiggy's sleeping head on mine. We didn't seem to be moving. Tonight, Declan was a gentleman. He decided to leave us alone.

Jamie was still staring at me intently, like he wanted to map me and explore me. It made me feel dizzy. And it wasn't just the firelight that was making me hot. He shifted his body closer to mine. The smell of the fire smoke on him, mixed with the woody scent of his aftershave, filled my senses to bursting point.

'I didn't know you could …' He faltered and stopped.

'What?'

'… look like that.'

'Oh, great. You say the nicest things.'

His lips curled into a smile. 'You know what I mean, Nina. I love the way you look. But tonight … I just …'

He reached out a hand to touch me. Every cell of my body tensed in anticipation.

'You don't look so bad yourself,' I admitted, secretly awarding myself the prize for understatement of the century. I wasn't sure how any of my synapses were still managing to function.

'We won't be here much longer,' he said. 'Afterwards, when it all goes crazy again, promise me you'll …'

He seemed to lose his train of thought as his fingers inched further towards me.

Three … two … one …

The door was flung open with a flourish. A sudden gust of air caused the fire to cower and crackle. Issy stood there, gazing down at us imperiously.

'Come on, lovebirds. Enough of that. Those boys are *terrible* at snooker. I can't bear to watch them any longer. We're going to play a game I used to play with my cousins at Christmas. We called it anchovies when we were little, but it's sardines really. You know how to play? Angus has gone to hide. Whoever finds him hides with him. The last person to find everyone has to swim in the lake tomorrow, and I assure you it's freezing, even in summer. One rule: no lights.'

I knew the game. At least, I'd heard of it, but you can't really play it in a small house in Croydon when the biggest cupboard is the size of a washing machine. In my house, it would last about thirty seconds. In this place … it could last days. Now I understood why Issy was standing there with that smile on her face. She was absolutely the sort of person who would love hiding in the dark.

Jamie sighed, but he was not the kind of person to avoid a game. And besides, we both knew Issy wouldn't let us.

'Come on,' he said, getting to his feet and holding out a hand for me.

Our sophisticated evening descended into chaos, shrieks and laughter, more like an eight-year-old's birthday party than a posh *soirée*. Running through the darkened rooms, up and down the broken staircase. Bumping into furniture and each other in unfamiliar places. Getting dusty searching under old four-poster beds; bravely opening creaking cupboards; standing, terrified, in pitch-black corridors, listening to the sound of pounding feet far away.

After a few minutes, the sounds died down. Some of the runners must have found Angus already. Was I the last? I didn't want to be the one to swim in that freezing lake. For a moment, I stopped to think more carefully. Where would Angus go? This house was enormous. There were any number of cupboards and spaces he could choose. I'd looked in all the obvious ones already. He was being clever.

OK. So narrow it down. If I was hiding, where would *I* go?

To the Fluttering Room. Because it was strange. And it

reminded me of twisted love.

And Angus?

To somewhere that reminded him of death.

I thought of the fascinated look on his face this evening as Issy described the priests' hole, and their discovery and torture. Where better than a priest hole, in fact? A space built especially for hiding.

Issy said it was in one of the oldest bedrooms – one with a big fireplace – and there were a couple like that on the east wing corridor, low-ceilinged and dark, with thick walls and inglenook fireplaces big enough for a person to stand inside them.

I was one staircase up, but I ran down it fast, treading lightly so as not to give away my position to the other searchers, though I had a vague sense of someone not far behind me. The first bedroom I tried was empty and silent, but somewhere close, I was sure I heard the sound of someone sneezing. In the room next door, the fireplace was even larger. When my right foot hit a creaky floorboard, I could have sworn I heard a giggle.

I walked up to the fireplace, and into it, ducking my head. To the left-hand side of the ancient grate, something pale and ghostly glowed in the darkness, level with my eyes. I gasped. It grinned. It was Declan's face.

'Come on!' he said in the faintest of whispers. I sensed bodies behind him, but couldn't tell how many.

'Who's there?'

'Angus and Issy.' He winced. I heard the sound of kissing. Another giggle. Something like a moan. Declan rolled his eyes. 'It's been nasty. Thank God you're here.'

More footsteps outside. The floorboard creaked again, and a darker silhouette appeared against the general darkness of the room. He stepped in close and I smelt the fire smoke on his shirt. My heart raced.

Jamie whispered in my ear: 'Hello.'

He must have been following me.

Now only Connor was still searching. We could hear him running around upstairs, thudding on the floorboards and shouting out. Issy laughed. There was the sloppy, slurpy sound of another kiss. Declan sighed in frustration.

All the time, Jamie was pressed up against me in the fireplace, his chest against my back, his arms around my waist so he could stay out of sight. His hands found mine in the darkness and it was like coming home. The feel of his breath on the back of my neck. The warmth of his skin, his smell, the chemical connection.

I knew why Issy had suggested this game. It was more for her benefit than mine, but the result was the same. I felt Jamie's heart, beating in time with mine. We said nothing. We did nothing, except touch. But what was going on between us felt a thousand times more exciting than the slurpy PDA going on behind Declan in the priest's hole. My temperature raced. My body was a silent fireworks display.

This is it. I'm gone. Off the precipice. In freefall. You idiot, Rory Windermere – of course this was going to happen.

Connor found us soon afterwards, ('Man, guys, it was like *Nightmare on Elm Street* out there – I'm never doing that again') and we all piled out of the fireplace, laughing.

We drifted back downstairs. Angus had his arm around Issy. Jamie reached his hand out for mine. I took it naturally and we walked down the staircase together. In the drawing room, Declan put on another record – something slow and bluesy. The fire spat and hissed. It wouldn't last much longer. I should do something about it, but Jamie's arms were around my shoulders now.

The lights were low and the room was full of moving limbs and the sound of guitar. Angus danced with Issy, and Jamie danced with me. I looked around at us all and realized this was one of those moments that would live for ever while the world kept turning.

We swayed gently, hardly moving, bodies close. Maybe this was wrong, but I was sure – absolutely sure – that it felt as natural to him as it did to me. Now the connection was made, we couldn't break it. He rested his hand on the back of my neck. We were soft skin and warm flesh and the world was a cocoon around us.

His head dipped. Warm breath on my skin. I raised my face up to his and ran my hand through his hair. Those lips. After about a hundred years of slow anticipation, they gently met mine, and it was as good as I knew it would be.

Kissing Jamie Maldon was like flying through the night sky, for ever. It was heady and dangerous and all I wanted was more.

For a while, there was nothing except him and me, and the taste of his lips, and the feel of his fingers on my skin, and the sound of our kisses.

Jamie Jamie Jamie Jamie. He wanted me as much as I

wanted him.

Then gradually, my other senses returned. The music was still playing. When we finally surfaced, the others were all watching us, smiling.

Jamie's heart was beating fast; his eyes were hooded with desire. He murmured in my ear, 'I've wanted to do that for so long.'

And so had I. Why hadn't we done it before? I couldn't remember. My brain fought through the fog of wanting him. Like this, with his arms around me, in about seven seconds I wouldn't be able to think about anything at all.

Then, with the roar of a banner going up in flames, I remembered what was really happening here.

This was the boy who could have anyone. Rock star. Temptation. Tragedy. The inevitable broken heart.

I'd fallen over the edge, but like a cartoon character madly running in mid-air, I thought maybe somehow it wasn't too late. I had to do something to save myself before I hit the ground, because I'd been there before and I couldn't do it again. Not like this. Not with him. When this stopped, it would hurt more than I could imagine.

I pulled away.

'I have to go. Upstairs. I—'

I couldn't think of a reason. I just knew I need some air. Away from the dying firelight, the hall was cold and dark. I shivered, pulling his jacket round my shoulders. He ran out after me.

'I know this is tough for you, Nina.' His breath was warm on my neck as he pulled me back towards him in the dark. 'What I am is tough for you. And it should be, because … I come with all this baggage, and you don't want it. It's why I love you so much.'

Blood pumped in my ears as my heart pounded. He said the L-word. I couldn't believe it. Boys *never* say the L-word. Not after just one kiss.

'I don't know … I'm sorry …'

He held my hands and pulled me back towards the drawing room, and the firelight, and the sound of blues guitar. 'Don't go yet. Stay with me. I love you, Nina. It's simple.'

'I … just … I can't … It's complicated.'

40

I ran up the stairs before I had any more time to think. My feet caught on the folds of my dress, tripping me with every step. I was Cinderella, running from the ball. There was even a clock chiming dimly from the kitchen.

It's complicated. It's complicated.

I ran down the corridor and to my cold, dark room, pressing my back against the rough surface of the ancient dressing gown as I shut the door behind me. My breath was ragged. My body ached.

It's complicated.

Except, now that I was here on my own and my frenzied mind was slowing, it wasn't complicated at all. In fact, it was so stupidly simple it took my breath away. I slumped to the floor.

I wanted him. And he wanted me. I wanted him so badly. Whatever the reasons for us being here, our skin was made to touch. We were a chemical reaction waiting to happen. He knew that, and what had I proved in the last five minutes? I'd just made two people unhappy. I had to learn to stop *thinking* so much, and just unlock my heart.

From where I sat, I could see myself by moonlight in the wardrobe's silvered mirror. I looked a mess. My smoky eyes were smudged and my hair was half falling down. I took out the clip Issy had given me and let it fall completely. Without really thinking, I fixed my eyes with a dampened finger while I worked out what to do.

I wanted him. When he kissed me, every cell in my body was happy. Something magical was happening, and I'd stopped it. For what? For no good reason at all.

I'd go downstairs. I'd say I'd just needed some air ... to fix my hair ... anything. I'd find a way to touch him again. I'd ask him to dance. Whatever it took. I could not let this perfect evening end this stupid way.

But halfway down the stairs, I heard them talking. Issy's voice, then Angus's, then Jamie's ... They were all together around the embers of the fire now. Their voices were low, but I heard my name. Shame flooded through me. It was like being back at school, after Jez. I'd made a fool of myself and now they were talking about me. I couldn't go on.

So I slunk back to my room and lay on the bed, wide awake with longing.

He said he loved me. How many boys say those words at all? What was I waiting for? A diamond ring? He gave a girl one of those once, and I thought it was ridiculous.

Idiot! Idiot! Idiot! I banged my head on the pillow. He must have thought I was such a little girl. I thought I'd got over Jez so long ago, but it turned out he'd messed me up more than I ever knew.

The moon shone pitilessly through the open curtains, leaving a pattern of cold blue light across the bed. I thought of us in the fireplace, fingers touching. The anguished look he gave me in the hall. Who said he would let me down? All he'd done so far was write me love songs.

Should I go to his room and wait for him there? I wanted to, but I couldn't bring myself to do it. Too many girls had tried to sneak into Jamie's bed over the last few years. If I went to him, I didn't want it to be some rock music groupie cliché.

So what should I do? I was burning up. I couldn't sleep. I grabbed a torch and wandered the corridor until I reached the Fluttering Room. I scanned the yellowed pages under the torch's weak circle of pale light, reading and discarding, until I found what I wanted: a poem by Yeats called 'Aedh Wishes for the Cloths of Heaven'.

> But I, being poor, have only my dreams;
> I have spread my dreams under your feet;
> Tread softly because you tread on my dreams.

That's what I wanted to tell him. I ripped the page from the wall.

Back in my room, I grabbed a pen from my desk – a red felt tip, the first one I could find. I ringed the words of the last line. They held my fears, my hopes, everything.

I'm sorry, I wrote. *It's simple. I love you. N.*

Pausing at the top of the stairs, I could still hear them talking. I went to his room and slipped the paper under his door. Tomorrow, I would do things differently.

41

I don't remember falling asleep, but I suppose it must have been shortly before the dawn. The sun was high in the sky when I woke up. The first thing I felt was the imprint of his lips on mine. I'd made a fool of myself last night, but today felt different. I had the strength to make it better. Besides, there was my note. By now, he must know I'd changed my mind.

I ran a bath, then slipped into an old evening shirt and a pair of shorts from the Chuck bag. I put my dirty hair up Issy-style, with a pencil. I was about to do my make-up when I noticed something strange out of the far edge of the bathroom window: a long, flat object seemed to be balanced in the air about three metres above the ground. It took me a moment to work out what it was: the tip of a rotor blade.

I looked closer. Sure enough, there was a helicopter parked on the grass outside. I could hardly believe I hadn't heard it land. I must have been sleeping deeply.

Windy was here. It was the only explanation I could think of. And even though his timing wasn't perfect, it would be so good to see him. He'd probably be annoyed when he found out about me and Jamie, but the other boys had seemed happy enough about it last night, so hopefully he wouldn't mind too much. I ran downstairs, hoping to catch him before the others woke up, so I could explain.

Orli was banging pots around in the kitchen, putting things away from last night. She looked glum. But then, she'd worked really hard to prepare the feast. Maybe she was still recovering.

'I don't think we thanked you enough for dinner,' I said, giving her a squeeze. 'It was incredible.'

'Oh!' She waved me away. 'It's what I do, Nina. I wouldn't do this job if they didn't ask me to be a bit creative.' She gave me an odd look. 'I mean, we're both here to do what we're paid for, aren't we?'

If I wasn't in a hurry, I'd have tried to make more sense of her grumpy mood. Orli never talked like that. I was sure they paid her well, but she never mentioned the money. Or my strange status here.

'Where's Windy?' I asked.

'Windy? He's not here. Why did you—?'

'The helicopter on the lawn. Then who—?'

But before I could finish my question, the door flew open. Issy came in, wearing Angus's slippers and a rose silk robe, with Angus himself not far behind her. She held out the glass cafetière.

'*Darling* Orli. We've run out of coffee. Would you mind

terribly …?' She froze when she saw me. 'Oh.'

First, I was amazed that they were up already. I was usually the first one to come downstairs, regardless of when we'd gone to bed. Then last night came back to me with full force. Those conversations they must have had about me after I'd run away. I blushed to the roots of my hair.

'Hi.' It came out as more of a whisper.

Angus gave me a long, steady look. 'This is going to be interesting.'

I had no idea what he meant. It must be something to do with the helicopter.

Issy looked super-awkward – the exact opposite of how she was last night. 'Yeah. Nina. Um … hi. Come and join us.'

'You go. I'll bring the coffee,' Orli said grimly, like she was announcing battle plans.

The atmosphere was weird and I could feel a ball of fear growing in my chest with every step as I followed the others to the dining room. If not Windy, then …?

I had come downstairs the back way, straight into the kitchen corridor, so I hadn't walked past the dining room yet. If I had done, I'd have heard the sound of loud voices carrying across the hall.

The sound of *one* loud voice.

'So where's the studio? I want to see EVERYWHERE! This place is just so historic I could DIE!'

I stumbled and nearly fell. Thank goodness Orli hadn't trusted me with the cafetière. I felt sick.

Sigrid Santorini was sitting at the far end of the table, facing the door. A designer peasant top that probably cost a thousand dollars hung loosely over one shoulder, emphasizing her skinny frame. Her shining hair was in braids. Her skin was tanned and sparkling. She looked like a visitor from another world.

Somehow, I crossed the hall and walked into the room. Jamie sat across the corner of the table from her, his back half-turned to the door. He didn't turn around when I came in. Instead, he raised his coffee cup to his lips like this scene happened every day.

It was clear from Sigrid's happy, happy face that they hadn't had The Conversation. It was clear from the way nobody looked at me that The Conversation wasn't even on the agenda. He and Sigrid were still together. I was just an awkward, embarrassing leftover from last night.

Angus and Issy slipped back into their seats, holding hands. Isabella Otterbury clearly had none of my hang-ups about hooking up quickly with a boy she liked. Although I suddenly felt grateful for all those hang-ups – every one. The best thing I'd ever done was say no to Jamie last night. I'd just been saved the most embarrassing moment of my life.

In favour of the second most embarrassing. Which was to be standing here, now, like this.

Sigrid looked up at me. Her perfect forehead crinkled in confusion. Her eyes flashed fire. She turned to Jamie.

'You didn't say *she* was here. Why is *she* here?'

Jamie's back was still turned to me. He was dressed in a crumpled tartan shirt and jeans, and his hair was ruffled, like he'd just rolled out of bed. I'd worn that shirt two days ago. A part of me still wanted to reach out and touch him. The rest wanted to disappear.

'Windy hired her. She's been helping us out,' he said dully. 'Issy, could you pass the butter?'

He didn't even say my name. My heart folded into a tiny ball and armoured itself in brass, like an unwanted snitch in a game of Quidditch.

'And 'ave you been here *aw*' the time?' Sigrid asked me, her mouth a tight smile, her eyes narrow. Still practising the Croydon accent, then. She hadn't lost her touch.

I blinked and nodded. I couldn't trust my voice.

'Windy thought she made a good assistant,' Angus said in a casual drawl. 'She walks the dog. Helps out with the housework ...'

Issy flicked me the briefest of pitying glances.

'Oh,' Sigrid said, 'Cause when I spoke to Windy, *several* times, he said there were no girls allowed here. No distractions.'

'Well, yeah,' Angus agreed, gulping from his favourite mug. 'Exactly. No girls. No distractions. Just ... staff. You know.' He shrugged. 'We've been working so hard, you wouldn't believe.'

Still, I said nothing.

'They played me some of their demo tapes,' Issy added. 'They're simply *gorgeous*.'

'And you just got here?' Sigrid asked her, focusing her suspicious gaze on Issy's calm, fine-featured face.

'Uh huh,' Issy said, not mentioning her earlier visit. 'Like I say, it's practically my family home. What brings *you* here?'

'Well ...' Sigrid said, relaxing slightly. 'I just *had* to talk to my Jamie. I mean ...' She cast Angus a nervous glance. 'After that story leaked out about the new *Backstage* series ... they got it all wrong. I had to reassure him.'

'So it isn't true?' Angus said sceptically.

'Well, yeah, it is, but it's gonna be nothing like the last one. I mean, it's gonna totally protect our privacy this time. No cameras in the bedroom. Nothing he doesn't want. But I knew my *darling* Jamie might be worried and I needed to explain ...'

'No need to explain,' Jamie said. He waved away all those reasons for breaking up with her with a single flick of his hand.

'Oh, but there *is*, baby. As soon as I signed, I had to talk to you. And I tried! But you weren't in any of the places they said you were. In the end I had Windy checked out. It took a while to find this place, but my guy had a hunch—'

'Which guy?' Angus probed.

'My private eye guy,' Sigrid said dismissively. 'Anyway, he just *knew* Windy wasn't visiting a sick old aunt up in Northumbershire, like he said to everyone. They can just tell, you know? So he did some more checks, and we worked out Windy'd hired Wutherington Manor for you, or whatever, and as soon as the director let me off the set, I got the first flight over from Vancouver. I gotta go back tonight, but it's worth it.' She turned to Jamie, the full force of her ice-blue gaze focused on his face. 'Thank God you're OK. I've been so *worried* about you!'

Jamie reached out and stroked her soft, downy cheek. 'I'm fine, babe. Absolutely fine. And don't worry about *Backstage*. It's your career. You do what you need to do.'

She leant in to him. He met her lips with his. As they kissed, she turned her eyes to look at me, still making sure of her prize. He didn't give me a single glance.

All this time I'd been standing at the table, about as significant as a hatstand, wondering what to do with myself.

It was always going to be bad, but he didn't have to make it *this* unbearable. Was he punishing me for last night? Or had he simply forgotten my existence in the sudden light of her presence? I felt as if I was falling down an endless elevator shaft at terminal velocity.

I told this boy I loved him, and now I'm the girl who walks the dog.

42

Orli arrived with the new cafetière. I took it from her and dumped it on the table, hard. Everybody jumped at the sound. I left the room without a word.

Back in the kitchen, I found Twiggy's lead and took her on the longest walk of her life. Past the *helicopter*, whose pilot was stretching his legs, admiring the view of the hills. Round the lake, through the woods and back again. Past the folly, and the sheep and the view of the distant mountains.

It's simple, he said.

It's simple if your girlfriend isn't around, and if there's a willing girl who's fallen in love with you, and is too stupid to keep her feelings in check, although goodness knows, she tried. It's simple if you know you're soon never going to see her again.

You just tell her what she wants to hear. You write her love songs … and when she becomes inconvenient, you go back to your stunning girlfriend and your real life.

By now even Twiggy was starting to drag her feet. I looked at my watch. We'd been out for nearly two hours.

I was distracted by the distant sound of voices, and lingered behind a copse of trees as they all came out together to watch Connor strip to his underwear and jump into the lake. I watched too, from my hiding place, as he ran out again quickly, screaming.

The others all laughed. Jamie was holding Sigrid's hand. As Connor raced back towards the house, wet and freezing, the others began to follow him. Then Jamie and Sigrid paused halfway to the house.

Good place for a Conversation, Jamie.

Instead, inevitably, their heads moved together. I forced myself to look. His lips lingered on hers. With the silhouette of her helicopter in the background, and his fancy historic mansion. How appropriate.

I want to go home. Now. Everything is spoilt. She ruins everything she touches. She's King Midas in reverse, but with the same result: misery.

I must stop thinking like this. I'm going mad.

Once they'd all gone back inside, Twiggy and I took the longest route I could think of back to the house, so we wouldn't bump into anyone.

The girl who walks the dog.

Not a girl girl.

I'd never make that mistake again.

Back in the kitchen, Orli was pounding at a lump of dough

on the table like it needed to be taught a lesson. She looked up as Twiggy took a long, loud drink of water and slunk off to her dog bed.

'You've tired her out!'

'Looks like it.'

'I didn't think that was possible.'

'She's not as tough as she looks.'

'None of us are,' Orli sighed. She wiped her hair off her face with the back of her hand. 'Look, Nina, I'm not sure what's going on. That ... *person* arrived here this morning and followed me up the stairs when I let her in. I didn't have time to warn Jamie she was coming.'

'He didn't look like he needed warning.'

'I know. But give him a chance. I've known that boy a long time. There's something not right.'

'Yeah. I'd noticed,' I said sharply. I didn't feel like conversation. 'Where are they now?'

'In the truck. Listening to the tapes.'

'I'll be in the garden. I have things to do.'

At least I knew, after years of experience, the best way to deal with these feelings. Which is to block them out. Get on with things. Make something. Grow something.

I went out to the walled garden this time, grabbing my tools from the greenhouse and setting to work pulling weeds, fixing poles, carefully attaching the spiralling tendrils of emerging beans and sweet peas to their tepee frames, getting my hands dirty.

I thought about Dad. How much he'd love this place. Especially with someone like Ed around to talk solder and valves and amplification issues. The twins would spend all day running in this garden, looking for sparkly unicorns. Ariel would be stretched out in the sun on the front lawn, listening to music and writing letters to her friends, while Josh watched his favourite shows on the ancient TV inside. Michael would pour trumpet music through the windows and Mum would stand near the lake, thinking of Aunt Cassie, and wishing she could be here, the way I wanted them all now.

Jamie, Angus, Connor and Declan would be … absolutely nowhere. They'd be gone. They'd be far away, getting married on a beach. Playing cowboys. Singing to a million screaming fans. Picking up supermodels. Telling the world their so-called favourite breakfast food. Breaking rules and hearts and leaving the scattered pieces in their wake. Because that's what rock stars do. It's their job. It's how they get where they are.

When I finally came back inside, I could hear voices in the drawing room. I knew I should be brave and say hi, but instead I sprinted to my room and pressed my hot forehead against the cool glass of the windowpanes.

On the front lawn, the pilot was sitting in the helicopter, looking like he was ready to go. Sigrid and Jamie walked out and lingered nearby. She stood on tiptoe and wound her arms around him.

This time I should really look away. I couldn't.

I sank down the window as I watched him kiss her yet again. His hand was wrapped around the back of her neck, the way he'd held me when we danced last night. The kiss was long and slow.

The last time this happened to me, 'Eden' was playing in the background. This time, there was silence. At least another decent song wouldn't be ruined for ever.

43

'It was a game, Nina! It was all a lie!'

'Nina! Nina! You've got to believe us!'

Two voices outside my door. Issy and Angus.

I felt groggy. I must have been asleep. The last thing I remembered was Jamie knocking and pleading for me to let him in.

Like that was going to happen.

He was there for a long time and at some point I must have drifted off. It was dark now. I'd been sleeping for quite a while.

'Open the door, Nina! Please!' Issy sounded desperate.

'No. Go away.'

'Oh, thank God you're awake! I've got to drive back soon, but please believe us.'

They wouldn't leave me alone.

I went to sit near the door and rested my aching head against it. 'You just said you lied,' I muttered.

'To her. To Sigrid.'

'You do get it, don't you?' Angus said.

'We thought you were brilliant. Oh, do open up, Nina, please!'

I opened the door a crack. Connor was in the corridor too, leaning gracefully against a doorway. Declan stood at Angus's shoulder, looking concerned. Jamie hovered in the shadows, pale as a ghost.

It was horrible, I felt claustrophobic with them all so close, staring at me. I grabbed the dressing gown and threw it round my shoulders, pushing past them and running down the wrong stairs, having to leap across the gaping hole.

'We thought you knew what we were doing,' Issy called out, following me.

'If she knew about you, she'd never have left us alone,' Angus said, from close behind. Could nobody take a hint? Not even him? I did. Not. Want. To talk about Sigrid Santorini.

Jamie outran them both. He caught up with me at the bottom of the stairs and put his arms around me.

'Please, Nina, please!'

My voice came from the bottom of a deep, dark well. 'Let me go.'

They all clattered down the corridor behind me as I ran into the Silk Room and shut the door, shoving the rocking horse against it and sitting with my back to it.

'She caught me off guard. I didn't have time to think,' Jamie shouted through the keyhole, sounding desperate. 'I just wanted to get rid of her. It seemed the easiest way.'

I hugged my knees and dug my nails into the palms of my hands. Funny how kissing a beautiful girl can seem the easiest way. If you're Jamie Maldon.

'How about telling her the truth?' I muttered.

If it *was* the truth. I didn't know anything any more. And the piece of me that cared was broken.

'Then she'd have stayed for ever.'

'We all knew it,' Connor called out, backing him up. 'She'd have tried to get him back. And you know what she's like. Nobody wanted her here. Jamie didn't even have to explain what he was doing. We just went along with it.'

Tears poured down my cheeks. I couldn't stop them. I didn't try.

They took it in turns to call through the door. She was clever, they said. And suspicious. (Which was true.) She'd have noticed if any of them hadn't played the game. They thought I played my part brilliantly, staying out of her way, behaving like the servant she wanted me to be.

Now they wanted to erase the last twelve hours and go back to exactly where we were last night. Or the part of last night, they implied, before I stormed off upstairs for no good reason.

But as it turned out, I'd had a very good reason. She had arrived by helicopter a few hours later. He had cooed over her coffee cup while my body and soul were vaporized two metres from his half-turned back.

'Look, I panicked. I'm sorry,' he said.

'We should have told you but we didn't have time,' Issy echoed. Please believe us.'

And, do you know what? I did. Eventually. Kind of.

The boys might lie to me, but I didn't think Issy would. Also, the story made its own strange kind of sense. Sigrid was clearly still obsessed with Jamie. She would have fought for him, if she thought she had to. They all seemed relieved that she wasn't here any longer.

I believed them, but it was too late.

I was back to being the girl who made pictures and walked the dog. My heart was an armoured snitch. I always knew that loving Jamie would hurt, and I'd tried it, and within twelve hours it had destroyed me. He was a star and I was just a little asteroid that burnt up as soon as I got too close. I couldn't put myself through that again.

No more Nina 2.0. I was done.

When they finally left me alone, I found Orli and told her to call Windy.

'I just need to get out of here. Now.'

The manager had said once that he was used to solving major problems before breakfast. Even though it was after midnight, it took his office less than an hour to get me on the next flight from Newcastle to London, and to book a car to take me to the airport in the morning. They didn't ask any questions. Either they didn't want to know, or Orli had already explained. As long as I didn't have to talk about it myself any more than was strictly necessary, I didn't care.

'This is for the journey,' Orli said as she handed me a package wrapped in a tea towel. I stood next to the taxi and thought of the boys inside – hiding, as usual, so the driver wouldn't see them. The Point was all about running and hiding.

'Thanks,' I said, trying and failing to smile as I climbed into the back seat. The car was a Skoda Octavia, I noticed. Dad had always had a surprising soft spot for Skodas, despite their absolute lack of cool. There was a distinct absence of helicopters this time.

Orli and Sam waved from the drive as I drove past the procession of cedar trees and out of sight of the Hall for ever. High above, a bird of prey hovered in the cloudless sky. For once, it wasn't raining.

Even so, I felt the dampness on my cheeks and wiped it quickly away. This was it. The dream had ended, as I knew it must. It didn't make it any easier, though.

Angus had kissed me on the lips and muttered 'Miss you, Leena', as he said goodbye. Jamie had simply said 'I love you,' very quietly, so only I could hear it. I wanted to hit something.

Once I'd gathered myself, I opened the tea towel to find a tin filled with singin' hinnies to keep me going. Suddenly the car smelt of currants and freshly-baked dough. The memories of our fancy tea-times flooded through me.

'You look a bit down, pet. Want some music?' the taxi driver asked. Without waiting for an answer, he turned the dial on his radio to the nearest music channel. They were playing 'Amethyst'.

Funny, that.

'I don't think so,' I said, wishing I had a gun so I could shoot the radio. 'I'll just watch the scenery, if that's OK.'

'Suit yourself,' he shrugged, turning it off again.

We drove on in silence for a while.

'No, I've changed my mind. Please turn it on again.'

I'd just inspired a whole album of break-up songs, I realized. It would probably be launched sometime in the next few months. I was going to have to learn to cope better than this.

44

By the time I got back to school, I'd missed the first two weeks of the new term. I told everyone it was glandular fever. I had a lot of English to catch up on, but at least my art A level was well on track. Windy asked if they could use my mural and a section of my photos for their album cover and publicity. I said yes. Why not? It helps your art school applications when your main project is the artwork for a bestselling band.

The story I told my art teacher was that I'd visited them for a couple of days through a connection of my sister's while I was off sick. And that's the story I told myself too: I'd been off sick. I was better now.

Tammy didn't know what to think.

'Either he's an evil, two-timing, cheating slimeball, or they were telling you the truth that night, in which case you're the one being totally unfair. I can't decide.'

'It doesn't matter anyway,' I pointed out.

Jamie was in a recording studio in LA, finishing off the final tracks. There'd been no news of a break-up, so Sigrid was probably there with him, sorting out real estate. She would make him unhappy one day, but that wasn't my problem now.

Mum gave me lots of work at the salon at weekends, which I was grateful for, because it kept my mind off things. Meanwhile, Ariel often took charge of the twins at home these days. She'd stepped into my shoes while I was away.

Ariel was older, taller, wiser. Her short, bobbed hair was pink from roots to tip, because she liked it that way. She had a new friend called Maddie, who didn't like The Point, and that was one of Ariel's favourite things about her. Even though I didn't tell her much about what had happened, she could tell the second trip had been a worse disaster than the first. She hated them for my sake, and though I was training myself not to care, not having to listen to their music daily made life a little easier.

Dad was fascinated by stories of Ed and the mobile studio. He wanted me to tell him everything I could remember about it, and I realized he'd missed his calling – instead of being a handyman, he should have been a sound tech for a band. I thought he'd be horrified when he realized I'd been practically on my own all that time with a bunch of rock stars, but he just looked into my eyes and said, 'As long as you're OK, love, that's all that matters.'

And I was OK. So everything was fine.

The fifth of November was my eighteenth birthday. Bonfire night. Free fireworks, courtesy of the council. Tammy threw a fancy-dress party for me and I danced the night away with friends, wearing a unicorn onesie with extra sparkles. I could be a party girl, no problem. I didn't even flinch when certain songs were played.

That morning, a letter had arrived for me, along with three dozen pink roses. Two blooms for each year of my life. The envelope was in Jamie's handwriting. I recognized it from his scribbled lyrics, like the ones I'd used in the collages when Sigrid fired me, and the ones on the songs he'd written for me.

I didn't open it.

The term came and went. I finished all my coursework and went to some more parties. Nobody would know there had ever been anything wrong. Anyway, they were all too busy commiserating with Clemmie since Jez had left her for a girl he met on a tour of Oxford colleges to care much about what had happened to me over the summer.

Lying around in Tammy's room one day, I saw a picture of a coat I liked the look of in one of her magazines. Next to it was the intro to an article with their 'Star of the Week', and before I could help myself, my eyes were scanning the lines.

As Backstage heads for our screens again, Sigrid Santorini talks about her love split, her new co-star beau, and the rumours that it was her break-up with Jamie Maldon that inspired the songs on The Point's eagerly awaited new album, Pilgrim Soul. *'What Jamie and I had was special. We touched each other in ways that were very deep. It's why I just had to let him go. It got too intense. We were like the Elizabeth Taylor and Tim Burton of our generation. But I am truly blessed. Toby and I are so happy now.'*

So they weren't together any more. Was it true that Sigrid had caused the break-up in the end? I didn't know, and didn't care. I knew both of them well enough by now to believe that anything was possible. But Tammy was furious on my behalf about the songs.

'Why doesn't he *say* anything? Those songs were about *you*, Neens. Why does everything always have to be about her? Why does he let her get away with this?'

She was really steaming. She'd hated Sigrid with a passion before, and now she hated her even more, and Jamie with it. He didn't give any interviews to correct the stories. Any thoughts of giving him the benefit of the doubt were gone.

I read, too, that someone had bought Heatherwick Hall. The reports didn't say who. I tried not to picture it being turned into a school, or a hotel, or a luxury pad, fit for a millionaire, with matching furniture and perfect plaster everywhere.

I was busy working on my application portfolio for an art-school foundation course, and I was using my pictures of the house. Page after page of sketches, photography, painting, and even a 3D model of the Silk Room. More than anything, I was trying to create the sense of unreality I'd felt while I was there. The perfect, damaged place for a damaged band and a damaged girl.

My Hall would always be slightly broken. It would have ancient windows that didn't fit their frames, and saggy sofas adopted as their own by leggy dogs. It would have chickens in the garden, and rooms with peeling wallpaper – an eerie background for unusual photoshoots. There would be horses and boats, and a festival in the grounds each summer – camping and lanterns in the trees and music. But at its essence, it would always be falling apart. The soundtrack to my portfolio was the blues.

Ariel came to find me a few days before Christmas. Her face was pale.

'You didn't tell me.'

I was busy working on a sky of stars on the ceiling of Pip and Lara's bedroom. I wasn't really concentrating.

'Tell you what?'

'This.'

She held up her phone. A tinny tune was playing through the earbuds. I could hardly make it out. 'What is it?'

She put one of the buds in my ear.

Like a bird, like an angel
Across the golden sky

Ariel
Take me there

'Ah,' I said. 'Oh, that.'

The band must have released the first single. In my eagerness to forget what I could about the Hall, I realized I'd forgotten to mention her song. It was bound to come out some day.

She put her face up close to mine. She wasn't happy.

'Yeah. That. Would you care to explain, by any chance?'

I shrugged. 'I told Jamie about you. How you cut your blue off, because of the way he treated me. He was sorry.'

Her face changed instantly, from fury to wonder. Her hand unconsciously went to her hair.

'So it *is* about me? Really me?'

'Mostly you,' I agreed. 'And a bit of Shakespeare, I think. He's a big reader.'

'Not the mermaid?'

'Absolutely not the mermaid. You, Lellie. Do you like it?'

She nodded dumbly. Her eyes were glistening. 'Yes. Can I tell people?'

'I'm sure he won't mind,' I said. 'Except—'

And then it hit me. If she told her friends the full story, she'd have to tell them all about me and Jamie. And so far that was, mercifully, a secret.

Was that why he hadn't corrected Sigrid, when she'd let people believe that she'd inspired all the songs? Because to correct her would require talking about me, and he knew that I wanted nothing to do with him any more? Was he trying to protect me?

Suddenly, I wasn't sure about him again. Wow, Jamie Maldon – he had seemingly endless power to unbalance me.

'Are you all right?' Ariel asked. She looked worried.

'Yes, I'm fine. And tell your friends if you want to. Maybe you could say I met him while I was doing my art project. It's kind of true. Hopefully they won't ask too many questions.'

She smiled. 'You're the only person I can imagine who's

hoping people *won't* ask her about Jamie Maldon.' Then the worried look came back. 'But should *I* be asking? What happened, Neenie?'

I told her then. And she held my hand and stroked my hair. She knew what it was like to love Jamie and lose him. I should have talked to her about him a long time ago.

45

Christmas Day was an endless feast. We ate so much turkey and trimmings we could hardly move. Afterwards, Mum and Dad offered to wash up. I knew they really fancied some time alone to chat. They'd been up until nearly midnight, wrapping things, and awake since dawn with the twins, unwrapping them again.

Michael disappeared upstairs to Skype his new girlfriend while the rest of us piled on to the sofas in the front room, watching *Doctor Who* and whatever other TV came on. In the evening there was a variety show hosted by Rose Ireland, who was one of Ariel's favourite singers, now she listened to other people in the charts.

'And now ... I can't believe it!' Rose beamed across the airwaves. 'I'm so excited! Here are some of my very best friends – fresh from recording their latest album. I've heard it, and it's incredible. Look! Here they are! Sitting right in front of me!' The camera panned over to the opposite sofa. *'The Point!'*

Ariel groaned and I felt my body go rigid, but Josh had buried the remote somewhere and we were too wiped out to find it. I wasn't going to waste my energy on The Point.

'They look pretty,' Lara said, watching from my lap.

'They do,' I agreed, because it was a simple fact.

Four famous hairstyles – the fourth one now being Declan's – sitting on a sofa, being interviewed. Déjà vu.

'D'you want me to turn it off?' Ariel asked. But she had Pip fast asleep on top of her, and the interview wouldn't last long. I knew what kind of thing they'd say anyway. I'd heard them often enough.

'No. Leave it.'

'First of all, how's George?' Rose asked them, with a concerned little frown.

'He's doing OK,' Angus said. 'Out of rehab now. He wants to thank everyone for their messages, by the way. He's taking it one day at a time, got a new band ... Nothing crazy like us.' Angus gave that rare and irresistible half-smile of his. 'Yeah. He's good.'

Rose smiled back. 'Now, I don't need to ask what you've been up to lately,' she went on, 'because I was lucky enough to catch up with you in LA. Look – here we are.'

The producers showed a picture of Rose on a night out with the boys. Their girlfriends were there too: Issy – skinny and balletic; Connor with a supermodel looking impossibly tall; and next to Jamie a crop-haired, athletic-looking girl I didn't recognize. His arm rested casually on her shoulder. The audience ah-ed at them all together, and applauded. Meanwhile, my heart discovered that there were further cracks and fissures it could endure.

'And like I say, I heard the album,' Rose went on gushingly. 'And it's a collection of love songs. Some of them are heart-breaking. Some are so tender. I have to ask – are you loved up these days, all of you?'

Jamie's face was unreadable. Connor blushed. Angus nudged him in the ribs and grinned.

'Well, the Love God's managed to hang on to a girl for longer than thirty seconds. Major personal record.'

'Congratulations!' Rose grinned. 'So, what's your secret?'

'Letters,' Connor said, his face cracking into a grin. 'Lots of letters.'

'Verushka says he writes like Tolstoy,' Declan laughed. 'Turns out it works. We all write letters now.'

'I find my personal magnetism generally does it,' Angus said smugly, only half joking. 'But we wrote our best stuff when we were single. You know, when you want someone and you don't know if you'll ever get them ...'

'I know,' Rose said, smiling. 'I've been there. I'm surprised you have, though.'

'Oh, we have,' Angus groaned. 'Well, Romeo over there has.' He pointed at Jamie. At which point they all joined in.

'There was this girl ... love of his life ...'

'Jamie lost her ...'

'Tried to get her back ... didn't work.'

'Oh?' Rose asked.

'Yeah. He had this grand plan. Total failure ...'

'He'd messed up too badly.'

'Hopeless with women, aren't you, mate?'

Angus cuffed his friend on the back of the head. Jamie hardly reacted. He hadn't said a word throughout this whole conversation.

My phone was already ringing. Tammy.

I answered it. 'Happy Christmas!'

'Whatever. Are you watching this?' she said. There was no need to specify.

'Accidentally,' I admitted.

'So. Two nights ago I was at this thing you wouldn't go to ...' ('This thing' was Tammy-code for a pre-Christmas party held by Clemmie, Jez's by-now-ex-girlfriend. Yes, I was more of a party girl now, but there were limits.)

'Yes ...?' I wasn't fully concentrating, as the TV screen kept distractingly showing a blown-up image of Jamie's stony, silent face. What was he thinking about? Or rather, who? Was it the crop-haired girl in the picture? Did he meet her in LA, after he split up with Sigrid? Right now, I had zero interest in Tammy's social life.

'... and she was talking about this so-called secret gig they're supposed to be doing at the Rialto. I just assumed it was a joke, or a tribute band, because ... the Rialto? But now I get it, Neens. Look at the boy!'

I had caught about one word in five of this. Tammy was talking way too fast — she must be high on her mum's brandy-soaked Christmas pudding or something — and she seemed to think I'd be interested in some event taking place in Croydon's second-largest music venue. I beyond didn't care.

'Look, Tam, can I get back to you? I'm kind of busy ...'

'Shut up and listen, you numpty. The Point. Are doing. A gig. In Croydon.'

'No, they aren't,' I sighed, shifting Lara over a bit so I could see the screen better. Because, obviously.

Tammy sighed back, louder and more huffily.

'Well I think they might be. You know them. Did any of them go to the BRIT School?'

'No.'

'Did they have lots of mates from there, who they constantly talked about?'

'Not that they mentioned.'

'Are they fans of Ikea? Do they love car parks?'

'Tammy! What are you *on*?'

'Say Clemmie's right. D'you think they chose this – much as I love it, but *hello*? – this *dump* for their secret gig because *a girl Jamie wrote a bunch of songs about lives here*?'

Oh.

But no.

Just … no.

I stared at the TV. By now, the boys were playing a live-broadcast world premiere of *Ariel*, with Rose Ireland guesting on backing vocals. They looked iconic.

'*There was this girl … Love of his life …*'

'N-no,' I stammered. 'It's not possible.'

'Fine,' Tammy sighed. 'They just chose Croydon for the hell of it. Because hey, it's an obvious venue …'

Was it true? Were they coming here for me? They couldn't be.

This wasn't good. I was back in the Silk Room, with Jamie

shouting through the door at me, and I didn't want to be. That was categorically the worst moment of my life – worse, even, than standing in front of Sigrid in the dining room, because then there was nothing I could do about it, but in the Silk Room I had a choice. I had to *choose* to keep him out, for the sake of my sanity. I hated myself then, too.

'There's only one thing,' Tammy mused, ignoring my total silence at the other end of the line. 'Why do it and not let you know? Look, are you sure he hasn't invited you?'

46

Back in my room, I looked around in a state of surreal confusion. Whatever grand plan Jamie had had, it was too late now – they'd said so. *'Tried to get her back ... Didn't work.'* And anyway, there was this other girl now. Maybe Tammy was wrong about the Croydon thing after all.

I didn't want to know, but I had to. I didn't want to do this, but I must.

The place was messier than usual. Bright Christmas wrapping paper was strewn all over the floor, teasingly revealing little piles of new presents and bigger ones of discarded clothes. My portfolio and sketchbooks covered the desk.

Where did I put it?

I paused in the sea of paper and clothes, and put my fingers to my temples.

I didn't open it, but I didn't throw it away.

Nothing in my desk drawers, or my bedside table. Nothing

poking out of the books on the shelves behind my bed ... *Where? Where? Where?* Eventually, I found it tucked in the second page of my portfolio. The envelope with Jamie's writing. I had no recollection of putting it here. But I hadn't really been thinking straight that day. I hadn't been thinking much at all.

Inside was a letter, on headed paper from an LA hotel. *So he wasn't staying with Sigrid then. In the house with the pool shaped like his guitar.* That was my first thought. His handwriting was strong and clear. I could hear his voice in my head as I read.

HOTEL LUCILLE
WEST HOLLYWOOD
LOS ANGELES

My darling Nina,

Happy Birthday! You see? I know the day now. One day it'll say so in your Wikipedia entry. Alongside the details of your famous art career, your celebrated garden, your family of dogs, your unique take on tweed and trainers. Your love of pancakes. It may even mention that once you went out with a pot-bellied guy who used to be a rock star. He knows he doesn't deserve it, but he'd love to be a footnote in your bio.

All I can think about is you

It's over with Sigrid, I promise. Here are two tickets to LA. Bring Ariel if you like, or your friend Tammy. There's something I want you to hear.

Tell Windy you're coming and he'll sort out everything you need. Please come. Let me prove you wrong about one thing at least. You said I'd forget your name, but I remember every word you ever said, every time you looked at me, the way you burned up when I nearly kissed you I said I could make you happy and I'm an egotistic idiot, but I still want to try.

I'll be waiting backstage afterwards, and if it's a scrum, just find Oliver or Windy and they'll bring you straight to me. I'm sorry my life is such a circus.

But I love you. It's simple. Always.

J

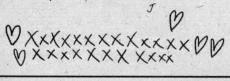

The bottom of the page was a forest of hearts and kisses, and the tickets he'd mentioned were nestling in the envelope. They were first class returns to LAX, and they had the price on them, and even though I'd travelled with a *rock band* it still made me gasp.

So Jamie had expected me to drop everything and fly out to California for him. Rock star. There was no mention of what event I'd need a backstage pass for, or where I was supposed to stay, but Windy would have sorted it out, I suppose. If I'd gone. If I'd wanted to go. But the tickets were for several weeks ago. Whatever he wanted me to hear, I wasn't there.

'*He'd messed up too badly …*'

Assuming it really was me they were talking about just now, I guess that was true.

I read his words again, and once again, and let my tears stream freely. The guy could write. And he wanted me. But didn't I always know that? Even if I'd flown all the way to California, would I have taken him back? Could I really have put myself through any of that pain again?

The answer was simple. No.

I should have burnt the letter. I should never have watched that show tonight.

Damn Jamie Maldon. There was no escaping him.

There was a knock at my door. A pink mop of hair appeared around the side of it. Ariel looked nervous. 'Can I come in?'

'Sure,' I sighed.

'I kind of … heard your conversation with Tammy.' She stepped inside, awkward and anxious, twisting the hem of her jumper with restless fingers. 'There's something I need to tell you.'

Oh my God. Tammy. The Rialto. Croydon – the other gig. I'd forgotten all about it, lost in Jamie's letter. That boy could fry my brain in ways I didn't think possible.

'Yeah, sure …' I muttered. 'Tell me what?'

Ariel mangled the hem of her jumper some more.

'I have a ticket.'

'You do?'

She saw the shock on my face. This was pink-haired Ariel.

The one who hated The Point.

'Mahika heard about it at school,' she said, all in a rush. 'She's a Pointer Sister like me... um, like I *was*. She was going with a bunch of people. Someone dropped out and she asked me if I wanted to go and ... I know he ... and you ... but ... I wanted to hear my song. Just once.'

She looked at me unhappily, with a kind of pleading glance.

'So it's true?' I asked. 'They really are coming here?'

She nodded. 'Mahika heard they booked the venue ages ago, under a fake name. I thought about telling you, but I know what Jamie did to you. At first I thought he'd invite you himself, but you didn't mention it so I assumed he hadn't. I didn't want to hurt you any more. I'm sorry, Nina. I thought it'd be easier if you didn't know.'

I stared at my little sister, so grown up now, trying to look after me. Her soul deserved a whole symphony, not just a song.

She happened to glance over my shoulder and saw the plane tickets and the letter scattered on my bed and her mouth fell open.

'He invited me to ... something else,' I said vaguely. My voice petered out. My mind was racing. My head ached.

'Are you going?'

'I can't. It was a long time ago.'

Slowly, my whirring thoughts arranged themselves into some kind of sense. Had Jamie pictured me going out to California in November, then bringing all my friends along to this gig after Christmas? Was *that* why he'd booked it here? I knew how he liked to plan romantic gestures. I thought Sigrid had messed up the dinner in Paris, but if I was right, that was nothing to what

I'd done now.

The ground underneath me seemed to be shaking and I put out a hand to steady myself. It had seemed so sensible and right to ignore his letter when it arrived. I was so proud of myself for shoving it out of sight. Now, suddenly, I wasn't sure.

'Come with me,' Ariel said, holding out her hand. 'I know we could get you in.' She looked into my eyes and I could see that she got the turmoil I was in. 'You don't have to do anything – just watch from the back. If you can't take it, we'll leave.'

I pictured his inscrutable face on the TV screen just now. I thought about the jagged pain of seeing the photo of him with his arm around another girl. I didn't know what to do, and I felt myself about to crumble.

'Please?' she begged.

I shook my head. 'I can't. It's too late. He's got someone else now … There's no point.'

'Jamie? Someone else? Who?'

'That girl in the picture they showed. The one with Rose. You saw her.'

Ariel wrinkled her brow. 'Charley van Schaal? The tennis player? That's Declan's girlfriend. They've been going out for ages. You really don't follow them any more, do you?'

I shrugged and sniffed. 'I guess not.'

'As far as I know, he's single,' Ariel said. 'Does that help? I really want to hear my song. And it's all because of you. Please come.'

'When is it?'

'The day after tomorrow.'

I nodded, wordlessly.

She threw her arms around me and hugged me.

Four boys, onstage at a dirty, sweaty venue in South London, full of a thousand screaming Pointer Sisters. No lasers or pyrotechnics or balloons. The band looked nervous and excited – like they used to, I guess, in the old days, before they played to stadiums of pixel-sized mega-fans.

The set list began with 'Pilgrim Soul' and that was hard, because it was about Jamie and me and I could picture exactly how I felt when I first heard it. He'd changed his look again, I noticed. The silk shirt had been replaced by an old, stiff-fronted evening shirt, half-untucked, like the kind I used to wear from Charity and Chuck. He was wandering the stage clothed in my memories.

The next song was hard too. Same story. Listening to Jamie Maldon sing anything, ever, was going to be difficult, I realized. I was just going to have to harden my heart.

Then Declan launched into a shimmering intro on drums, and Jamie sang:

I let you down
You cut your hair

And already I was crying. Ariel turned to me with wet cheeks too. It was so beautiful and sad and heartfelt. Boys' hearts get broken too, he'd told me. He sang like a boy with a broken heart.

The crowd were transported. They seemed to love each song more than the last. Windy didn't need to worry – it was clear they had a new set of hits on their hands.

Song after song. Old ones, new ones. Each one packed with special memories. Each one harder to bear than the last.

But Ariel was in paradise. She was back to her old self – a Pointer Sister to her core, surrounded by her soulmates. And we were too crammed in to think of moving, even if I'd had the heart to pull her away.

'As you know, we always do a cover,' Jamie said eventually, standing in the spotlight. This must mean the gig was nearly over. 'This one's by Derek and the Dominos. It's about a girl. Hope you like it.'

From the first seven notes of Angus's riff, I knew it. They launched into a wild, zinging, heartfelt rendition of 'Layla', one of the most passionate rock songs ever written. It was one of the songs we used to listen to at the Hall.

As Jamie howled into the mic, I was back there, by the fire, and trying so hard not to be. The feeling was like a fire inside me. Happiness, joy, love. So much love. More emotion than a body could contain.

Angus's sweeping solo came close to expressing it. For a while, I was transported by the fireworks of his guitar. Then Jamie came back on vocals and the rawness of his emotion cut right through me.

Jamie Jamie Jamie Jamie.

Just because someone smashes your heart on the rocks, it doesn't mean you stop loving them, unfortunately. I was lost. Nothing had changed.

As the last notes died away, the crowd screamed and stomped like never before. Jamie stood there, soaking up their reaction for a while. Then he walked up to the front of the stage, spotlight on his face, mic in hand.

'This one's for someone I used to know,' he announced quietly, guarding his emotions, staring at the floor. Connor played a riff on bass and Angus joined in. I recognized the tune as one they'd been working on, but they hadn't turned it into anything by the time I left the Hall. Now Jamie raised the mic to sing.

A little bit broken
A little bit beautiful
That's who we are,
Aurora

A little bit broken
A little bit lost
But I found you
Tread on my dreams
And I'll take you to
A place that no one knows
Just me and you

And there it was. A song with the words I'd given to Jamie when I told him I loved him. He'd read the words and kept them. It must be the thing he wanted to me to hear. But I still didn't really understand. *Aurora* was the name of the broken boat on the lake. It could refer to any girl, or any broken thing – it didn't have to be me.

After the second verse, Declan moved on to keyboards from the drums. He accompanied Angus and Jamie as they played a long instrumental, a bit like 'Layla' – a journey in music that reached inside me and played me like one of their guitars. It was the best thing they'd ever done. Perfectly beautiful. Did Jamie simply want to give me this song?

Then, as the last notes died away, there was a coda. Jamie stood, alone, in the spotlight to sing it. The words of this final, unexpected verse reminded me of 'Layla', too. I wondered if that was why he'd chosen that cover just now.

> I'm on my knees now
> I'm begging you, please now
> You said you loved me
> Please don't walk away

His voice was raw. It gave me goosebumps.

When he'd sung the words, Jamie stayed staring out into the crowd, while Declan went back to his drums and the other boys played quietly behind him. Angus strummed a few simple chords. Declan took the drums down to their softest shimmer. Connor let his bass hang on its strap and gave Jamie a mock 'go ahead' bow.

Jamie spoke to the crowd. 'You look good tonight, Croydon. I want you to do something for me.'

Applause. Random cheering.

'There was a girl. I messed up. I probably made it worse, because she hates attention. I mean, she *hates* attention. But I needed a big gesture.'

More cheers. Yells of sympathy.

Ariel looked at me. My skin started to prickle.

He opened his arms out to everyone in front of him. 'It didn't work, but it's kind of a tradition for this song now. Will you sing for me?'

'Yes!' There was some cheering from the front rows.

'I *said*, will you sing for me?'

'Woo! Woo! Woo!' This time, the cheer ran round the venue.

'OK. It goes like this …'

Angus played the notes on guitar, then Jamie sang, unaccompanied:

I'm on my knee-knee-knees, now

He gestured to the crowd to sing. They sang back.

I'm on my knee-knee-knees, now

He made them sing it a few times. I didn't join in. I was still trying to understand what was happening. I reached out and clutched Ariel's hand.

'Now this side …' Jamie crouched down and indicated the audience to his left.

I'm on my knee-knee-knees …

'And you …' He got the audience to his right to sing one note:

Now

And that was it. He got them to repeat it, over, and over –
the left side, then the right, conducting them like a choir.

I'm on my knee-knee-knees ... Now

He made them sing quietly, so it almost sounded like a
lullaby, or a prayer. He had them in the palm of his hand, just as
he had in New York. That same magic.

On the fourth or fifth time, I heard it.

My name.

If you didn't hear the word every day, you wouldn't notice.
But there it was, floating above the crowd.

Ni-Ni-Ni ... Na
Ni-Ni-Ni ... Na

He let them sing. Listening to the sound, his face finally
relaxed into that faraway look he got when he was lifted by the
audience's energy.

It wasn't a coincidence. It wasn't a mistake. Jamie Maldon
knew the power of words too well. A while ago, I'd told him
that he wouldn't remember me. Now, a thousand people, without knowing it, were singing my name.

Ariel heard it too. She turned to look at me, her eyes wide
with wonder. I couldn't do anything or say anything. When a
thousand people sing to you, even if they don't know it's you
they're singing to, the magic is powerful.

I closed my eyes. I don't know how long they sang for. It was
probably less than a minute. It felt like for ever. A thousand

voices, blending together. My name, my name, my name.

When it was over, Jamie sank to his knees and sang the last line of the song:

> You said you loved me
> Please don't walk away

And then silence.

He stayed on his knees as the people cheered, and blew a kiss to the crowd.

'Thank you, Croydon. You were beautiful.'

A thousand-voice-choir apology.

Rock star.

And still in love with me.

Not every boy is Jez Rockingham. As I stood there watching him, alone under the spotlight, the armour around my heart peeled off and fell away.

HEATHERWICK HALL, NEW YEAR'S DAY

They'd been here two days, and he was already regretting his decision. When he wasn't working these days, the Hall was the only place he wanted to be. But he'd invited the rest of the band for New Year's Eve, and they'd invited other people and ever since they got here it had been a raging party. His head hurt. The noise was constant – a different dance tune in every room. Snooker balls and party games ... Beautiful people, having a beautiful time. He didn't know who half of them were.

It was five in the afternoon, and already pitch black outside. He went to the kitchen to make himself a sandwich. A girl in a bikini top, spangled hotpants and platform boots (why? – it was Northumberland) was giving a massage to a shirtless boy leaning forward on the kitchen table, and the room smelt of patchouli oil. He missed the aroma of Orli's roast chicken. And Orli herself, who couldn't come and cook for him because she was on holiday with Sam. He missed everything.

Avoiding the half-naked couple, he made his sandwich on the far side of the room.

'Jamie! Jamie! This place is so *fantastic*!' the girl said, ignoring her massage partner for a moment to focus her bright green eyes on him. Who was she? Had they met last night? He couldn't remember. 'Just imagine what you could do with it! I was thinking just now ... You could knock these walls down and put in some picture windows. Get rid of that old stove and install some decent fridges that do ice, you know? And a big TV with Sky up there in the corner. I do interior design. I could help you remodel it.' She batted her extra-long lashes.

He nodded and mentally ignored her, quickly finishing his sandwich and walking away. Ever since he got here, people had been telling him how great the house was, and how to change it. Take this down ... make that better ... sell all the old stuff ... make it look like every other luxury pad they'd ever stayed in. He nodded to them all and hated them.

She would have made a cup of tea and curled up on the sofa beside him, and laughed at them with him. And he'd have leant in to kiss her, and her cheeks would have flushed with the anticipation ... his blood quickened at the thought of it, even though she was just a memory.

It all made sense with her. It only made sense with her.

He passed the dining room, where he'd smarmed all over Sigrid, and all the time he was killing *her* just a little bit, and he hadn't known it. He should have done – she'd warned him. Her heart was a delicate mechanism, like his. You couldn't smash it with a hammer and expect it still to keep working.

He hadn't been in the room since. The table had been dismantled and now the space was full of people dancing. Verushka was doing a hot routine to the loud approval of several guests. He didn't recognize most of them.

The hall throbbed with music he didn't like. Someone had raided the cellar and dropped a bottle of vintage wine on the marble flagstones. The pungent smell was turning acrid. But the beautiful people simply walked through it, as if it wasn't there.

He would sell Heatherwick as soon as he could, he decided. This whole idea had been a mistake. Meanwhile, nobody was going to clear up that stinking mess. Nobody cared about the little things here any more. Nobody *made* things. He went to the utility room behind the kitchen to find a cloth and bucket. When he got back, a girl in skinny jeans and a micro-top wandered in from the drawing room, clutching one of the wooden boxes that had once held Windy's records.

'Hi Jamie,' she cooed to him, with a take-me smile. 'We ran out of stuff for the fire. It's nearly out now. We can use these, can't we?'

He looked beyond her, to see the old albums scattered carelessly on the floor.

Get out! he wanted to yell. *All of you! Leave me alone.*

Instead, he simply shook his head. 'No. You can't. I need those.'

But she wasn't listening. She was heading to the front door. 'Did you hear something?' She opened it and peered outside. 'Can I help you? It's someone from the village, Jamie. Oh! Snow! Hey! C'mon everyone! It's *snowing*!'

She shouted loudly and a crowd of people rushed past him, through the hall and out of the front door, following in her laughing wake. A flurry of cold wind made him shiver.

The crowd disappeared. He looked out into the darkness. And

there she was. In a coat, with a suitcase. Looking quite out of place at the party. And totally at home.

'*Nina!*'

He ran down the steps towards her. She was shivering, and there were snowflakes in her hair. She must have been out there for ages, while nobody heard the bell over the music. He put his arms around her and held her close.

'Windy t-told m-me you were here,' she said, through chattering teeth. 'N-no signal ...'

He bent his head down to hers, and hesitated. She had a history of reacting badly to his attempts to show her how he felt about her. Restraining the powerful urge to kiss her, he murmured, 'But ... you read my letter. You didn't reply. You didn't come to the gig ...'

She looked up at him and shook her head. 'I d-didn't read your letter. Not until a week ago. I went to the gig at the Rialto, but I didn't have a p-pass. I c-couldn't get backstage. T-too many people. Then I didn't know where you were.'

'You could have called me.'

'D-didn't have your number,' she said. 'And Windy wasn't answering his calls. Until yest-t-terday.'

'I thought I'd blown it.'

'You had.'

He couldn't believe she was really here. 'I never lied to you about Sigrid,' he told her urgently pulling back, so he could look at her. 'As soon as we left the Hall, I flew out to her and told her it was over. She wouldn't believe me for a while. Then she wanted to keep it quiet. I was a mess, I was busy, I didn't care. When she finally told everyone it was over, she made it seem like ... In Sigrid's world, nobody leaves her. It's not possible. I wanted to tell you the truth. But I had to make you trust me first.'

She simply nodded. 'I kn-know.'

Something had changed in her. Though she stammered with the cold, the flicker of uncertainty was gone. Now she was all fire, despite the snow. Oh God, the snow. She was freezing. He quickly led her through the open door and reached out a hand to brush the melting snowflakes from her hair.

A group of raucous people spilled out of the dining room into the hall and stared briefly at the girl in the coat before turning their eyes to him. 'Come and dance, baby!' Verushka cooed seductively, holding out her hands and undulating to the music.

Not again ...

But before he could answer, he felt Nina's arms snake around his waist. 'Don't dance,' she said. 'Not yet.' She pulled him in close.

'I wasn't going to,' he murmured. He looked into her eyes, amazed. She was smiling. Hope, and something stronger, sparked in his chest. 'You were wrong, by the way,' he said.

'What about?'

'I remembered your name.'

'Oh that. I noticed.'

'And your birthday.'

'You did, didn't you?' she grinned.

'Forgiven?'

The last time he had tried to kiss her here, she had pulled away. This time, ignoring the watching crowd, she looked at him with heavy-lidded eyes and pulled him to her.

The world disappeared. Even the sound of Angus laughing in the background didn't matter. 'Finally. *Finally* ...'

Kissing Nina Baxter was hot, and fierce, and wonderful. Time exploded into a million precious moments. For ever started now, and it was beautiful.

CODA

SIX MONTHS LATER

A beach wedding, on an island in the Caribbean. The bride is one of Rory Windermere's favourite people, he says. No expense has been spared.

Today, I'm wearing a long, strappy dress by an American designer. At least this time they've been given my proper dimensions. It fits me with almost indecent perfection.

Warm breeze. Bare feet on silk-soft sand. The smell of frangipani flowers, twisted in our hair. Issy and Verushka stand beside me. Declan's girlfriend couldn't make it – she's playing in the quarter-finals at Wimbledon.

A steel band plays 'Can't Help Falling In Love' by Elvis Presley, and we start down the sandy path to the waiting groom. Jamie catches my eye and gives me The Smile. I return it, shyly. I'm starting to get used to it.

When Orli reaches the top of the aisle, the other bridesmaids and I go to our allotted places. Jamie takes my hand in his. It's a beautiful wedding and Orli looks more angelic than ever in her flowing white dress, with her thick golden hair. She gazes at Sam with a mixture of laughter and devotion. He's lucky to have her and he knows it.

In a way, I envy them. Being a rock star's girlfriend sucks sometimes. I know there are a dozen paparazzi cameras hidden in the bushes, and they're all focused on Jamie and me, not Orli and Sam. Tomorrow, all the stories will be about us, and when we'll follow in their footsteps. But I have no plans in that direction. I'm eighteen, with my life ahead of me. Who knows what will happen next?

Jamie thinks he does, but then, Jamie is the most romantic boy I know. He has the soul of a poet, and poets dream big dreams. He wanted to settle down in a house by the sea with Sigrid and the Malteser diamond, until he discovered who she really was. He's crazy, but I love him.

Will we survive the stories and the lies on the internet, and the girls who'll follow him on tour while I go to art school? I can't be sure. But twining my fingers into his on the beach today, I want us to.

Sigrid tried to break us apart. She gave a big interview soon after our relationship leaked out, saying I was her assistant and I'd 'stolen' Jamie from her. She was angry and hurt and it was obvious she was still in love with him.

Watching her rant and rave online, and all the comments mounting up underneath, defending me and criticizing her, I felt almost sorry for her. Almost. But I only had to remember that day in the dining room to find that my pity evaporated pretty fast. The support from the Pointer Sisters, meanwhile, means more to me than they will ever know.

Being a rock star's girlfriend has its compensations.

Jamie standing in the kitchen at home, singing Ariel's song to her, a cappella, solo. She nearly forgot to breathe.

Taking my whole family on holiday with his mum, to an island not far from here that was so beautiful I'm not sure I'll ever recover.

Planning a mini-festival at the Hall next year, for fans of the band and local families. All those dreams we had about the place – he wants to turn them into reality. (Except the cheese part. He was joking about the cheese part.) Maybe one day we will.

He has the greatest smile in the world. This is official. It is even mentioned in Wikipedia. It still melts me every time.

The thing is, I melt him too.

'Nina Nina Nina Nina.'

He sings my name under his breath, while Orli and Sam look lovingly at each other and say the vows he helped them write.

I rub my fingers against his. Rough and smooth. Skin against skin. That chemical rush never ceases to amaze me. It may break them, sometimes, but love is what hearts are for.

Some of his lines run through my head. They're for my sister, and me, and for Aunt Cassie, and Orli today, and for everyone who has ever loved – like a love song should be.

And now you're flying through the air
Like a bird, like an angel
Across the golden sky

Take me there
Take me anywhere

THE END

PLAYLIST

There are two critically important songs in this book: 'In My Life', by the Beatles, and 'Kashmir', by Led Zeppelin. I've known all the Beatles' music all my life, but I only encountered 'Kashmir' properly recently, sitting quietly with my eight-year-old, and the spellbinding effect on us was similar to the one it has on Nina. I can still feel the chills.

All the songs mentioned in the book are important to me in one way or another. Here they are, along with some others I'd love to have included. I hope they get you dancing like nobody's watching, and inspire you to make new discoveries of your own.

The Beatles - 'In My Life', 'Within You Without You',
'Come Together', 'Norwegian Wood', 'Paperback Writer' (for
obvious reasons), 'Lucy in the Sky with Diamonds', 'Dear
Prudence' (this song for Prudence Farrow, Mia Farrow's sister,
partly inspired Nina in the book)

Blondie - 'Rapture'

Nirvana - 'Lithium', 'Smells Like Teen Spirit'

The Rolling Stones - 'Gimme Shelter'

David Bowie - 'Fame', 'Fashion', 'Heroes'

The Cure - 'Lovesong', 'Friday I'm In Love'

Led Zeppelin - 'Kashmir'

Robert Plant - 'Shine It All Around'

Muddy Waters - 'Baby Please Don't Go'

The Velvet Underground - 'Oh! Sweet Nuthin''

Talking Heads - 'Psycho Killer'

Derek and the Dominos - 'Layla'

Jimi Hendrix - 'Little Wing', 'Hey Joe'

Pink Floyd - 'Comfortably Numb'

The Pretenders - 'Brass in Pocket'

The Go-Go's - 'Our Lips Are Sealed', 'We Got The Beat'

Duran Duran - 'Save A Prayer', 'Rio'

Blur - 'Song 2'

Foo Fighters - 'Times Like These', 'The Pretender'

The White Stripes - 'Seven Nation Army'

Ed Sheeran - 'Thinking Out Loud'

Mark Ronson - 'Uptown Funk'

CHECK OUT SOPHIA'S PLAYLIST ON

Spotify®

ACKNOWLEDGEMENTS

Writing a book is a solitary process, but I couldn't possibly have written this one without the help and inspiration of many wonderful friends. Thank you all.

To Theresa Waterlow, for donating Nina's name. And Orli Voght-Vincent for donating her own name – a prize she won in a short story writing competition. I hope you both like who you became!

Melita and Rosella Gostelow for believing in Nina's story all the way through, and Emily and Sophie Bennett, Freddie Rawlins, Archie, Alice and Eliza Reed and Louisa Hughes for helping me to find my way to the end.

My fabulous friends in the Sisterhood, the Yoga Girls and the Walkers. Especially, this time, Keris Stainton, Keren David and Susie Day, for your help when the story was a patchwork of scenes, and I hadn't even decided on a tense.

The Reeds and Mark and Belinda Tredwell for giving me precious space to write.

The Year 8 girls at The Abbey School, Reading, for all the insightful comments and title suggestions. You were brilliant.

Adam Norsworthy for tips on band life when I really needed them. Keith Richards, Hunter Davies, Stephen Davis, Rod Stewart, John Taylor and Jo Wood for writing such entertaining and fascinating autobiographies and biographies. Rock is a foreign country: they do things differently there.

Professor Jim Al-Khalili and Professor Mark Miodownik for a fascinating discussion on Radio 4's *The Life Scientific*, which introduced me to the importance of making things in the art of being happy. This strongly influenced who Nina was in the book, and how she coped, and is a recipe I use myself when I'm feeling low, and which I cheerfully pass on to my readers.

Jenny Savill at Andrew Nurnberg Associates for believing in Nina from the start, and Rachel Hickman for her support all the way through. Barry Cunningham, Rachel Leyshon and everyone at Chicken House. Helen Crawford-White for my cover, which actually helped me finish the book. And Bella Pearson for being an utterly brilliant editor, whom I'm so lucky to work with.

To Freddie and Tom for putting up with me when I was spending more time in Nina's world than in my own.

And Alex. In the immortal words of another epic band, thank you for the music.

ABOUT THE AUTHOR

Sophia Bennett would have loved to be an artist, fashion designer, or the lady who does costumes for Jane Austen films. However, not being able to draw or sew very well made those careers unlikely. Luckily, she also loves to write. She is the author of the internationally successful *Threads* series, as well as *The Look*, *You Don't Know Me* and *The Castle*, and has written for *The Times* and *The Guardian*.

She lives in London with her family, and is known for her shoes and her writing shed. You can find out more about her on her website: www.sophiabennett.com

🐦 @sophiabennett
f SophiaBennettAuthor

Page 303 W.B. Yeats: from 'Aedh Wishes for the Cloths of Heaven' from *The Wind Among the Reeds* (1899)

THE THREADS TRILOGY

Nonie's passion is fashion. Humanitarian Edie wants to save the world. And budding actress Jenny has just landed a part in a Hollywood blockbuster.

But when these three friends meet a young refugee called Crow, wearing a pair of pink fairy wings and sketching a dress, they get the chance to pool their talents and do something truly wonderful, proving that fashion fairy tales really can happen.

'Great fun. It goes at a cracking pace and girls will love it.'
JACQUELINE WILSON

'. . . the next Princess Diaries — only hotter.'
THE TIMES

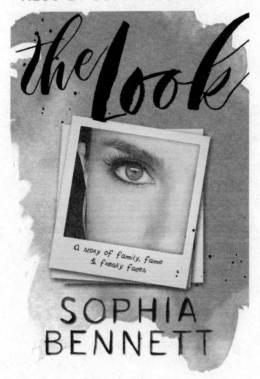

THE LOOK

Ted is tall. Freaky. When she's spotted by a model agency, she can't believe it. At the same time, her gorgeous sister falls seriously ill.

With her world turned upside down, Ted must choose between fame and family. Can she be a supermodel *and* a super sister? All in five-inch heels?

'. . . one word, BRILLIANT. A difficult topic, sensitively handled.'
CATHY CASSIDY

Paperback, ISBN 978-1-910655-72-6, £6.99 • ebook, ISBN 978-1-908435-16-3, £6.99

YOU DON'T KNOW ME

Me and Rose. In a band. Singing together, all the way to the live finals of Killer Act.

Only to be told one of us must go. But no girl would drop her best friend in front of millions . . . Would she?

If this is fame, it sucks.

Everyone's talking about us, but nobody knows the truth.

'. . . her best yet.'
AMANDA CRAIG, THE TIMES

Paperback, ISBN 978-1-910655-73-3, £6.99 • ebook, ISBN 978-1-908435-80-4, £6.99

THE CASTLE

It's not just the bridesmaid's dress that Peta has a problem with – it's the whole wedding. How can her mum remarry when Peta's army-hero dad isn't dead?

When Peta receives clues that seem to prove he's alive, she sets out on a crazy mission. Somewhere across the sea, her father's being held in a billionaire's castle.

Dad would do anything to save her – and now it's her turn to rescue him.

'. . . a fun, frolicking, and increasingly frightening adventure.'

TERI TERRY

Paperback, ISBN 978-1-909489-78-3, £6.99 • ebook, ISBN 978-1-909489-79-0, £6.99